THE LICENSEE

HUGH COLLINS was born and brought up in Glasgow and in 1977, after a lifetime of crime, was sentenced to life for murder. He was released in 1992 after serving sixteen years of the sentence. His autobiography, published in two parts, *An Autobiography of a Murderer* and *Walking Away*, covers his time in jail and his struggle to cope after release. He is now married and lives and works in Edinburgh as a sculptor and writer. *The Licensee* is the second part of his Glasgow crime trilogy. The first novel, *No Smoke*, is also published by Canongate Crime.

Also by Hugh Collins

Autobiography of a Murderer
Walking Away
No Smoke

THE LICENSEE

Hugh Collins

First published in Great Britain in 2002 by Canongate Crime,
an imprint of Canongate Books Ltd, 14 High Street,
Edinburgh EH1 1TE

10 9 8 7 6 5 4 3 2 1

British Library Cataloguing-in-Publication Data
A catalogue record for this book is available on
request from the British Library

ISBN 1 84195 244 3

Typeset by Palimpsest Book Production Limited,
Polmont, Stirlingshire
Printed and bound in Great Britain by
The CPI Group

To the memory of Karen McNee

To Caroline, my wife. Brian McEwan. George Kerevan. Andy and Lorraine Dick Arnott. Linda, Jim and Derek McNee. Jake Arnott of The Long Firm. Dr Jane Goldman, Gus and Roberta. Big Norrie Rowan. Special thanks to Andrew Brown. Kevin Williamson, Paddy Hill and John McManus. Jamie, Karen, Pru, Sheila, Stan and all the staff at Canongate. And Bob Dylan, for his companionship throughout the long lonely hours of writing . . .

'There is no such thing as society.
There are individual men and women . . .'
                                    Margaret Thatcher

And here he comes . . . watch out.
                                    Hugh Collins

Part One

Chapter One

THE WEE GLEN Bar sits like an oasis in the middle of a desert; locals have a 'bevvy' the day the giro lands behind the door. Millionaires for a day, they hog the bar of the only pub in the area likely to give tick, at least to regulars under sixty.

Rounds of drinks depend on who's been paid, and then there's the wee 'kerry oot' and back to a house until the ritual repeats itself the following day – it's the story of their lives up the Garngad – 'Much dae a owe ye?'

Televisions are in most bars these days, but here, the black box still has some novelty value; it's a gimmick, a conversation killer, but helps distract those bleary staring eyes from depressed visions; the endless flow of repetitive game shows give way to flashy cars, but yet another contestant walks off with the enamel mug, relieving the tension throughout the bar's mandatory audience – 'Away ye go, ya fuckin haufwit, ye! See wit a mean? Ada won that fuckin motur there!'

Today, though, the viewing is different: today all eyes are riveted to the huge television screen, eyes filled with excitement. News bulletins, flashing by the hour, have broken the hypnotic hold of prize-winners screeching from another world. True life drama is on their doorstep, disaster involving locals, possibly neighbours – 'Jesus, eh. The whole faimly deid?' someone mutters amid the stunned silence.

Nicotined fingers curl around half-filled pint glasses of flat beer, while cleaner, more manicured fingernails drum on the table in the corner.

'S'keepin this cunt?' the tallish, thinly built bespectacled figure behind them thinks. He glances up at the door from behind his glass of Coca Cola. He looks at his wristwatch and glances up again while ice cubes crash impatiently around the glass – 'S'keepin this cunt?'

Only the drumming can be heard in the bar as commentators continue the update on the news – 'Three generations of the family were wiped out as fire swept through the house during the early hours of the morning. A police spokesman said today the fire may be connected to the recent violent incidents involving rivalry between local drug barons. The police state that they are following definite leads but have launched an appeal asking the public to come forward with any further information.'

The man sitting at the table in the corner is paying no attention to the television news report but his thin lips smile slightly when he recognises the tough-looking face of the police spokesman – 'The Hammer, eh.'

A bedraggled tracksuit in cheap trainers walking through the door catches his eye. A nod directs the figure into the only other chair at the table. He has 'junky' stamped all over him – 'Pat! Honest, man. Sorry, man, sorry am late, man,' he stammers.

Pat points to a bag of brown lying in the ashtray – 'Here, square yersel up an en wull huv a wee blether,' he says quietly.

'Aw-w, Pat. Thanks, man, thanks. M'rattlin. Noa be a wee minut. Back inna sec'nd, mate.' The dilapidated athlete's outfit burns the tracks to the toilet.

Pat looks to the barman, pointing to his glass: the untouched Diet Coke is immediately replaced without a drop spilling onto the table — 'Get Davy a pint as well,' he drawls lazily.

The barman nods obediently — 'Right, Pat. A pint, Pat. Aye, Pat. Nae bother, Pat.'

Davy reappears looking more composed. The tracksuit, transformed beyond that lived-in look, bounces across the floor to take a pew. Now that those screaming veins have been burned the world seems a better place; dark, hollow sockets take on a yellowish gleam as a mild glow creeps from the soles of his feet to touch base at the back of his head — 'Whoof. Wa-ow,' he whispers through a shudder. He winks as he sits down at the table — 'S'dun. Nae problem, man.'

Pat lights a cigarette — 'Aye?' he asks, inhaling.

Davy downs half a lager — 'Aye, Pat. Av telt thum a heard that mob talkin in here last night aboot daen a frightener. A said tae thum it aw musta went wrang ur sumthin. A don't think thur givin a fuck wit happened. Jist wanted the statement an names. Goat a bit heavy, know wit a mean, man.'

Pat is listening attentively, watching every move, asking occasional questions, going over every detail, checking, re-checking to make sure Davy isn't lying. He trusts no one — 'Sound, Davy. Sound, wee man. Get ye squared up shortly, okay.'

Davy breathes a sigh of relief — 'Magic. Pat, listen, kin ye, eh, geez a wee bit noo?' he asks.

Pat looks to the floor — 'S'there, it yer feet. Keep ye gaun. N'listen, nae booze, right?' he orders — 'Booze's fur bampots.'

Davy's confidence soars — 'Aw, Pat. C'mon, man. S'Davy, man. A know the score. Nae danjur ey me yappin tae eny cunt. Yer insultin me noo, man. C'mon, eh? S'wee Davy!' he says with outstretched arms — 'S'me, man!'

Pat smiles – 'Sure, Davy. Sound, wee man, sound,' he winks.

Davy had been rehearsed over and over until the statement came tumbling out like an overspill of ramblings from another junky who had heard something about the fire. The information had been crafted into the perfectly pre-empted 'plant' in order to kill two birds with one stone, or, as transpired, seven down with two to go for life. Torching the house had been simple: kids and an oil drum at the front door; knock, knock – who's there? Whooosh! Guy Fawkes Night would never be the same in this district, but this was the Eighties – few things would ever be the same, anywhere.

Davy picks the bag up from the floor – 'Magic, Pat. Magic, man. S'thur enathin else ye want me tae dae?' he asks.

Pat remains silent, thinking. Anything more to do? No, he doesn't think so: not right now anyway. He looks around the bar, dragging on his cigarette. There appears to be an argument about the murders, someone is upset. The finger is being pointed already, it seems. Friends or neighbours of the dead family, unable to contain their outrage at the mindless slaughter are making accusations, the person refuses to hear otherwise – 'Fuckin Woods bruthers!' he's shouting – 'M'fuckin tellin ye! Fuckin dugs in the street know they dun it!' People try calming him down but the guy's emotions are swimming in the remains of that giro – 'Bastards! Shood be taken oot n shot!'

The Woods and Johnstone families had been rivals for a number of years: police had been aware of their activities and although there was growing concern over the more recent escalation in violent incidents involving guns, their crackdown operations had been futile.

The guy shouting storms out of the bar – 'Fuckin polis, eh! Don't gie a fuck fur people like us! Ordnary people urny important anuff ur they? Noa like that fuckin cow,' he's roaring. People turn; he's pointing at the television – 'Aye! Awright fur these cunts!'

Margaret Thatcher is leering down from the screen – 'Substitute the role of the mob for the rule of the law?' She looks demented as she deflects allegations that a coal-miner had been truncheoned to death – 'The Prime Minister was unequivocal in her support of the police amid today's allegations,' states the news anchorman – 'Mr David Jones died during clashes between police and strikers,' he continues, as footage of the mass demonstrations depict policemen laying into miners with sticks amid clouds of tear gas – 'In what looks the beginning of the end for the coal industry, police mounted the biggest anti-riot operation ever following the closure of Ollerton Colliery, Nottinghamshire. As talks today broke down between Mr Scargill, President of the NUM, and Mr McGregor, Head of the Coal Board, the government introduced emergency powers as police prepare to meet the potential for further trouble,' the anchorman concludes as the Premier recedes, grinning, clutching her handbag, and staring fixedly at her audience. She doesn't hear the tirade directed at her in the pub – 'DIE, YA FUCKIN COW, YE!' He's still screaming as he turns straight into the jukebox by the door – 'Oof. Ya fu-uucker, ye!' The pent-up emotions in the bar explode into laughter as he staggers to the door, his ranting now drowned out by the punk rock music screeching from the jukebox, deafening the whole bar.

'I AM THEE ANTI-CHRRISTA!

I AM THE ANARKEEYA!
AND NO-OWA!'

Davy's on his feet pogo-dancing all over the floor with other teenagers, screeching out

'THE GARNGAD TEAMAAAAA!'

Pat remains still, unmoved by the commotion. No, there was nothing more to do but watch events unfold. The Woods brothers have problems, he thought. He'd had little doubt that they'd be the main suspects: he'd merely exploited their rivalry with the Johnstones and raised the stakes. They'd be lifted by midnight: the coppers would want to maximise all that publicity. He'd hang around awhile maybe, watch the arrests. The Hammer would be plastered over every newspaper in the country. Davy had been told to specifically ask for the copper; he'd to make the statement to him, no one else. Pat reckoned a case like this would accelerate the copper's career through the promotional stratosphere. Detective Chief Inspector Ron McGhee. Yes, had a nice ring to it, he thought. An Inspector no less – in his pocket. The Hammer, he smiled, another fucking wanker.

Davy pogo's back into his chair – 'Bampots, eh,' he winks – 'M'gonny get a bitta fresh air, sweatin like a fuckin pig, man.'

Pat looks at him – 'Aye, Davy,' he grins – 'Sound, wee man, sound.'

Chapter Two

RAB WOODS IS still tired as his bare feet hit the linoleum, but he has a lot of work to do today. Angelena, his wife, stirs as he nudges her awake – 'Here. C'mon, get up.' Puffed eyes scowl back at him from the pillow.

'Time's it?' she yawns.

Rab pulls his jeans on – 'S'efter twelve, so c'mon, fuckin move. Get a cuppa tea,' he barks at her. Angelena pulls her housecoat around herself while he rolls a joint.

'Time did ye get back?' she asks. 'Never heard ye comin in.'

He hands her the joint while he pulls on socks – 'Fu-ck knows. Hauf four ur sumthin. Eh, any calls when a wis oot?'

She shakes her long black hair – 'Naw, did it go awright then?'

Rab nods – 'Aye, two kilo. Right, c'mo-on, get the tea oan. S'at urra cunt up yet? See if he's moved an get um up,' he snaps – 'Tell um tae get movin, hen.'

John, Rab's younger brother, is crashed in the living room, stuck to the sunken leather sofa: the television, hissing and crackling, has been on all night. Videos lie scattered all over the floor amid roaches, crisp packets, empty plastic bottles filled with floaters and other unmentionable piles of debris. A house-fly hovers around his open mouth for a moment before landing to investigate the layer of mushy bacteria caked to the surface of black stumps once resembling teeth. After shitting and vomiting on the shrunken greenish gums it flits further down that black hole, until an eruption of phlegm sucks it down a slide of spasmodic spluttering and swallowing.

Angelena's face screws up as she tiptoes past – 'Smell this fuckin place. That fuckin fire's been oan aw night tae,' she gags. She switches it off as she passes him to get into their tiny kitchen. She lights a cigarette while waiting for the kettle to boil – 'Och, hurry up. Right, tea bags, tea bags, the fuck ur they?' she mutters. She finds them in time for the kettle boiling – 'John!' she shouts – 'Jo-oohn! Jo-oohn! C'mon! Up! Yer tea's oot, so move!'

John snorts as he climbs from oblivion to semi-consciousness – 'The fucksat daen aw the shoutin, man? Time's it? Fuckin knackered, so am ur,' he grumbles – 'S'at tea yer makin, hen?'

Rab's fully dressed when he appears in the living room – 'Here, John, c'mon,' he says, passing a freshly rolled joint – 'Got that gear tae get cut. A want it bagged an oot the night, so c'mon, UP!'

John takes a deep drag – 'Go awright en?' he asks, blowing a smoke ring – 'Much did they huv?'

Rab pulls open the veranda door – 'Fuckin stinkin in here you, ya cunt. Ye been eatin? Deid rats ur sumthin?' he sneers – 'Fucksake, man. Here, yer squarin this pitch up by the way. Yer takin fuckin liberties wi hur, John.'

John throws the joint at him – 'Be fuckin right! S'fuckin hur that makes the mess. Yer fuckin missus, noa me,' he exclaims. He picks up an empty packet – 'Maltesurs! See! Fuckin blamin me fur every fuckin thing. Under the thumb! That's your problem, son! Right under the fuckin thumb, so ye ur. Aye, eh. Noa sayin much ur ye?' he asks – 'Av got tae fuckin laugh. Eh? Makin a fuckin mess? Be fuckin right . . . cunts.'

Rab pokes him in the ribs – 'S'the matter, son? Ye got a sore heid? Aw. Angelena, es got a sore heid. Aw, wit a shame, eh,' he mocks, climbing on top of him.

John pushes him away – 'Right, ya cunt! Chuck it! Ye know am tickly! Hauw hauw! A promise! Aw, c'mon! Al noa say anythin again! Naw! Aw, c'mon, chuck it, ya cunt!'

Rab lets him go – 'Right, en. C'mon, start gettin ready. Here, there's a wee tester. It's good kit. Get that up yer nose n wull get movin. A bought two kilo but wur still due a cuppla grand. S'nae bother. Gerrit oot early an fuck that urra mob. Here, by the way, they've aw hud a faw oot. Wee Mick Rosinni telt me last night when a got the gear aff um. Said they fucked um fur ten grand, wanted an in wi us.'

John catches the bag – 'Magic. Where's she wi that tea, man? Widye say tae um? Av nae problems wi um. S'a good grafter. Pat McGowan an him noa pals?'

Rab shouts through to the kitchen – 'Hauw! S'happenin wi that fuckin tea? S'like the fuckin desert in iss pitch!' he winks – 'Hauw! S'happenin, en? Naw, McGowan's noa interestit. The quiet man, eh. Pat the rat. Anyway, fuck him, prick.'

Angelena appears with the three mugs – 'Och shut it wull ye, fur fucksake. M'tryin tae listen tae the fuckin trani there,' she snaps – 'S'been a big fire ur sumthin. S'oan the news. Here, take yer cups afore ye get fuckin roastit, spillin aw o'er the place. That's great kit, by the way, John.'

John clears a space on the glass coffee table: he flips the bag onto the surface, chops it up with a cigarette coupon and then rolls it into a snorter – 'Aw-w. Jesus,' he gags, as vomit spills down his tee-shirt – 'Fuckinhell, man,' he gurgles.

Angelena turns away – 'Aw, Jesus,' she sighs – 'Al get a cloth fur that. Some kit, eh.'

Rab laughs, dragging the joint – 'Told ye, son, heavy fuckin stuff.'

John leans back – 'Fuckin hell,' he grins – 'S'hut me right away. M'fuckin steamin, so am ur.'

Rab hands him the joint – 'Aye, needs cut.'

John's trembling – 'Heavy, right enuff. Where is it anyway? N'the lock up?'

Rab feels bursts of energy surging through his system – 'Aye, the lock up. Swally that tea an en wull get movin,' he says – 'M'fuckin jumpin I'ready, man.'

John's feeling it too – 'Some kit, eh. Jumpin ma fuckin self man. We jist cuttin it doon there?' he asks – 'Aye, eh, saves aw that fuckin kerry oan watchin the door.'

Rab agrees – 'Aye, John. Angelena kin take orders in fur the night. Shood be finished fur tea time. Get these cunts squared up an get some peace. Fed up wi thum cummin tae the fuckin door aw the time. Anyway, c'mon. Square yersel up an get doon there an wull get it done.'

Angelena begins tidying up while her brother-in-law traverses the pile of towels on the way to the toilet: the living-room begins to look habitable with the rubbish cleared, the drawn pink ruched blinds hanging like knickers, hiding bacteria breeding in the whitish shag rug spread before the feature fireplace with its imitation brick – 'Aye, al get this place tidied up fur ma Maw,' she mutters – 'S'like a fuckin midden.'

The Constable *Haywain* print hanging above doesn't sit right with the array of brass ornaments and the inevitable line-up of silver-framed family photographs, but it's only a horse and cart anyway, so who cares?

Housework involves taking furniture polish to the huge

black television humming in a corner and the expensive sound system with its massive speakers occupying half the living space. The black leather three-piece suite plays host to nits the size of dogs – a species suspected in a mysterious outbreak of cattle rustling – bugs happy, however, to be home feeding on smack at night-shift sessions.

Angelena's proud of her home. You don't see many folks with houses decorated with blue velvet wallpaper: the patterned gold stripes may well be fading but a scarlet red border? No, you don't get this kind of thing around these parts. Her man's spared no expense, unlike some people, living off the dole. Her man's looked after their whole family, even paying for holidays. No, she's done well, she thinks, polishing their new Capo Di Monte.

Rab watches her once-beautiful figure fill the silk housecoat he bought her: she loves silk underwear, and he loves buying her sexy lingerie. Not many guys would do that for their bird, he thinks, but she's a real diamond and deserves the very best – 'Hmm,' he smirks – 'Check that arse.'

Angelena can read him like a book – 'He-ere, you. Think a canny see ye?' she grins.

Rab feigns surprise – 'Wi-it?' he laughs – 'Jist lookin hen, jist lookin.'

From her twenty-three-year-old face, once so pretty, dead eyes look back at him – 'Aye, right. Don't you start gettin ideas en, son,' she grimaces.

Rab's pinned pupils don't see the ravages of just 'dabbling'. Angelena's not a junky. She can't be: you only have to look at the house. Junky's don't live like this. There're no needle marks on her arms: he would never let her start that shit. Sure, she takes a line, but who doesn't these days? S'cheaper than booze. No, she dabbles but that's it and anyway, once she gets pregnant she's chucking the smack.

John reappears in a black shellsuit, arranging gold chains around his wrist – 'Y'ready, Rab?' he asks – 'Check ma eyes, man. Look like a fuckin vampire.'

Rab pulls on his black leather 'bomber' – 'Aye. Let's go,' he says, pulling a bundle of bank notes from his pocket – 'Here, hen. Cuppla quid. Av left some kit there. Square ye up. Fire doon the toon an get yersel some new gear ur sumthin.'

Angelena takes the money – 'Ma Ma's cummin up so a might take ur wi me. Make ura bag tae take hame fore ye go. Aye, she likes a wee bit fur daen the hoosewurk. Keeps ur aff the drink tae.'

John pulls a bag from his pocket – 'Gie ur that wan, it's fae the urra day, noa as heavy as that kit there. Auld Kitty, eh, be oan ur arse wi that stuff, hen,' he laughs.

They're all laughing at the idea – 'Anyway,' Rab says, giving her more money – 'Take the auld yin doon the toon an buy ur sumthin, okay? Wull be back later than a thought, probably efter twelve ur sumthin. Kin stick that stuff oot the morra. Time wi get it cut an at, know wit a mean.' He puts an affectionate arm around his brother – 'S'you, ya cunt, takin ages tae get ready as usual, eh?'

John takes the bait – 'Wi-it? Me? Don't fuckin start, you. Right, hen, see ye later. This cunt, eh? Fuckin wind-up merchant,' he laughs – 'M'bitin like a fuckin fish tae.'

Rab kisses Angelena – 'See ye later doll, okay? John,' he says turning – 'Yer lace. Yer lace's open. Fucksake, never learn, dae ye?'

A wee boy guards their Porche – 'Awright en, Rab?' he

grins – 'Nae cunt's touched it.' he reports cheekily – 'They noa al battur thum.'

Rab bungs him – 'Tenner, er ye go, wee man. Yer a good yin, son. See ye the morra n mind, don't spend it aw in the wan shop!' he sniggers – 'Fuckin weans. Wee widos.' They drive off, oblivious to the looks of anger, but catch the unusual number of police cars driving around.

'Lotta bizzies, eh, Rab?' comments John – 'Probably sum cunt's been chibbed ur sumthin.'

Rab looks in the rear-view mirror – 'Aye, probably the weans. Fightin ur sumthin. Aw here, wait tae ye see the motur-boat av seen. A cracker. Ye kin moor thum up n Loch Lomond. Ye fancy gettin wan? Be a good laugh.'

John leans back – 'Aye, s'up tae yerself. Aw Rab, that's some fuckin kit, man. Cut the stuff right doon, don't want these cunts turnin up in a close. Bodies eh, that's aw wi fuckin need. See they fun some cunt the urra night again, anurra O.D.' He laughs – 'They fun sum cunt the urra day, lyin up a close, wurks stull in es erm.'

He lobs an imaginary hand grenade at the Wee Glen – 'The Johnstones, eh! Cop that ya pricks! BANG! F-U-C-K-K-I-N W-A-N-K-U-U-U-R-S! HAUW! HAUW! HAUW!'

Davy watches as the car speeds past the bar – 'Oh, aye. They two pricks stull oan the loose?' he murmurs to himself – 'Fuckin bams.'

Pat shrugs when he's told – 'S'at right? Magine that, eh,' he grins.

Davy laughs too – 'A know, wankurs, eh. No be shoutin thur mooths aff the night. Aye, eh. Wait tae ye see thur fuckin faces when they get jailed-up, the fuckin bams.'

Pat smiles – 'Ach, well, wull see wit happens. Listen, a think ye shood maybe lie low tae things die doon. Manchester might be a good idea, keep ye oot the road tae their trial comes up. M'needin somebody doon there anyway, some cunt reliable.'

Davy can't believe it. Manchester? Reliable?

Manchester means work, real work, shifting gear. Pat, he feels, trusts him now: doing the statement had given him a chance to prove himself. Manchester: Pat's definitely giving him an 'in' at last. This isn't the usual thing, doing his 'runner' for other guys. No, this is it: he's in with a real top outfit – 'Aw, Pat. Fuckin hell, man. When? You're the boss,' he declares, filling his narrow ribs with pride – 'Jist say the wurd, man.'

Pat winks – 'Sound, Davy, sound. Gie it a cuppla weeks an al get ye aw sortit oot. Wit aboot yer missus?' he asks.

Davy laughs – 'Wee Ina? R'ye kiddin, man? Catholic's Pat, canny tell thum anythin,' he declares – 'Wantey confess every fuckin hing, man.'

Pat signals the barman – 'Right, Davy. Tell hur nuthin, okay? The less she knows the better. Wumin, eh?' he grins – 'Canny keep thur mooths shut.'

Davy's bursting with pride: the barman looks at him with a new respect as he's given instructions – 'Davy's a lager. Nuthin fur me, an listen. Run Davy a tab oan the bar fae the day an square um up wi kit,' Pat orders, looking at his watch – 'S'that the right time? Phone Derek, tell um tae come roon. Am leavin in a minute.'

The barman nods – 'Aye, Pat. Right, Pat, phone Derek an a lager? Right, Pat, s'nae bother.'

Davy escorts Pat outside a few minutes later – 'Thanks, Pat. Al noa let ye doon,' he promises – 'Am a good grafter, Pat.'

The BMW is parked at the kerb: the sleek black door is

open, waiting for the owner to step inside – 'Okay, Davy. Keep yer ears open an yer mooth shut an ye'll dae okay. Al be in touch, an here,' he says, palming him a bung – 'Stick that in yer tail wee man an mind noo, don't get greedy.'

Davy's delirious with self-importance: his jawbone clenches as he watches his 'gaffer' slip into the passenger seat. He pockets the wad of banknotes – 'Fuck me, man,' he mutters – 'Fuck me, man. Am wanney the boys.'

John, the barman, disappears down into the cellar before palming a bag to Davy – 'OK, Davy? A lager, Davy? Bring it right o'er, Davy,' he nods – 'Two seconds.'

Davy drums his fingers on the polished surface of the table – 'Sound man, sound,' he mutters – 'Fuck me. The heavy team, man. Am wurkin fur Pat McGowan. Pat fuckin McGowan.'

Kitty arrives at her daughter's around seven o'clock – 'Sorry am late. S'yer faithur's eh, it's es anniversary, hen.'

Angelena's confused for a moment – 'Anniversary? Widdy ye mean, Ma?'

Kitty blows her nose into a handkerchief – 'Well. It's thirteen years the day since that bastard murdured yer Da. Av been up at the cemetery aw day. S'terrible so it is, that bastard's still walkin aboot tae. S'aw wrang ye know,' she sniffles.

Angelena chops up a line: her mother's obviously upset, but there's no point in going over and over it – 'Aw, c'mon Ma, s'awright. Here, take that, try noa tae think aboot it. A know it's noa easy,' she sighs – 'A mean, a miss ma Da as well. That bastard'll cop it wan day. Jist you wait n see. Rab'll put a contract on um.'

Kitty wipes tears from her eyes, fingering the gold wedding band, hidden almost amid the gold sovereigns adorning her nicotine-stained fingers – 'A know, hen, but a canny help thinkin aboot it wi that murderin bastard in the papers every week. That Special Unit's aw wrang, so it is,' she sniffles – 'Treatin thum like celebrities tae an gien thum televisions. S'noa right. Yer faithur never hermed a fly in es life. Ma John wis a hard-wurkin man.'

Angelena, too, feels the tears well up in her eyes: her father, murdered, tortured by money lenders – for a measly tenner. The memories flood back now; having to help her mother through the trauma afterwards. Her mother's in the right of course; that murderer with his sculpture, and having the neck to publish a book claiming innocence. Her mother knew the truth: her husband nailed to the floor, forced to watch them raping her before they killed him in cold blood. How could she forget the aftermath: those nightmares suffered by her mother, screaming as she relived the terrible visions of her husband being castrated and seeing his balls forced down his throat. God, she shudders – 'Ma,' she says, handing her mother the snorter – 'Here, Robert left that fur ye, so take it the noo. Thur's a bit tae take hame wi ye as well, get ye a sleep. Listen thuv left ye a few quid, so ye takin me doon the toon? Go fur a curry ur sumthin? S'your turn, hen,' she smiles.

Kitty's smile is feeble, but the heroin breaks the image of the painful memories: nerve endings melt into a warm glow – 'S'terrible, eh? Sixty-five n takin drugs,' she cackles as the heroin disappears – 'Oor John wid go mad if ey knew. Oh, God, it's quite strong intit? Aye. A wee bit'll put me tae sleep the night. V'no been sleepin well at aw the noo, thinkin aboot yer Da,' she sighs – 'Aw the laughs wi hud thegither. Oh, hen, dae ye mind that time wi took you tae Cyprus? Ad got drunk an left ye oan the beach. Yer Da gaun mad? An me steamin!'

She laughs – 'Oh, yer Da wis a good laugh, so ey wis, knew how tae huv fun wi people. Oh, an ey cood tell ye stories tae, ye know. He knew aw the real gangsters, so ey did. Aye. Knew Reggie Kray, so ey did.'

Angelena's smiling, remembering; her father, lifting her onto his knee, laughing – 'Av still goat the photies fae that holiday. Look, Ma, that wis the gold chain ey bought me in Cyprus. Mind ey it?' she asks, fingering the gold bracelet – 'Al always keep it, Ma,' she promises.

Kitty's blinking slowly, nodding off as her daughter's voice soothes her troubled heart, feeling the pulse of her body beside her. Angelena and Divina, her two lovely lassies. Her two angels, they were everything; her past, her future, her whole life – 'Aye, hen, aye,' she mumbles gently as two little girls in white dresses float up before her mind's eye – 'Aye, hen, aye. S'yer Holy Communion the day. Ye's look lovely tae.'

A rush of energy brings her back, lifts her mascara'd lids to find her oldest girl staring at her with those beautiful pale blue eyes – 'Oh. Hullo, hen,' she smiles.

Angelena takes her hand – 'Ye okay, Ma?' she asks – 'Gouchin away there, eh. C'mon, wull hit the toon. Get fucked up eh an enjoy wurselves.'

Kitty chuckles – 'Yer a good lassie, so ye ur, hen. God, this stuff eh, it makes everythin disappear, dintit? Okay then, c'mon wull go doon the toon. Am aw fulla energy again. Wit a relief jist tae furget fur a wee while eh, hen?'

Angelena pulls on her leather coat – 'Aye, Ma. A like it fur ma bed. But oor Divina's a pain in the arse aboot it,' she moans – 'Och, she's oan ma case aw the time callin me a junky. V'goat tae laugh tae, hint ye?' she sniggers – 'Hur an that bampot ey a man ey hurs, stuck in frontey the telly every night eatin sweeties? Don't tell ur anyway cos she jist geez me a sore fuckin heid.'

Kitty looks at her daughter knowingly – 'Oh, Christ! Ye kiddin? She'd go mad!' she giggles – 'Aw she means well, hen, but a know wit ye mean.'

Angelena humphs, opening the front door – 'A know, but fur fucksake, Ma. She wis up last week gien me sore heid aboot puntin. A mean, Rab's good tae that Tony. But oh naw, she never complains aboot takin the money, dis she? Wit's she all about?'

Kitty shrugs – 'Och, a don't know. Robert's a good boy, so ey is. Pity that man ey hurs didny get up aff es arse an earn some money. Least Robert an John are oot tryin thur best. Noa like that Tony. Aw ey talks aboot is socialism n politics.' She giggles – 'Yer faithur always said thur wis sumthin wrang wi um. That Robert n John tae, callin um Josuph Stallin. They two up tae the day, anyway?' she asks.

Angelena pushes her into the waiting cab at the close – 'Away daen a wee message, wee bitta business,' she whispers – 'Ye know they two, Ma.'

The driver adjusts the rear-view mirror – 'Yes ladies? The toon? Bitta late shoppin? Oot spendin yer man's wages, eh?' he jokes – 'Aye, yous wumin, eh.'

The passengers laugh too – 'Aye. That'll be right. That's your tip away, by the way!' Angelena laughs – 'Wit a cheek, eh? Noa that when ye aw want yer suppers, eh?'

They pass several police cars – 'So-orry, girls! Only kiddin there. Helluva lotta polis the night, eh? Heard sumthin aboot a fire up this way somewhere,' he says.

Angelena and Kitty look around too – 'Aye, a jist missed

it oan the news. A fire up the road ur sumthin. Anyway. Right Maw, where dae ye fancy?'

Kitty nudges her daughter – 'Mani's? A like it in there. Thur nice tae ye as well. Wull see aw the gangsters tae,' she grins – 'Eh, Mani's, driver. S'Glesga Cross. Aye, it's an Indian. Ye been there yersel?' she asks.

The driver grins into the rear-view mirror – 'Mani's? Aw c'mon, hen. Ye kiddin? Thuv the best curry in Glesga. Aw pure gentlemen in there.'

Angelena takes her mothers arm, snuggling into her – 'Aye. Mani's, then. C'mon, wull huv a right good night. Rab an John won't be back tae late anyway. Might as well get oot while wuv got the chance, eh Ma?'

Kitty feels the warmth of her daughter's body seep into her – 'Aye, hen, eh. A jist wish a could, och well, nevermind. Aye, Mani's. Handsome, so ey is, that boy.'

Chapter Three

DEREK, PAT'S DRIVER, slams his foot down on another stretch of road – 'S'happenin en? S'it hame?' he asks as they pass Barlinnie Prison – 'How'd Davy get on by the way?'

Pat looks out of the window – 'Aye, nae problem. Done the statements. That Woods mob took aff aboot an hoor ago. Be away tae thur wee secret lock up, eh? S'if naibdy knows. Woods say anythin last night?' he enquires.

Derek frowns, recalling the deal – 'Naw. Wee Mick telt um we'd aw fell oot. Said thit ey wis gaun o'er tae Belfast. Naw, Pat, ey definitely didny tipple. Stull due a cuppla grand, but eh, a don't see that happenin, dae you?' he sniggers.

They both laugh – 'Ey kin always pay it aff es canteen,' Derek cracks, nodding toward the notorious jail – 'Tell um tae send oot es wages, the cunt!' He pounds his big ham-fist on the steering wheel – 'Aye! Fuck! Ey'd probably stull owe us money by the time ey got parole!' he roars.

He's still curious – 'Sure Davy telt the coppers? Aye? Aw, well en. Be bran new if ed chuck the smack, es a good wee grafter, so ey is,' he concedes.

Pat agrees but it's winter in that black heart – 'Aye, Derek, the statement's done. The Johnstones, eh, wantey be gangsters. N'got thur fingers burnt,' he sniggers – 'Aye, aw the gangsters, eh. But Davy? S'a loose end, big yin.'

They lapse into silence: after thirty years of graft together they feel totally comfortable with silences, thirty years of petty crime, gangs and dope, and now – arson. They had no secrets.

Pat had married Derek's sister, Janis. Laura and Zoe, their two teenage daughters, were at private school but knew the score about their father: they'd visited enough jails to understand.

'Cut o'er tae the Victoria Club, Derek. Wull stay visible the next few days. Get a laugh wi aw these auld fuckin wumin up there. The Heavy Mob, eh. The Armani Connection!' he sneers – 'Fucksake, eh. Aw they daft wee burds hingin oan tae thur erms tae. The gangsters. Fuckin embarrassin. The God Blethurs. Cosa fuckin Nostra,' he continues – 'M'gonny tobur thum up. Times've changed. Aw past thur sell-by dates.'

Derek glances at his partner: he knows he's deadly serious – 'Fuckin bampots. Kiddin thurselves on. Ad plug every fuckin wanney thum,' he shouts – 'Wan right in the heid. BA-ANG! BA-ANG! BA-ANG!' he roars out the window, popping pedestrians – 'PO-W! Aw, sorry er, missus! S'awright, hen, yer only wounded!' he laughs, blaring the horn at stunned pedestrians – 'Terrible, so it is. Bloody drug dealers!'

Rab and John are about finished cutting the smack – 'Fuck, Rab! S'that the time? At's hauf twelve man. C'mon, am gaun doon the toon the night.'

Rab looks at the pile of bags – 'Dae fur the night. Dae the urra kilo the morra. Righto, time tae head up the road. Angelena's heid'll be nippin, bet there's been cunts at the door aw night,' he sighs – 'Need tae get anurra hoose fur graftin ootey.'

John laughs – 'Aw strung oot tae. Hope Johnstone's nae gear. If thuv aw fell oot thur fucked fur puttin stuff oot,' he says – 'N'wee Mick won't take any shite affey any thum. S'a gem wee cunt, ye know. Anyway, c'mon. A wantey get changed an back doon the toon.'

Rab nods, scooping the huge piles of bags of heroin into a hold-all – 'John, stick that message in the boot,' he says, pointing to a corner.

John turns, lifting a sawn-off pump-action rifle – 'Bang bang bang. Caught ye, eh. Am seein a guy next week, by the way, cuppla haun guns,' he says – 'That thing jams aw the time. Saw a .357 Magnum, by the way. S'a fuckin cannon, man.'

Rab's listening but checking they've got everything – 'Aye, right. Think that's us, eh?' he asks – 'Ye got everythin? Better wi a Glock – s'a good haun-gun, never jams.'

John's looking around too, stuffing the gun into the bag – 'Aye, Rab, let's go. Ye wanta break? Me drive?' he asks, but his older brother just smiles – 'You? Ye aff yer fuckin heid? *Whacky Races* wi you ya cunt. Fuckin coppers wid pull us fore wi hut the M8!' he laughs – 'Nae fuckin danjur!'

John's feeling good – 'Aw, c'mon, man. M'no that bad. Promise, al take it easy. You're tired man. C'mon eh, wan wee shot up the road. Be nae coppers aboot at this time,' he pleads.

Rab's insistent – 'Nae fuckin danjur! Right, c'mon. Naw John, yer not on. A jist don't want a pull wi the bizzies. Ye kin take the motur doon the toon wi ye, okay?'

John rubs his hands together – 'Yer a diamond, big yin. M'nippin a wee burd so al be careful, okay? Anyway, am noa that bad a driver. The bizzies, man. When did ye start worryin aboot they cunts? This Angelena again?' he taunts.

Rab ignores the dig about his relationship – 'Naw. Jist bein careful son. Angelena's a good burd by the way. We might huva wean, wur jist noa sure yet.'

John laughs – 'Fuckin knew it! Fuckin real yin! A wean? Wit aboot me? That me oot the hoose? You an hur daen yer

Wee Hoose n the Prairie? Aye eh, fuckin smelt it. Al bet ye she's been bendin yer ear, eh? Aw that shite aboot the mess, eh. Yer under the thumb, son! A told ye!'

R ab pulls the garage door down behind them as they're leaving – 'Och, turn it up! Yer fuckin heavy man so ye ur. V'no planned nuthin yet so calm doon!' he laughs.

John shrugs his shoulders, getting into the car – 'Aye, very good. No planned nuthin yet,' he mimics – 'Think am a bam? calm doon, eh. S'it a jelly baby?'

Rab switches on the ignition – 'Well, it's jist a thought . . . be you an uncle,' he sniggers.

John stomps his feet – 'Aw, nae mer, man! An uncle! Fucksake, man!'

They roar off, singing and howling into the night – 'Baby Luv! Ma Baby Love!'

They're still singing as they reach the front close – 'Right, John. Al take the bag up an you keep that message ready, jist in case,' instructs the elder brother – 'Sum ey these cunts wid rob thur grannies fur a fuckin hit.'

John stays at his brother's back, the gun inside his open jacket – 'S'helluva quiet, innit? Thought thur widda been a queue ootside the close,' he says – 'S'late right nuff, innit? Hope that urra mob huvnae fucked us up. S'at you, y'ready en Rab?' he asks, looking around – 'Right. Nae cunt aboot, right, on ye go.'

Rab looks straight ahead as they fire up the close – 'C'mon, John. S'cool. Nae cunt at thur windaes either.' he murmurs – 'S'quiet right annuff, eh.'

Cold, authoritative eyes observe their every move – 'Two suspects have arrived. Two male. Over and out,' a voice crackles over a radio channel.

'Remain in position. Over and out,' replies the second voice — 'Command control. Repeat. Remain in position. Over and out.'

Rab and John's movements are being monitored by a whole network of coordinated wires set up around their building. Curtains twitch in the dark deserted street, but not a soul is to be seen — it's late, but not *that* late.

Detective Sergeant Ron 'The Hammer' McGhee first sees a taxi turning into the street and opens the lines of his radio — 'Attention. Remain in position. Two females in black taxi. Angelena Woods and an unknown person have arrived. Prepare to move. Remain in position. Steady now. Prepare to. Right! GO! GO! GO!'

Angelena's still hanging their coats as the front door comes in — BA-ANG! Straight off at the hinges; the door crashes down on top of her, pinning her body to the floor. She is barely breathing — 'DON'T MOVE! DON'T MOVE! STILL! STAY STILL!'

She's handcuffed behind her back and on her way to a local police station before she regains consciousness — 'RAB! RAB! OH, FUCK! RA-ABB!'

Rab barely downs the bag before an old familiar terror grips his insides, freeze-framing him between the noise recognition and moving — fast. He's unable to pull his thoughts out of the irrational — 'Who furgot tae lock the door?'

Steel bites into his wrists as a voice suddenly roars — 'STILL! STILL! DON'T MO-VE!' Kitty is being lifted in a bundle; black knickers flash before his eyes, thick pubic hair pushes through a tiny tear at the seam. His mother-in-law's bush is still registering in his brain when the voice screams — 'STILL! DON'T!' — BANG!

The sound is of a watermelon exploding as soundwave meets matter – SPLAT! Someone groans; a long sigh follows, and then there is complete silence for what seems an eternity.

'MOVE THEM OUT! MOVE THEM OUT!' voices bark.

Rab's head's forced down as he's dragged upward by the wrists: a training shoe catches his eye, the lace is undone – the foot is not moving. He tries to call out to his brother but his brother can't hear him, his brother can't hear anything, he's long gone. The Boom Boom Boys have taken him out – one in the head. John's final thought has no end; the lightning beam flashing through his skull leaves life behind as steel penetrates the eye socket, travelling at a hundred miles an hour – BANG!

The sudden exit leaves the bullet lodged in that scarlet border; blood and grey matter decorate the rich gold pattern.

Tabloid headlines make it clear where they stand, put public feelings into perspective.

ONE DOWN! TWO TO GO!
HANGING TOO GOOD!
DEALERS IN DEATH! BRING BACK THE NOOSE!

There will always be the questions. Was he going for the gun? Rab knew his brother, he wasn't crazy. The coppers later claimed that they saw his hand reach for the gun. Who knows? Maybe he had just grown up, perhaps it was the lace he reached for? Maybe not. One thing that was definite. A dead brother negates the possibility of corroboration in any alibi. Dealing guaranteed an average ten-stretch without parole: six-and-a-half years and it's done, no big deal, but six murders?

Rab Woods is in trouble. Traumatised beyond all recognition, his psychological frame falls back in on him. The disfiguration kills all emotion, leaving a gaping hole staring at four yellow walls on the bottom landing of C/hall.

'R'you stull here?' a voice asks, as an eye appears in the middle of the steel door – 'You're a fuckin monster. That's aw you are, son. Away n join yer bruthur in hell.'

Barlinnie Prison has strict policy on suicide observation, but today they're making the exception. Rab stares at the rope lying on the floor, but he can't do it. Under present circumstances it would be a valid option, but he didn't kill those people.

'Right! Get up! Move! Surgery!' a voice shouts as the door slams back – 'Up! Fuckin move!' it's shouting – 'C'mon! Surgery! Doctor tae see ye!'

Rab staggers to his feet; the voice drops to a whisper in his ear – 'Jist you fuckin wait. Jist you fuckin wait,' it says as the source pushes him into the direction of a prisoner. Piss stings his eyes as the contents of a pot are thrown in his face, he smells the shite in his nostrils before he hits the deck with a broken jaw.

'Musta fell boss, eh?' a voice laughs.

Rab regains consciousness in the hospital wing; observation here is around the clock until he is fully committed for trial. The white smock and plastic slippers he's wearing are splattered in blood.

'Fish tank tae the doctur sees um,' someone is explaining.

'S'that him?' another asks.

'Aye. Fuckin monstur,' is the reply.

A television blares through the main ward, but he can't hear it, the sound muted by an extraordinary thick glass wall. Rab can only stare at the screen as the viewers lounging in pyjamas stare back at him. The cut-throat gestures inform him of future intent, but the sudden appearance of his mug-shot on screen brings home the significance of the day's brutality – the funerals of the Johnstones.

Out in the main ward the voice of a news reporter informs the captive audience of the depth of feeling within the local community – 'A community is in mourning today as they bury a family brutally murdered in their homes. Among the dead was eighteen-month-old baby, Tara Johnstone.'

A voice from the news desk breaks through – 'Mark. What are the feelings of people? It's understood that two people have been questioned and charged by the police. Are there any further developments concerning the shooting that occurred during those arrests?'

The Hammer's face fills the screen as a microphone is thrust under his square jaw. The reporter fills in the gaps – 'Yes, Shareen, indeed. It's understood that the two people questioned about the fire have since been charged. D.S. Ron McGhee is with me now.'

Big Ron's statement is filled with all the appropriate solemnity usually reserved for bomb tragedies – 'Today the, the Garngad community is in shock,' he says, pausing, gulping for effect – 'Aherm, ah-erm, he-rm, herm, hrmm.' Composed once more, he resumes – 'Today, at six hundred hours, the police questioned and charged two suspects with the brutal murders of the family of Agnes and Thomas Johnstone. Among the dead, ah-erm, the body of an eighteen-month-old baby was discovered.'

The hardened cop fights back those tears – 'Today, Robert and Angelena Woods were charged with the murders. Unfortunately, during the arrests of four armed suspects, one man was shot dead by police. A report will be submitted in due course to the procurator fiscal. As the officer in charge of the case there is nothing more I can add at this point in time. Our thoughts, as one can appreciate, must lie with the surviving relatives of this terrible tragedy.'

The reporter's face reappears – 'Mark Geissler. Back to you at the studio.'

The news desk anchor-woman shuffles papers around as she appears on screen with another backdrop depicting a riot – 'Thank you, Mark. And now for today's other news. Today police were gathering evidence as they began their enquiries into the fatal stabbing of police constable John Blackwell. The constable, who was married with three children, was killed during last night's rioting on the Broadwater Farm Estate in London. The recent months of tension erupted into violence after police denied allegations of a 'cover up' in the enquiry into the death of black activist Cynthia Jarott. Mike Edwards joins us live at the estate. Mike?'

Mike Edwards pauses for a moment before answering – 'Shareen. The mood here today is tense as police begin their enquiries into last night's tragedy. The Broadwater Farm riot has been described by police as the greatest threat to social order since the Fifties and the nuclear bomb. The Metropolitan Police claim that due to a lack of manpower they were ill-prepared and unable to deal with the rioting that resulted in one police officer being slashed and another being killed. With me now is spokesman Alex Marnoch of Special Patrol Group. Mr Marnoch, can you tell us what happened?'

* * *

Fingernails drum on a table top as jaws around the bar hang open, their owners listening intently to the news reports. No one is pays any attention to the drumming noise.

'Jesus, God. Six people dead? They should bring back hanging.' someone says.

'Aye. That would sort the lot of them out,' another agrees, but not all.

'Hm. Gernged? S'thet some old housing scheme?' asks an older, more eloquent voice – 'Tregic, tregic for the families. Henging, however, doesn't necesserily work old chep, not in ey civileysed society.'

Nothing like burnt remains to keep an audience glued to television screens – 'Thet poor child, burnt.' The British public have become accustomed to the occasional cop-killing, nothing new in that these days – 'Probebly overkim by smoke inheletion, the poor little blighter. Such ey tregidy.'

Pat clocks the pastel colour scheme propping up the brandies and half-pints of lager, spread along the mahogany. Marks and Sparks, he smiles. His plain black suit looks like a blot on the pinkish clothes-scape as red-veined noses snort in agreement over the community in mourning.

'Tregic. Forced to live like thet, like wild enimels.'

Pat adjusts the tape-recorder under his jacket; the background music floats gently into oblivious ears, but causes no interference with the machine – perfect. He rewinds the tape, and waits – 'S'keepin this cunt?'

The Hammer's pale blue jumper hangs loosely over those khaki polyester trousers but that fifty-year bulge struggles against gravity with every step. He's sweating profusely as he enters the bar – 'Drink, Paddy? Sorry am late, bloody journalists.'

Pat pushes the nearest chair out – 'Naw. Aye, saw ye oan

the telly there.' He watches the copper down a double whisky at the bar; the record button clicks, just as the cop heaves his body into the vacant chair.

'The news? Oh?' he wheezes – 'Oh aye, n that traffic. Nice wee place, eh?'

Pat pretends interest, glancing around – 'Aye, s'awright. Long ye drank here? S'ita coppers pitch?' he asks.

Ron downs the double – 'God, a needed that. Th-is place? Naw, ye kiddin? Bad enough huvin tae work wi thum,' he laughs.

Pat leans across and gives him an affectionate nudge – 'Big Ron McGhee. Wi'wid we dae withoot ye, big man, eh?'

Big Ron looks over a shoulder – 'Oh a noa. W-ell Paddy, the money's good, eh. Know wit a mean,' he winks – 'Right, listen, doon ey business. Kitty's been tossed, made a statement. She's nae problem, wee bitta verbal an that. Panicked, she won't change ur statement at the trial. Davy's the problem, ye sure ey him? Seemed awful panicky at the station.'

Pat avoids implicating himself – 'Auld Kitty? Slung? S'that right she's fulla smack tae? Jesus, yer ain Maw oan smack? S'it aw comin tae, eh?' he says, shaking his head in apparent disgust – 'Don't worry aboot the rest. Happened tae the bruther, by the way? Go fur es gun?' he asks, laughing – 'Beat tae the draw?'

Big Ron rolls his eyes at the ceiling – 'Jesus, wit a sight. The shooter wis lyin oan the table. The Rab wans frozen, canny move, the face's chalk white tae. The burd hud mer bottle. Honest. Kicked an screamed the whole fuckin way! But that daft brother?' he laughs – 'Firearm teams take nae prisoners! Jesus! That John wan moved, jist a fraction. Bang! Es brains aw o'er the place.' He leans over – 'Ma division told the firearm team that they were tae be on thur toes fur trouble. Next thing, bang! Coodny fuckin believe it. Right through the eye as well, instant skylight n the back ey es heid.'

Pat sips his Coke – 'The Rab wan, s'happenin wi him? Caved in yet? Heard es oan protection. Gangsturs fur ye, eh? Anyway, listen. A canny stay long the day. We kin meet up efter the trial,' he winks – 'V'got a bank lined up fur ye. Al put four guys oan it an gie ye the wire nearer the time. Here Ron, there's five grand, ye earned it. S'happenin wi the promotion, by the way?'

Big Ron palms the bundle into his wallet – 'Oh, nuthin yet, but we-ll, expect thull wait tae efter the trial. A bank?' he smiles, raising his eyebrows – 'Hmmm. Thur's a pal ey mine as well, jist needin a wee turn. Al introduce ye an ye kin sort sumthin oot wi um. A trustworthy guy, fifteen years n the force. Never opened es mouth wance,' he says, frowning – 'Wis a pity aboot the wean, but that's the way things go, probably a turned oot like the faithur anyway. Aye well, maybe it'll be Inspector next time a see ye, eh? Right, listen then, gie me a buzz in a cuppla weeks.'

Pat gets up to leave – 'Sound, big man, sound. N'listen, by the way. Mick Rosinni's in daen the Garngad. S'ma gear. The Garngad's mine noo,' he states – 'N'Wee Davy'll be daen a bit, so gie um a clear run, n don't worry, es sound.'

Big Ron takes his hand as they part ways – 'Right, Paddy, nae problem. Okay, n'al see ye inna cuppla weeks. N'make sure that wee yin shows up fur the trial.'

Pat smiles – 'Aye, sound. N'listen Ron, dae me a favour wul ye, cut oot aw this Paddy. Sounds like sum bampot. S'Pat, Pat McGowan. A hate bein called Paddy.'

Big Ron laughs as he orders another drink – 'Right,

Pat. Double, son. Naw, nae ice.' he calls to the barman – 'S'right, nae ice.' He feels the bundle of notes in his pocket as he watches the black suit disappear through the doors – 'Toe-rag,' he mutters, as he picks up his drink – 'Think ey'd buy a decent suit wi the kinna money he's makin.'

Pat grins as he slides into the car – *'Right, Pat. Double, son. Naw, nae ice.'* Click. He throws the tape-recorder to the driver – 'Right, Derek, deposit box wi that.' He's so pleased with himself – 'Derek, d'ye fancy a holiday? Take Janis n the weans? Kin be back fur the trial. Everythin's tied up noo anyway, so. Take a wee break wi the faimly?' he repeats – 'Aye, get tickets sorted oot, nae point sittin aboot waitin.'

Derek agrees – 'Aye, Pat. Due a break anyway. Turkey again?'

Pat nods – 'Aye, sound, big yin, sound. Sunshine. Book it fur a cuppla month. Don't think the trial's gonny last that long. Thuv nae alibi, an corroboration puts thum in the frame so thur dun.'

Derek pats the tape on his lap – 'Big McGhee tied up en?'

Pat grins – 'Big Hammer? Up tae es fuckin eyes innit. S'jist Davy.' He examines the tape recorder – 'A camcorder. That's wit we need noo. McGhee's got anurra copper fur us,' he explains – 'Wull gie thum that bank as soon as this trial's finished.'

He thinks to himself for a moment – 'Derek. Who's due oot the jail? Shood try'n get a lifer fur the bank, thur always desperate fur money, int they? Anyway, keep yer ears open fur wanney thum gettin oot,' he says – 'Jist get this trial oot the way, an en wi really start spreadin wur wings.'

Derek nods – 'Aye, nae bother. Wee Davy'll be bran new. Big McGhee eh, big fuckin prick,' he grumbles – 'Ad luv tae put wan in es fuckin heid.'

Chapter Four

WEE DAVY'S RELIEVED the trial is finally over; all those months of worrying – but six life sentences? Angelena didn't take that too well, screeching at him – 'GRASSSSSSSS!' He could still hear her screeching throughout his evidence – 'GRASSSSSSSSSSSSSS!' Auld Kitty stuck them in too. All he'd said was that he'd heard them talking in the pub the night before the fire. Fuck, Kitty backed the coppers' story. A grass? Davy had to laugh, a grass? This was the Eighties! Who gives a fuck? She'll get parole. That Rab though, fainting in the dock? Imagine that! Fainting, for fucksake? He'd have spat in the judge's face if they'd given him six consecutive life sentences. What did you have to lose? Parole? No, he'd have taken it like a man, spat right in their fucking faces. Fainting like some first offender. What an embarrassment, the prick. Deserves all he gets after that performance. Well, that's it, it's all over. A fortnight and no one will remember anything. Rab Who?

Davy brushes down his brand-new black shellsuit. All he wanted now was a pint and a wee thingmy-jag. All that talking, going over and over the same fuckin thing. Their defence counsel had dragged him across the coals, calling him an addict. So how did he know that? Grasses? Who did those two think they were kidding? He's desperate for a pint but looks at his new expensive watch first – 'Na, better noa. Pat'll smell it, too wide. Get wan efter av seen um,' he mutters to himself.

Pat had smiled faintly at him from the public gallery –

'Sound, Davy. Sound, wee man,' he'd seemed to say – 'Sound, wee man.' He'll be pleased to see him – 'M'wanney the boys, noo,' he smiles – 'Wanney McGowan's Mob.'

The Wee Glen's packed but no one is at the table. Davy looks around – 'John! S'Pat been in?' he shouts to the barman. He feels eyes upon him, but nobody says a word. Davy's one of the boys now – 'Here, c'mon, move. Ha-uw, fuc-kin move tae a get in there,' he snarls, as the barman waves him over.

John whispers in his ear. It's a message from his gaffer – 'Wit? Right, right,' he's nodding – 'Right, John!' he calls over the general noise, making sure everyone hears him – 'JOHN! TELL INA AM DAEN A MESSAGE FUR PAT! WI-IT? MEETIN PAT! WI-IT? AYE, RIGHT, GET ME A CAB!'

John nods – 'RIGHT, DAVY! S'OAN ITS WAY, DAVY!'

Davy swaggers through the front door to wait for the taxi – 'Sound, big yin, sound,' he mutters to himself as a car pulls slowly up to the kerb.

'R'you Davy Wilson, pal?' asks the drives.

'Aye, Davy, that's me, son,' he replies getting into the back – 'Pat tell ye where wur meeting um?' he asks.

Davy doesn't hear the reply; the first bullet penetrates his cheekbone and exits from what was once an ear. The second bullet breaks through his teeth, before ricocheting upward, leaving the back of his skull like a sunroof. The silencer jams, but there is no hurry. The driver drags the body from his car, and slams it against the wall of the pub before pumping the four remaining bullets into the back.

'It's Johnny, by the way. Here. Message fae Pat,' he laughs.

Pop! Pop! Two in the head! Sound. Pop! Pop! Pop! Pop! Four in the back! Sound, wee man!

Johnny later strips the protective bin-liners and Sellotape from his arms, and throws them all into the car — 'Guy's face,' he thinks, torching the old banger — 'Es fuckin jaw wis stull yappin as well.' He sniggers, checking his hands for any powder burns — 'Right, that's it. See Derek an hame. Guy's face, man,' he chuckles.

Angelena's staring at the ceiling in her cell; her mind is beginning to recover from the shock. Thoughts tentatively tiptoe back into reality; flashes of the funeral and the trial begin falling into a more coherent sequence of events. The appeal against conviction holds little hope for her in the face of the publicity. They're not going to waste energy on their case after all the coverage about being heroin dealers. Who is going to care about a possible miscarriage of justice? This is Britain. Anyway, they were dealing in heroin. This will always be the argument against retrial — 'Wit umma gonny dae?' she wonders.

Rational thinking; it's her only way out of the nightmare. The confused images are connecting — 'God. Oor John,' she thinks — 'Murdured.' She can still see his coffin — 'Poor Rab tae, fucked up,' she remembers — 'Greetin es eyes oot. Jesus,' she cries — 'Wit a fuckin mess.'

The funeral was a relatively quiet affair by comparison to the communal watershed of the previous mass dig; a family affair but with half of the police force grafting bonanza bonus pay under the guise of high security, all forty of them — 'Fuckin sick bastards.' Those prison warders too; fighting for endless overtime — 'Fuckin animals.' They've more potential than North Sea Oil. Sweat money. That's all it is, she thinks. The graveside mobbed too; there was more security there than in

Northern Ireland – 'Did Divina believe me?' she asks herself as the lights are dimmed – 'She's ma only hope fur the truth.'

Ina's screaming outside the Wee Glen – 'GET A FUCKIN AMBULANCE! PLEASE! O-HH PLEASE! SUMBUDY GET A FUCKIN AMBULANCE! ES STULL BREATHIN!'

Davy's breathing is faint but he's survived six bullets, for the moment anyway – 'Get a priest . . .' he's mumbling through bubbles of blood – 'Priest, Ina. Priest . . .'

The parish medicine man arrives before the ambulance; he prepares the last rites for Davy there and then – 'Quiet, my son, quiet,' he whispers – 'Do you renounce your sins before God?' he asks, while making signs of the cross – 'I now absolve you of sin. In the name of the Father, the Son and of the Holy Ghost.'

Davy's gurgling throughout the sign language – 'Lies. Told lies, lies, Father,' he tries to explain, but too late – 'M'sorry, Father. Lies . . . Murdur trial . . .'

Ina's on her knees beside him, completely numb; her husband is now in the past, his conscience clear but unheard in the night.

No one is listening but the medicine man and a young widow. Gunshot sounds aren't exactly an invitation to see what is going on outside a bar; the television seems louder than before.

'Yeees! A told ye that wis the answer!' someone roars – 'A cooda won that fuckin motur!'

The 'Shooda Known Better' look on Davy's face is permanent, fixed forever with the clear message – 'Just Say No-Thing.' No one will pursue his death; having perjured himself to become a major face, he becomes just that – a momentary headline for the punters at the bar before being forgotten. Two people though, will never forget him, nor that claim from the dock – 'A frightnur, that's right, sur.'

Rab's being handcuffed, but has no idea where he's to be taken. He knows not to ask questions.

Six huge warders stand silently watching as he's shackled – 'S'him ready. S'the hall clear? Aye? Right, let's go.'

Inspector McGhee beams as the prisoner is pushed into an interview room – 'There es there! Robert, son! How ye daen, then? They treatin ye awright, kid?' he bellows.

Rab's stunned. *Son?* He takes a seat – 'Bran new. Widdy you want?' he demands to know – 'Ye up tae gloat? You fuckin fitted me up, ya cunt.'

Big Ron nods to the warders – 'S'awright. Noa be any trouble, wull ye, Robert? A wee cuppa tea then? Naw? Aw, well,' he smiles.

Rab almost falls off his chair when the copper gets to the crunch – 'Wee Wulson. D'ye know enathin? Might help yer situation if ye come clean?' he asks.

Murdered? Rab doesn't believe it. Shot six times? Brilliant, he thinks. Wee Davy, eh. Peaced off. Fucking brilliant. He can still see him – pointing the finger straight at him. He'll never understand why, but the evidence still rang in his ears – 'A frightnur, that's right, sur.'

Rab could remember every detail of the trial; the jury, horrified by the photographs of the charred remains of the baby, people hissing and spitting from the public gallery, a voice screaming as they are sentenced; buried alive, up to their necks in concrete for life, by one perjured statement – 'A frightnur, that's right, sur.'

GRASSSSSS! GRASSSSSSS! GRASSSSSSS! GRASSSSSSS! GRASSSSSSSS!

Big Ron brings him back again – 'A don't blame ye, son, but if you organised a contract, an admission wid clear oor books withoot too much trouble. A mean, let's face it, yer no gaun anywhere, so?'

Rab remains silent, but the copper prods him, until it hurts – 'Angelena's takin it hard eh,' he grins – 'Oh, well. A suppose thull let ye write tae each other wance it aw dies doon. The methadone's helpin but the lassie needs mer support. S'lotta big dykes in that Cortonvale.'

Angelena and Rab have had no contact since being sentenced, but he knows from his previous prison sentences that there are avenues – 'Here, fuck you, ya'n arsehole. Your mob fitted me up an am gled that wee grass copped it. N'don't send fur me again cos av got fuck all tae say tae any yous cunts,' he sneers – 'N'listen, by the way, am gonny fight ma case tae the end. Am fuckin innacent an you fuckin know it, so don't come up here askin me fur favours, ya prick!'

Big Ron signals the warders – 'Oh, well then, thought ye mighta wanted tae dae yersel a wee bitta good here,' he sighs, getting up – 'Aye, that's us finished lads.'

Rab's escorted back to his tomb. The sun's rays scorch the retinae of his eyes; the layer of nerve fibres forming the eyeball are over sensitive to light after the long months of solitary confinement, but he manages a chuckle – 'Wee Davy, eh.'

Six life sentences, he thinks. Six fucking life sentences, because of that wee bastard's statement. He felt no pity at the demise of Davy Wilson – 'Hope that wee fucker roasts in hell.'

Chapter Five

PAT'S GLASGOW PALLOR'S gone; he looks tanned, revitalised lounging there on the patio of his sixty-grand bungalow – 'Good tae be back, eh, big yin,' he says, sipping his iced Coke.

Derek, too, is refreshed – 'Aye, but it wis good, eh. Ye need that wee break,' he replies.

Pat leafs briefly through the backlog of tabloids to check the daily pillaging, rape and murder statistics before pondering the broadsheets to assess the stock market – 'Here, Derek. Check this. S'Wee Wulson. Check they photies, man,' he laughs.

The *Daily Record*'s pinned the usual underworld yarn to the shooting incident. Davy's photograph depicts him during his pre-hypodermic life; the face of an altar boy smiles back from the black-and-white picture, accompanied by an appeal from the distraught young widow – 'Ma Davy didnae deserve this. Everybody liked um. A hope the polis find these murdururs.'

Derek laughs too – 'Check they fuckin curls, man! Here, listen tae this shite. Sayin the deceased made a confession, possibly identifyin wan ey the killurs, s'fuckin shite!' he roars – 'A know fur a fact . . .'

Pat casts the paper aside – 'Aye, well. Noa be sayin much noo,' he grins.

Derek agrees – 'S'worth that thurty grand. A hope McGinty tortured that wee prick,' he snarls – 'A confession – pish.'

Janis, Pat's wife, emerges to prepare the barbecue – 'Derek, keep yer voice doon, the weans kin hear ye,' she remarks casually – 'Steak n mushrooms dae ye's the noo?'

Derek looks over his sunglasses – 'Oops. Sorry, furgot there,' he apologises.

Pat barely glances up – 'Aye, plentya mushrooms, hen,' he drawls – 'N'leave plentya blood in ma steak.'

Janis's Armani sequins glitter in the sunlight; the contours of her figure look sculpted in her immaculately cut outfit. She could have been beautiful, but for the indifference in her demeanour; her ash-blonde spiky hairstyle accentuated weary eyes that seemed greyish-blue. At thirty years old she was an enigma; no one knew her exact age, no one dared ask, not even her husband – 'Derek? Well done?' she asks.

Derek timidly nods – 'Aye, eh, any onions instead, hen?' he asks his sister – 'Ye know wit am like wi mushrooms, Janis.'

Janis draws him a look – 'Always got tae be different, eh?'

Derek and Janis had never got on with each other; being the elder of the two he may have had the upper hand in childhood rivalry, but those days were long gone, not that it bothered him. She had her house and the kids. Together, they had joint investments in Pat – 'Creative hen, creative,' he mutters.

Pat interrupts the possibility of bickering – 'Janis, don't bite, hen. Jist gie um a fuckin fryin pan an let um dae es ain onions.'

Derek fans himself with a newspaper – 'Aw, here wi go,' he yawns – 'Where's the two weans by the way?' he asks.

Janis doesn't bat an eyelid – 'Don't waste yer breath, they don't like onions,' she says sarcastically – 'Anyhow, thur vegetarian.'

Pat lies back, enjoying his brother-in-law's discomfort — 'Kin read ye like a book, big yin,' he chuckles.

Derek slaps him with the newspaper as he gets up — 'Ach, yous two cunts. Morticia an that urra bovril. Da! Do! Do! Do! Da! Da-raa! Da! Do! Da! Ra! Da! Ra-raa!' he sings to them, snapping his fingers — Click! Click! — 'Da! Da! Da! Duum! Boom! Boom! Da! Ra! Ra! Ruum! Boom! Boom! The Adams fami-lee!'

Pat and Janis look at each other — 'Creative?'

Janis laughs — 'Told ye, a nutcase.'

Derek waltzes off to find the kids — 'Geez a shout. Mind, don't burn the onions, nippy,' he calls over his shoulder — 'Laura? Zoe? Ye's there, hen?'

Laura and Zoe have been in their den listening to music; they're on their way outside as he's coming in — 'Where's Daddy?' asks the elder of the girls — 'In the garden? Is he finished reading his papers?'

Derek lifts her in his arms — 'Aw, s'ma wee darlins! Laura, pal. How ye doin, pal? Listen. Yer uncle needs a wee favour. Noo, dae yous like onions?'

Laura's blonde pony tail swings from side to side — 'No-o! Where's Daddy? Is he out in the garden?' she repeats.

Derek gives up — 'Ach, you two, paira sooks, so ye ur,' he says pulling a face — 'Aye, es stull readin es papurs. C'mon, wull go oot an annoy um.'

Janis brushes her fingers through her daughter's long blonde hair — 'Hair's needin done again, Laura. Want Mummy tae style it fur ye this time?' she asks affectionately — 'Ye shood get it cut shorter,' she suggests against the usual protests.

'No-ooo Mummy!' Laura shrieks — 'No-ooo! Everybody at school has their hair long!'

Janis mimics her — 'O-ooh! Everybody at school hus thur hair long! Right then, darlin. Get Daddy a Coke fae the fridge. Uncle Derek'll want Irn Bru. Won't ey uncle Derek?' she says — 'Uncle Derek's creative, int ey.'

Zoe leaps to her feet first — 'I'll get them Mummy! A Coke for Mr Cool!' she giggles.

Derek laughs — 'A wit? A Coke fur Mr Cool?'

Pat beams — 'S'right. Mr Cool, innit, hen?' he chuckles — 'Uncle Derek's noa gettin any, sure es noa, darlin!'

Laura drapes herself around her father; she's all over him — 'Daddy, can we go out? Take us somewhere nice? Daddy? Hmmm? Can we? Hmmm?'

Zoe returns with the iced Coke and joins the chorus — 'Yes, Daddy. Can we? Hmmm? Daddy? Hmmm?'

Pat's melting; he loves his two daughters — 'Aye, darlin, sure. Jist let me finish readin ma papurs furst, eh darlin? Five minutes, darlin, wull aw go doon the toon, okay?'

He's putty in their hands, thinks his wife — 'C'mon, let Daddy finish readin. Spoilt rotten, you two. Listen, let yer Daddy get some peace. Dy'es noa fancy the toon wi yer Mummy? Al buy sumthin nice?' she asks.

Laura and Zoe are squealing with delight, but want a family trip — 'Ye-ees! But Daddy too! Oh, come on, Dad.'

Derek puts the petted lip on — 'Uncle Derek noa comin? Nah, leave Daddy n me here. Wuv got lotsa wurk tae dae darlin,' he smiles, pulling a bundle of banknotes from his back pocket — 'Zoe, here darlin. Pick a nice shirt fur me, wull ye? That Laura yin gets the wrang colour aw the time, so she dis. Here, there ye go, darlin.'

Pat looks up from his papers — 'S'awright, Derek. Al take thum doon the toon masel,' he smiles — 'S'nae bother. Gie

Derek that back darlin, probably charge interest rates, ye know wit es like.'

Laura and Zoe didn't need gifts of money; they had bank accounts and always carried at least a grand in their pockets. This wasn't so much to do with values, but to become acclimatised and unafraid of money – 'Never let people impress ye wi money,' they'd been told by their father – 'You'll always huv mer than urra people.'

Janis pats his head – 'Naw, Pat, five minutes n they two'll huv ye demented. Anyway, a might look in at the shop, see wit's been happenin. See how that new stylist's gettin oan. Jist you sit an read yer papurs – Mr Cool.'

Pat chuckles – 'Aye, eh. Mr Cool.'

Janis's Mercedes sports car crunches slowly down the gravel path – 'Pat! Al be back aboot hauf six okay!' she waves – 'Right cheerio!'

'Cheerio, Daddy!'

Derek pretends the huff – 'Wit aboot me? S'noa fair!' he roars. Laura and Zoe love it when he teases them.

'Uncle Derek!' they laugh, sticking up two fingers – 'Bye-eee!'

Pat picks up his paper – 'That bank sortit?' he asks – 'Meetin they coppers later oan the night, mind.'

Derek's still waving – 'Aye, s'aw set up,' he replies – 'Cheerio, darlin!'

Janis looks back in the rear-view mirror; her two daughters are waving, they really do love their father – 'C'mon girls, settle down,' she says – 'Laura! C'mon, noo! Don't get wide noo.'

Mr Cool right enough, she thinks. Jeez, if they only knew. Still, there were no phoney pretentions with him about what he might be. Patrick, she knew, was a thug: his philosophy, bleak but simple and effective – anything goes. He disregarded all the old criminal codes as weakness – 'Thur jist copyin the upper classes,' he'd once said to her – 'N'things huv changed.'

A bone of contention was his obsession with anonymity, refusing to buy any new suits or anything else which might draw unwanted attention. She smiled wryly, thinking to herself; the property, the bank accounts, everything – all in her name. Aye, McGowan she thinks – 'Nae flies oan that yin, eh.'

Father Joseph Kennedy too had read the *Daily Record* – 'Dear God in Heaven. Celtic lettin us down again. Ach, well,' he'd sighed as he flipped through the pages – 'Dear. David Wilson? Wasn't that the lad I administered to awhile back?' The hair on the back of his neck had risen upon reading about the role of the dead man during the trial of that unfortunate family, the Johnstones – Dear God! Had the lies he spoke of been his testament? His evidence in court?

He had physically balked at the very thought of the confession – 'Oh, God. Does this mean that those two people were innocent? God forbid!'

Derek adjusts the lense of his new camcorder – 'Ye-es, excellento, magico,' he mutters as he focuses on the three men sitting at the table – 'Right Pat m'boy. S'up tae you noo, son.'

Big Ron's holding court – 'Pat, s'Bert Spears. Bert, s'Pat McGowan.'

Pat accepts the outstretched hand – 'How ye doin, Bertie? Pleased tae meet ye.'

The middle-aged cop smiles sheepishly – 'Pleased tae meet ye, son,' he replies.

Derek's steadying the camera on the window of the car; he is no more than a few feet from the door of the bar; the cops have no idea of his presence. He can see them but they can't see him through the open door, they're all too busy talking. He spreads a folded newspaper over the camera; the television section, it doesn't interfere with the view in any way – 'Hmm, s'oan the night?' he wonders, glancing at the programmes – 'Aw here! S'fuckin *Rawhide*!' he snaps, slapping his thigh – Crack! – 'Yip! Rollin! Rollin! Rollin! Keep em doggies movin! Keep em camera's rollin! Rawhi-de!' Crack! – 'Yip! Ride em up! Head um up! Move em out! Am rollin! Rawhi-ide!'

Big Ron gets right down to business – 'So? Ye wur sayin ye hud a wee bank lined up fur us Pat?' he asks – 'S'the story then?'

Bertie doesn't believe his ears as the details spill onto the table – 'Crow Road. Two on the dot. Four guys. Monday, next week,' states Pat coolly – 'S'aw set up. Sound, big man, sound.'

Big Ron slaps him on the back – 'See Bertie? Widida tell ye, son?' he grins – 'Anurra double then? Pat, a Coke?'

Pat dismisses the drink – 'Right, Ron, listen. Deflect any complaints comin in fae any private cab comp'nies. Thur mine noo.' he says flatly – 'Need tae shift some money.' he explains, briefly.

Big Ron's surprised – 'Private cabs? When did ye buy intae that?' he asks.

Pat blandly replies – 'The morra. Am buyin thum oot the morra. S'legit business but ye know the score, so make sure your mob's lookin the urra way. Am takin the whole lottey thum o'er the next cuppla weeks.'

Bertie's bewildered – 'Jesus. So haud oan. Two at the

Crow Road?' he asks – 'That's definite then? Any shooturs involved?'

Pat hands five grand to the cop – 'Here Bertie, drink money. Right. Two oan the dot thull be inside the bank. You work your end oot. Aye, thull be tooled up. Thur jist fur bluff. Fucksakeman,' he chuckles – 'Nae cunt uses a shootur n a bank fur fucksake. Well, that's it. Al be in touch shortly, okay? See ye's later.'

In the car, Derek supresses his delight – 'Yes, Paddy boy. S'it son. Pass – that – money – NOW! YEEESSSS! Got ye, ya fucker!' He pounds the wheel – 'Yes! Yes! Ya fuckin beauty,' he squeals – 'Rollin! Rollin! Rollin! Right Paddy boy, oot ye come, son. That's it ma man, hame tae Daddy!'

Bertie lifts the flat bundle – 'Jesus! S'five grand! Ehm, thanks, Pat,' he exclaims with disbelief – 'S'five fuckin thousand pounds, Ron!'

Pat picks up his cigarettes – 'Okay, Bertie. Nice daen business wi ye. Good news wi yer promotion big man, eh, sound. Inspector Ron McGhee,' he smiles – 'Okay. Al see ye's later.'

Big Ron's laughing as Pat leaves – 'Widda tell ye? Bertie, yer in! Noo it's cash *and* yer promotion! Mer kin ye ask fur? Preventin a bank robbery? When wis the last time ye captured a bank robber? The Sixties, eh?'

Bertie's dizzy with the wad, but there's still some hesitancy in his voice – 'Jesus! Ron, thur's five grand there, five fuckin grand man! V'never even *held* that much money in ma fuckin life! But haud oan. S'innit fur him? A mean, that's some money.'

Ron grins smugly – 'S'pennies, son. Three million a week – that's the incentive. Bertie, thur's three million a week in smack alone. Hauf the population's dabblin in it. That's serious money,' he states – 'Escobar there wants the lot.'

Bertie's not so easily convinced – 'But Ron, fur fucksake, man. Five grand? Wit dis he expect fae me fur that amount a money? That's wit's worryin me. Wit am a supposed tae dae fur him? A mean, settin up a bank?' he protests – 'N'fuckin guns?'

Big Ron's smooth, reassuring, seductive – 'Bertie, this boy's a new breed. Jist wants a clear run tae put away any rivals. Look at it this way. We know everythin there is tae know,' he purrs – 'He keeps us informed, n we make serious arrests.'

Bertie keeps looking over his shoulder – 'But Ron, this is heavy. Christ, it might even be danjerus,' he squawks – 'Think aboot that.'

Big Ron lights a cigar – 'Bertie, Bertie, Bertie, listen tae me. Look son, this is the new way. This is man management. Instead ey drug barons aw o'er the place n terrorisin the public, wi keep wan man in a strong postion. Things huv changed dramatically in the last few years. Results ur wit matter these days. Look at the wage rises wuv hud under this government. Dae ye think thur's noa a price fur that? F'ye don't get instant results these days yer career's finished.'

Bertie feels that five grand – 'Ach. A suppose yer right, but five grand? Here. A might get maself that wee Sierra!' he laughs feebly – 'Aye fuck it, am in noo anyway.'

Big Ron slaps him on the back – 'Bertie! That's the boy! Number One! Yev got tae be ahead in this game. Look after Number One, that's the namey the game noo – Numero Uno!'

*   *   *

Pat slides into the passenger seat – *'Jesus! S'five grand! Ehm, thanks, Pat.'* Click. The camcorder captures that smile for posterity – 'Deposit box wi that, big yin,' he says, grinning – 'S'anurra yin in the bag.'

Derek pulls into the traffic – 'Pat, wit a machine. S'got thum tae a tee. Ye kin see the look oan that bampot's face. Five grand? S'wit ey said winnit?' he asks – 'This wee camera's fuckin brulliant.'

Pat lights a cigarette – 'Aye, sound, sound. Right, head hame noo. Make sure these pricks ur ready fur next week. Who's the lifer by the way?' he asks – 'Dae you know um?'

Derek drums his fingers on the steering wheel – 'Ach, a bampot. Sixteen-stretch fur a stabbin. George McKay, fuckin lunatic. A mad escape artist.'

Pat looks at him – 'Aye? Where'd ey escape fae?'

Derek frowns – 'Ach, fuck knows. A met um years ago daen a wee sentence. S'heid's nippin, says ey wis in the SAS. Been oan the trot fur aboot a year noo. Wanney they bampots, thinks es an assassin.'

Pat lies back – 'Aw is ey a legionnaire? Sound. S'gonny get plentya action noo, eh?' he laughs – 'Keep that fuckin mob happy fur awhile tae.'

Janis is watching the television when they get home; she doesn't ask where he's been with her brother, up to no good no doubt – 'Back early, eh?' she says.

Derek flops down into a huge leather armchair – 'M'knackured, man,' he yawns – 'Aye, Manchester the morra tae. Need tae get up early.'

Pat looks around – 'Right, hen. The weans in bed? S'at yer watchin?' he asks.

Janis flicks the television off – 'Rubbish. Aye, ach they wur tired. Thuv thur school in the mornin anyway. Ye gaun wi him tae Manchester?'

Pat settles into his chair by the white marble fireplace – 'Me? Nah, too much oan. A don't know, how? Ye needin me fur sumthin?' he asks, pulling a book from the steel tubular bookcase – 'Meetin McGinty, then that's me, how?' he repeats.

Janis shrugs her shoulders – 'Naw naw, nuthin. Jist wunderin, that's aw. Laura's got ur exams this week.'

Derek laughs – 'Exams? Ur wee heid'll be nippin. Am keepin right oot thur road then fur the rest ey the week.'

Pat and Janis laugh – 'Aw c'mon you, she's noa that bad! S'you thit winds ur up aw the time. She's great wi urra people,' continues Pat – 'Fuckin cheek, hint ey? Laura's heid's nippin? Listen tae him eh?'

Derek throws his arms up – 'Aw listen tae Mr Cool!'

'Who's this McGinty fella?' asks Janis.

'McGinty? Och, wanney that auld mob. Ran aboot the toon a few year ago. Bran new, dis a bitta graft,' replies Derek.

Janis picks up the black triangular clock to break the deadlock – 'Set the alarm fur six then? Time ye leavin fur Manchester?'

Her brother shrugs – 'Ach, early. Be drivin straight back so, aye, six,' he decides.

Janis adjusts a portrait of the girls on the wall; their primary colours complement the series of family photographs occupying the house – 'Right, then. Right, m'away up tae ma bed. Mind put aw the switches aff,' she says.

Pat looks up – 'Aye, be up shortly, hen. Gonny read fur a wee while. Al get the lights an dae the security alarms. Night, hen.'

Janis pads across the immaculate white rugs in her gold slippers – 'Night. N'leave the hoosekeeper's money, mind.'

Derek smirks – 'Hoosekeeper, eh? S'like Dallas in here wi yous two cunts. Goodni-ight en, darling.'

Pat nips him in the bud before he causes a fight – 'Kin always get ye a wee flat if yer noa happy here? Naw? Aye, wull jist shut it en. Night, doll,' he drawls.

Janis blows him a kiss to make her point – 'Night, doll. Al be keepin the bed warm fur ye darlin.'

Derek sniggers in the silence – 'Aye, eh. Right, better hit the sack masel. Some ey us ur wurkin the morra. Night en – Boss.'

Pat sniffs into his book – 'Amazin, eh? Didye know that the chimpanzee's oor nearest relative? Evalution's amazin, innit? Long ur your erms, by the way?' he asks, lighting another cigarette – 'Aye, evalution,' he repeats, as his brother-in-law ambles upstairs to his bedroom – 'Aye eh, evalution, sound man, sound.'

He remains reading below his angle-poise lamp, but that brain is going over the plans and preparations for the next day's propositions. He needed more legitimate avenues to launder his income. Janis's hair salons provided a decent front but he had to create plausible businesses to handle the bulk of the profits from heroin; the private cabs, he believed, had potential. They'll put up a struggle, he thinks, but he had confidence in his outfit – 'Jist leave it tae ma wee sojurs,' he decides – 'They enjoy this kinna work anyway.'

Chapter Six

McGINTY LOOKS COOL in his double-breasted suit; the beautifully cut crombie coat hung below the knee, but he had the height to carry it off – 'Mornin! Meetin Mr Steen. Ten o'clock?' he chirps at the sullen-faced secretary – 'S'ey here yet?'

She looks down the list of appointments on her desk – 'Aye, right. S'here. Take a seat, then,' she replies as yet another call comes through – 'Tch. Hullo, Steen's private hire. How kin a help?' she sighs wearily, until she notices the smartly dressed figure going through the office door to see her boss – 'Eh! Here you! Eh! A wee minute! Fuck!'

Johnny walks into the office – 'R'you Mr Steen?' he asks lazily – 'Aye? Right, en. Am representin a Mrs Janis McGowan. S'a contract fur you tae sign. She's buyin Steen's Cabs.'

Arnie Steen doesn't believe this – 'Wit? Who the fuck're you? Mrs who? Listen son, a think yer gettin me mixed up wi some urra firm. Am no sellin,' he states – 'So excuse me, but am busy.'

Johnny smiles, throwing polaroid snaps onto the table – 'Seen these en?' Mr Steen recognises his daughter; going into school, leaving school and going home. Penned circles drawn around her breasts send a chill through his bones – 'Ad get ur ready fur the implants,' the coat sneers viciously – 'Never know wit might happen, dae ye? N'by the way. The next time ye call me son yer jaw's gettin broke. An when am leavin here, you shout it wis nice daen business wi ye, Mr McGinty.'

Mr Steen looks at the powerful physique; that cropped, red-haired head, slightly tilted to the side, waiting for his answer, waiting to explode upon him. He can't say what it is that scares him more – the photographs or the calmness of the threat – 'Eh, listen. Look, this business is eh, right nevermind, a get the message,' he stammers – 'Where dae a sign?' he almost weeps.

The secretary watches him leave – 'S'like Marlon Brando that guy int ey, kinna busted up version.'

Mr Steen wheels round on her – 'You shut the fuck up! The fuck d'ye let him through fur, ya stupit fuckin cow, ye!' he roars in her face – 'Ye fuckin stupit?'

She's stunned – 'Wit the fuck! Who dae you think yer talkin tae?' she shouts – 'Don't think because yer ma boss ye kin talk tae me like that, ya cheeky swine ye!'

His eyes are bulging out of his head – 'WI-IT?' he spits, dragging her out of her chair by the hair – 'AL FUCKIN KILL YE, YA STUPIT CUNT! GET OOT!' he screeches, as she tries to break free – 'GET TAE FUCK OOTA HERE! YER SACKED! FUCKIN SACKED!' The secretary lands face first on the pavement – 'N'DON'T COME BACK!'

Mr Steen isn't taking it too well at all – 'BASTARDS! BASTARDS!'

Pat takes the telephone call at home a few days later – 'S'dun, Pat. Steen's wurkin fur yer missus noo. Pickin up aw the details later. Gie thum tae Derek. S'that okay?' the caller asks – 'Ye got ma wages ready?'

Pat's pleased – 'Sound, big man, sound. Derek'll square ye up wi yer wages. Did'ye get any resistance at aw, Johnny?' he asks.

Johnny sounds surprised – 'R'ye kiddin?'

Pat laughs down the line – 'S'sound, big man, sound,' he says, hanging up.

Janis is watching a newsflash about a bank robbery that's happening – 'Pat, listen tae this. S'Crow Road. These guys ur haudin hostages inside a bank.'

'Aye? Magine that. Listen, ye own they private hires in Ruchill. Guy folded,' he says – 'S'happenin here?'

Janis continues watching the news – 'Aye? Fine. Och, s'a bank robbery,' she replies.

Pat nods – 'Aye, Calton's next. Any bodies yet? Nah? Well. Al be ootside anyway,' he says, picking up his morning papers – 'See who's been dun, s'the same shite every week innit? Murder n rape.'

Janis laughs – 'Aye, aye. Listen tae this. S'gettin like America. Lo-ok at that bampot, es staunin there wi es microphone tae! Oh, a don't know, wit? Aye, Pat, they guys ur inside the bank the noo!'

Pat perches on the arm of her chair – 'Aw a see. S'happenin right noo? A thought it wis jist a report fae the urra day ur sumthin like that,' he laughs – 'Aye, fuckin bonker cases. Be a right laugh if that daft reporter gets grabbed intae the bank, eh? Anyway, geez a shout if anythin happens, al be readin ma papurs, hen.'

Janis is hanging onto the edge of her chair – 'Aye, Pat. Right, right.'

Mark Geissler's there live on the scene; he's whispering – 'Yes, Shareen. It's believed a teller pressed the alarm immediately the men entered the bank.'

The bank tellers are absolutely petrified – 'SHUT IT!' the hooded figure with the shotgun is screaming at them – 'DON'T

MOVE! YOU TWO! DOON OAN THE FLER! NOO! GET DOON! AL BLOW YER FUCKIN BRAINS OOT! JIST BE FUCKIN COOL! NAE HEROES'

Two hooded men are behind the counter while another watches the door. The fourth man, standing on the counter, is still screaming – 'STIY N THE GRUN! WIT YE FUCKIN LOOKIN IT? GET YER FUCKIN HEID DOON! DONT LOOK UP! FUCKIN HERO HERE!'

A masked face glances outside the door – 'Here,' he whispers, almost laughing – 'Yer noa gonny believe this! Thur's cops aw roon this fuckin buildin! Wit? Naw, am fuckin serious!' he laughs hysterically – 'Thur aw o'er the place, fur fucksake! Wanney these cunts've pressed the alarm. Aye, thur jist waitin fur us comin oot,' he sighs, resigned to the fact – 'The fuck dae wi dae noo? S'us fucked.'

Little did they know. Bertie Spears's tip-off had been fruitful; the police had files on the four men. They were all known criminals, but one in particular concerned them much more than the other three, the lifer, George McKay – 'McKay's a fantasist. Dangerous in a situation like this, and could be unpredictable if he panics. Absconded a year ago from Saughton Prison. Chief suspect in a spate of armed robberies.'

The Boom Boom Boys take up positions on the rooftops opposite the bank; their high-powered rifle scopes, which can tell the time at a hundred yards, point directly at the hooded heads inside the bank – 'In position. Over.'

McKays freaking out – 'WITSAT? COPS? WHERE? THE ALARMS?'

He bears down on the faces lying on the floor, his lifer flashes through his head as reality penetrates, freezing the adrenaline rush, rooting him to the spot. They'll bury him alive in security, solitary confinement – death. He has nothing to lose. Trembling, he roars – 'WIT WANNEY YOU CUNTS WIS IT?'

The others begin pulling off their hoods; they're professionals, they take the bad with the good – 'The fuck's up wi him?' asks one laughing – 'Ye screamin fur, George?'

The figure at the door turns to McKay – 'Och, shut the fuck up wi the screamin, man. Wur fuckin dun, that's it. R'ye tryin tae get us shot? This isnae the fuckin IRA,' he snipes, pulling off his hood – 'Fuckin headcase.'

BANG! McKay fires the sawn-off shotgun at point-blank range; the head of his buddy splatters across the wall behind him as the torso slumps to the floor. He jumps down to the floor, dragging the first teller to the door – 'MOVE, YOU CUNT!' – BANG! BANG! There is an eerie silence as the teller's body lands on the pavement – THUD!

McKay's screaming – 'NOA TAKIN ME ALIVE!'

The dead brain of the teller is showered in bright lights as the first atoms escape to fly in the eternal cycle of life, and death. Only fond memories of consciousness remain left behind.

The shots ringing out from inside the bank startle the reporter, making him jerk back involuntarily – PING! PING! PING! – 'Whaugh? Shareen! I'm sure you heard that back at the studio?' he yelps – 'I think it . . . yes, yes, yes, it was shots! Shots have been fired from inside the bank!'

He regains his composure – 'As we speak, police marksmen are moving into position. In fact. Wait. There is something happening just now. It looks like. Yes. One of the hostages has been – GOD! The hostage has been shot!' – THUD!

A .44 Magnum rifle focused on the figure at the door of the bank, fires off a single shot, hitting the head of the masked man, bringing him down like a sack of potatoes – 'Man down,' a voice reports matter-of-factly – 'Over.'

Janis leaps to her feet – 'Fuckinhell! Pat! C'mere n see this! Pat! Fuck me!' she's shouting – 'Pat! Pat! C'mere! Where ur ye? Pat!'

Pat's sipping his Coke – 'Good day, Mr McGowan!' calls a neighbour walking his dog. Mr McGowan, eh? he thinks. When you're treading the floorboards of poverty, no one calls you Mister. He observes the man and his dog, a huge Alsation. He watches with disbelief as the owner scoops the dog shit into a bag, and smiles over his shoulder at him – 'Nice day for golf, isn't it?'

Golf? These people, he thinks; they think they're the fucking aristocracy, they believe they're different from him. They're fucking desperados, chancers trying to flee those fucking floorboards, with their cultivated morality – 'Yeah, sound, nice.'

Pat looked at life through black-and-white lenses. Look at him, he thinks; trapped in some contrived class hoax, mimicking the ruling classes. Those bastards were tough. They had to be to hang onto power, but this lot? – 'Nice dug there.'

The professional castes; doctors, priests and coppers, that's what they are. They're a lynching class; they'd fucking hang you for stealing a button. But to look at them, with their pastel jumpers, the dog, the golf – picking shit off the ground. It's all to preserve their fairytale lives, their hereditary accents – 'Deddy breeds them.'

Deddy? These fucking bampots, fooling themselves. Their lives are totally dependent on other factors, things outwith their control; inflation, mortgage rates, interest rates. These people had more to worry about than people with nothing at all, they're three meals from the pavement — 'Aw, a see.'

Pat smiles; the laws of evolution were a combination of risks and action, power was the reward. More people are killed at work than in the criminal world, killed through taking risks to keep their bosses in luxury. Risking their lives for what? Some annual holiday to escape their worries? A pension for old age? Like lambs being led to the slaughterhouses of angina and heart attacks — 'Deddy, eh?'

There is only one language; power. Power has to be taken, and by whatever means necessary. You only had to look at history. Man is a violent species — a predator. Mister McGowan, is it? Pat has more respect for the huge dog — Deddy won't last two minutes on the street when he's bankrupted, he thinks, scratching the dog's thick fur. Bite the hand that feeds you boy, bite it off right now and swallow it whole — 'Hiya pal, geeza paw, c'mon son, geeza paw, s'a good boy.'

Janis finds him on the patio — 'Pat! Ye'v missed it! The polis've shot two guys! Aye! thur wis a hostage as well, shot in the bank! Oh, hullo,' she smiles — 'S'the news. It's on the news.'

Pat turns to the neighbour — 'Janis, ma wife. S'why we moved tae Bearsden. Thur's terrible things happenin these days.'

The neighbour frowns — 'A what? A bank robbery? Which branch? Did they say?' he asks, tugging on the chain — 'C'mon Simba, c'mon.'

Pat waves him off — bite, Simba, bite the cunt. Bite Deddy's hand off — eat him.

Pat and Janis watch heavily armed police surround the bank;

two men are rushed in a bundle into separate police vans parked on the pavement outside the bank.

'There are two men dead,' exclaims the reporter – 'And now back to you at the studio.'

Janis hits her husband's knee – 'Tch, wuv missed it.'

The two guys remained with their hands in the air, as coppers finally stormed the bank – 'STILL! DON'T FUCKING MOVE! NOW! DOWN ON THE FLOOR! MOVE!'

The hoods knew not to move an inch; this was shoot-to-kill territory – Britain. A police statement was enough to exonerate an officer from prosecution – 'Suspect was wearing a ski mask.' That the corpse may have been on snow made no difference. The public's thirst for blood had been increased by mainland bombings – 'Well, it *could* have been the IRA.' A previous conviction was enough to have a mistaken identity dismissed as an accidental manslaughter these days – 'Well, he was a criminal after all. The police are only doing their job.'

Big Bad George is horizontal; dead eyes stare into a vacant space where there are no prison recalls, no security measures, no solitary confinement – and definitely no more fantasies of that big job; the flights of fancy are no more – gone. There was no medicine man whispering by his side, no lamentation about the souls of the faithful departed finding mercy; being prison property the bad man would be planted behind D/Hall of Barlinnie. A stone would bear the inscription – 'Here Lies A Jail Yarn For Posterity – Rest in Peace.'

Pat shakes his head – 'Oh, well. They two're in trouble, eh.'

Janis agrees – 'Fuckin liberty tae. They two guys, deid. They tellers, wit they thinkin? S'noa even their money. They think thur heroes?' she asks — 'A mean thur's wanney thum deid. Think anybody cares? Ye heard him there, askin wit branch?'

Pat hears the telephone ringing — 'Aye, bampots. S'the phone. Al get it,' he says.

Derek's calling from Manchester — 'Right kerry oan, eh? Two deid?' he laughs — 'That McKay, the prick. Anyway, twenty tapes, s'rock. Fuckin yardies, black bastards, tried tae hit me wi that urra shite.'

Pat laughs — 'Aye, Bertie'll be shitin es troosurs. Naw, s'awright, am meetin thum the night anyway. Bung um n shut um up. Right, listen, al see ye when ye get back later. M'gaun tae pick the weans up fae school. S'at?' he asks — 'Naw. S'awright, al meet thum maself. Big Ron'll be there, keep that prick fae panickin. Ach, fuck thum. Thur in too deep so don't worry aboot it.'

Janis looks up — 'Derek? Everythin okay?' she asks — 'Time's ey comin back?'

Pat nods — 'Aye. Twenty kilo, back the night. Wee Rosinni n the boys'll put it oot the morra wance it's been cut. McGinty's got that cab pitch by the way,' he says — 'You're the new gaffer.'

Janis laughs — 'Aye, ye wur sayin. Christ, Pat, many accounts am a gonny need noo? Wit aboot garages? Never thought aboot garages?' she asks.

Pat frowns — 'Garages? Here, brilliant, hen. Garages, aye. Fucksake, that's right. Al fix sumthin up,' he smiles — 'McGinty's daen the rounds wi these private hires. Al put sumdae else oan it. Garages, aye, sound.'

Janis looks at her gold watch — 'You gettin the weans, d'ye say? Right then, al get the tea oan. Ye gaun oot the night?' she asks — 'Wer ye gaun? Al pick up the weans if your meetin somebody. A kin make yer supper later if ye want?'

Pat picks up his jacket — 'Aye, okay then. Al head off then in case thur waitin. Witsat? Naw, naw,' he says — 'Al be back early, jista wee bitta business. Right, c'mon al get ye oot. Yer keys an at, ye got thum?'

Janis brushes her hair before checking herself in the hall mirror — 'Aye, fine. Right, al see ye later okay, geez a kiss,' she smiles — 'N'watch wit yer daen, mind.'

Pat pecks her cheek — 'Fucksake, turn it up, man, am n a hurry. Wee guy's gonny be n a panic if am late,' he laughs — 'Fuckin wumin wi thur wee kisses.'

Bertie's been in a state of severe shock all day, since hearing the news — 'A shootin?' he'd squealed — 'A fuckin shootin? Oh, Jesus Christ! A fuckin knew it! A knew it!'

Pat coldly greets the two cops sitting in the corner of the bar — 'Hullo. The fuck's aw the panic aboot?' he demands — 'The fuck's wrang wi your face?'

Big Ron raises his eyebrows, glancing at his partner — 'Aye, Pat. Och, s'nuthin. Bertie hud a touch ey the jitters,' he says — 'Kin sort it oot.'

Bertie feels the penetrating stare of the man opposite; there's something about him he can't handle — 'Jitters? Aboot wit?' the guy asks, staring at him — 'Aboot wit?' he repeats — 'Ye fuckin deaf?'

Bert tries to pass it off — 'Naw, Pat, naw. Eh, it wis eh, thingmy, they wur eh, askin me questions, aboot ma source n the bank. Wit? Naw, av no said anythin. Naw, definite. A jist felt a bit under pressure, dae ye know wit a mean?' he pleads – 'They kept askin who you wur an how a got the tip aff aboot the bank.'

Pat looks at him – 'You puttin the squeeze oan me fur money, ya prick?'

Bertie shrinks; his head's buried inside his shoulders – 'Wit? Naw, Pat! Naw! S'jist a didnae know wit tae dae, know wit a mean?' he squeals – 'Naw, a wis jist panickin at furst, dae ye know wit a mean, Pat?'

Pat doesn't know what he means – 'Ron, ye better talk tae this prick. Cos al leave um up the fuckin Campsies,' he states, going to the bar – 'Coke please, wi ice.'

The Campsie Hills? Bertie doesn't need an interpreter to work it out – 'Jesus, Ron!' he whispers – 'The Campsies? Ron! Who the fuck is this guy? Es jist threatened tae kill me! Did ye hear um? The Campsies?' he squirms – 'Ron! Av got the fuckin horrors! Say sumthin, fur fucksake!'

Pat watches from the gantry mirror as the older cop puts an arm around the shoulder of the other – 'Look Bertie, jist reassure um yer okay. Yer jist in a panic. Wance it aw blaws o'er it's finished,' he's saying – 'N'listen, you don't huv tae reveal sources. Ye shood know that. Jist put this doon tae experience. Nuthin's gonny happen tae ye.'

Pat turns; the head nodding indicates it's sorted out.

'Aye, Ron. Aye, okay,' the cop's whimpering – 'Right, Ron, nae problum.'

Bertie looks up as he returns to the table – 'Pat, listen, eh. Am really sorry. S'ma first time wi this sorta thing, dae ye know wit a mean?' he pleads – 'It'll no happen again,' he swears – 'A promise ye.'

Pat's face breaks into a smile – 'S'better, Bertie. Nae need tae panic. Here, take yer faimly a holiday ur sumthin,' he says, throwing a bundle of notes onto the table — 'Yer under too much pressure. Jist phone in an say yer sick. S'sound wee man, s'sound.'

Big Ron picks up the bundle of banknotes — 'There ye go. See? S'anurra three grand er. Fucksake, the bank? Be furgot by the weekend,' he says — 'Wait n see.'

Bertie doesn't refuse the cash — 'Three grand? Ye kiddin? Fuckinhell, Pat. Listen, av jist been in a panic,' he says — 'Wis the teller gettin shot, but well, roll on the weekend, eh?'

Pat laughs — 'Ach, Bertie, ye'll get used tae that. S'nuthin, disnae even get headline space these days. Lucky if it gets page three. N'listen, don't be stuck fur money, okay? Thur's plenty fur every cunt.'

Bertie's forgotten the teller already — 'Ach, Pat. Yer right. S'that teller's ain fault innit, tryin tae be a fuckin hero,' he laughs — 'A Dick Barton.'

Pat buys two double whiskies — 'Right, Ron, huv tae move. Garages, by the way. Aye, buyin thum oot as well. Any complaints fae the private hires?' he asks — 'Nah? Well. S'good. Straight pegs, they jist collapse.'

Big Ron downs his double — 'Cheers, Pat! Right then, stay in touch, son. See ye!' he waves as the black suit disappears through the door — 'Bertie, Bertie, Bertie,' he says to his partner — 'Sumthin ye need tae learn aboot these types.'

He furrows his brow — 'Drug dealers are noa like thiefs. They tell ye everythin. That's the beauty, they've transformed oor careers. Look at me? Dae ye think ad a made it chasin low life?' he asks — 'An inspector?'

He signals the barman — 'S'your round. Naw, criminuls ye see ur different. They think twice aboot violence. Thur's nuthin innit fur thum, cept maybe mer time. But yer drug dealers? Murdur an violence means nuthin. They designate a rocket tae dae the dirty wurk. Then, if it suits thum, set him up fur a dive. That's the way they work — and they wurk fur us,' he winks — 'We canny lose. Let thum kill each urra.'

Bertie's listening intently — 'Aye, Ron, but that poor teller. A mean, it's a human bein. Dis ey noa count?' he asks.

Ron completely ignores the question — 'But yer criminul? He'll take a heavy sentence before grassin, even if it's only an associate. Where dis that leave us? S'aw that auld-fashioned pride, wi thur codes a honour, fuckin haufwits. Oh! They're above aw that! Sellin dope? Oh, no! Aw thur daen is mimickin the upper classes! That's the paradox ey the criminal world,' he continues — 'Thur fuckin snobs. That's gonny be thur downfall ye know, they canny keep up wi the times, become extinct, like fuckin dinosaurs,' he laughs — 'Fuckin dinosaurs.'

He waves an arm to illustrate his point — 'The landscape's changin wi new technology, security cameras everywhere, criminals canny get movin. Believe me, fore ye know it we're redundant, a spent force.'

Bertie's nodding — 'Aye, aye, right, a see wit ye mean, but he's fuckin heavy, int ey? A mean that guy's fuckin danjerus.'

Big Ron laughs — 'Pat the Rat? A-ch. S'there fur the usin Bertie boy. N'remember we kin put him away anytime. He works fur us, we're police officurs. N'fur the bank teller bein a human bein?' he asks — 'In name only son, name only. Human bein's ur quite content tae sit back an watch each other suffer an die. Thur only interestit in number wan, that's the name ey the game noo son, Numero Uno.'

Bertie's feeling the whisky — 'A suppose yer right. S'us that ur in control,' he says to his partner — 'Aye, eh. Numero Uno.'

* * *

Pat jumps into the BMW – '*Yer right. S'that tellers ain fault innit, tryin tae be a fuckin hero.*' Click. He lets the brake off – 'Pricks,' he thinks – 'Right. See Mick an hame,' he decides, pulling the car out onto the M8 – 'See how much es got fur me.'

Mick Rosinni's cutting a kilo of soft black when he hears a knock at the door – 'Ha-uw! See who that is. Tell um tae come back in an hoor,' he shouts, picking up a butcher's knife and hacking off a nine bar – 'Fuckin pests. Canny get a fuckin minute. Here, get a cuppla joints bult, Nerdy.'

Jimmy Kinnaird, Nerdy, believes he's the fastest roller up the Garngad – 'Many ye want, Mick?' he asks – 'Wull a dae a few?'

A 9mm lying on the table is loaded, bullets lie scattered around – 'Och, S'Pat! How ye doin, mate?' he winks on seeing who it is – 'C'mon in, man.'

Mick laughs uproariously – 'Fucksake! S'ready tae plug ye there, man!'

Pat takes the outstretched hand – 'Sound, wee man, sound,' he smiles – 'Bothur?' he asks, noticing the gun lying on the table.

Mick throws his arms open – 'Borra? Me? Ye fuckin kiddin?' he roars – 'Ach. S'sum mob supposed tae be gonny nip me. S'bams fae up the road – dafties fae Blackhull. Nae problemo. Anyway, how ye daen?'

Pat looks around the living-room.

'Pat. Haud oan a minut tae a chase these cunts.' winks Mick – 'RIGHT! OOT! C'MON! COME BACK IN AN HOOR!' he roars – 'HAUW!'

Nerdy leads the wee gang of soldiers out of the living-room

— 'Right. Mick? D'ye want enathin fae the shops, sweeties ur wit?' he asks.

Mick slaps him on the back — 'Right, Nerdy. Sweeties fur yerself, ya cunt,' he laughs — 'Nah, back in an hoor, okay?'

A pitbull lies sleeping at the fire. Pat gives it a friendly nudge with his shoe — 'S'auld Tyson, eh. Stull eatin weans?' he laughs — 'Ye got anathin fur me?' The dog looks at him for a moment and begins licking its balls — 'Auld Tyson, eh,' he smiles — 'Wrufff.'

Mick leads him through to the kitchen — 'Check this wee hide oot, eh,' he winks — 'The mob've turned me o'er twice n never fun it. Magic, eh?'

Pat's amazed; half the floor appears to lift up like a trap-door beneath the sink.

'Noo check that. Used tae be a plumber when a wis a boy,' Mick explains — 'S'aw concrete underneath there, Pat. A hollowed it oot first day wi moved in. The dug sleeps there tae, eh?' he grins proudly — 'Here Pat. Grab that, wull ye?' he says, jerking a pillow-case from the hole in the floor — 'Al jist slide that back — ooof!'

Pat takes the pillow case — 'Aye, sound. Right Mick, much's here?' he asks.

Mick does some mental arithmetic — 'S'thurty there. V'flooded Blackhull n Riddrie tae, takin time tae get the money in so a shood huv aboot unara twenty grand fur ye at the end ey week. S'that okay? Ye wanta cuppa tea, by the way?' he asks.

Pat looks at the kitchen — 'Naw Mick, yer awright, son. N-aw, that's sound. Wit're ye daen in Blackhull? S'only a cuppla streets fur fucksake. S'at wit the bother's aboot?' he asks — 'Who is it?'

Mick shrugs his broad shoulders — 'Ach. Thur fuckin

bampots, man. Place's been dry fur weeks noo. That drug squad mob crash in a few doors n thur aw panickin. S'like Operation Frankie fuckin Vaughan!' he roars, heading back to the living-room – 'Thur aw bampots. Fuck thum! Am puttin gear oot – end a story.'

Pat laughs – 'Sound, wee man, sound. Thur's kit the morra fur ye, much ye want? Ye needid mer hash?' he asks.

Mick shakes his head as he strokes the dog – 'Na, Pat. V'stull gotta cuppla kilo lyin in there. Nae jellies?' he asks, stroking the dog – 'Tyson! Up, son! C'mon, son. Kiss fur yer Da. At's a good boy!'

Pat watches the dog licking its balls then lapping Daddy's face – 'L'see wit a kin dae fur ye. Listen, Mick, am needin sumbudy fur a wee bitta rough stuff. Put pressure oan garages. Aye, buyin thum oot kinna thing. S'Nerdy like wi that kinna wurk?' he asks.

Mick bursts out laughing – 'The monkey? Och, he's fuckin nuts! Good grafter, but noa got a brain, Pat!' he roars – 'Don't get me wrang. Nerdy's solid, dae the damage fur ye – jist nae mannurs. Listen, let me sort sumthin oot. Where's the garages anyway?'

Pat doesn't bat an eyelid – 'Where? The lottey thum, many as ye kin,' he replies – 'Am jist usin thum fur fronts.'

Mick lights a joint – 'Aw right, a see. Wull look, leave it wi me, right. Al fire a cuppla guys in an see wit happens, okay?' he coughs – 'Fuckin lungs, man. Right, jist gie the ownurs a tenner ur sumthin like that? Ach, nae borra. Fuck, Nerdy kin dae that. Naw, the way ye wur talkin a thought ye meant ye wur buyin thum, legally kinna thing.'

Pat smiles – 'Well, kinna legal, innit? Anyway, think that's the door. Be yer wee mob wi the sweeties. Right, Derek's back later oan so let um know wit yer needin.'

Mick is at the door. He rolls his eyes – 'S'aw that cunt eats, man, sweeties,' he says – 'Right Pat. Al gie ye a phone. Mind the jellies, eh? Tell Derek, okay?'

Pat waits as he fiddles with the numerous locks, bolts and snibs on the front door. A railway sleeper completes the barricade – 'Aye, Pat, fuckin right. Makes it harder fur that mob tryin tae put the door in.'

Nerdy and about a dozen pals are waiting for the door to open – 'Pat, ye leavin? Av got sweeties fur ye as well,' he grins – 'Aw well, see ye again eh?'

Pat thanks him – 'Sound, Nerdy, sound pal. Right, Mick, geez a phone. Send Nerdy ur sumebudy doon fur they jellies. Okay, boys, see ye's,' he smiles.

A chorus goes up as he walks down the stairs.

'Right, Pat.'

'See ye, Pat.'

'Nae borra, Pat.'

'Aye, Pat.'

'Cheerio, Pat.'

Pat laughs to himself as the bolts and snibs rattle, and the door's barricaded with the old railway-track sleeper – CALUNKK!

Mick picks up the butcher's knife – 'Right, let's get rollin. Who's got the cling? Malky dae the bags fur the morra. Sammy dae hash deals fur the night an en at's us. Nerdy, thur's a wee job fur you n Gerry. Get a talk wi ye later oan. Right, s'that fuckin joint?' he asks.

Nerdy looks up – 'Wit joint? Oh – this joint?' he grins.

Mick snatches it – 'Geezat, ya cuntye.'

*   *   *

Derek's at home when his brother-in-law returns – 'How ye doin? Got back aboot hauf an hoor ago. Aye, bran new, everythins sortit oot. S'happenin, en?' he asks.

Pat hangs his jacket in the hall – 'Aye, how ye doin? Saw wee Rosinni. Es wee rockets ur aw geared up. Aye, dozens ey thum, comical as fuck,' he laughs.

Derek frowns – 'Trouble?' he asks – 'S'it aw aboot?'

Pat shrugs – 'S'took Blackhull n at. Aye, thur noa gien a fuck. Oh, by the way, case a furget, thur lookin fur jellies.'

Derek throws his hands up – 'Jellies?' he laughs – 'Aw, here wi go. Wait an see, Pat. Be fuckin bodies aw o'er the place, jellies n straight in. Wee Nerdy there? Aye? Wur ye talkin tae um? Nuts eh, disnae gie a fuck. Wit aboot they coppers?' he asks.

Pat looks around – 'Janis n ur bed?' he asks – 'Honest a coodny keep a straight face the day. Am sittin ootside talkin tae wanney they bampots up the road n she's runnin aboot shoutin aboot the news.' He throws the car keys to Derek – 'Here, thur's some money, stash it oot the road fore ye go tae yer bed. Janis'll bank it later oan. McKay eh?' he chuckles.

Derek slaps his knee – 'NOA TAKIN ME ALIVE! POP! Fucksake man, eh. Coodny stop laughin when a heard.'

Pat's giggling too – 'A know, didye hear it oan the news? Janis kept sayin, look thur inside the bank! S'actually happenin!' he laughs – 'She kin be comical.'

They try to control the giggling – 'Shsshht! Fucksake, don't waken ur up. That Bertie, fuckin panickin. Naw, gied um a cuppla quid. Thur in too deep. Anyway how'd it go doon the road?' he asks.

Derek's delighted to elaborate – 'Fuckin kerry oan man.

That Yardie mob tryin tae hit me wi crack. Thought it wis gonny get heavy. Och, this cunt, oot es box but a put that message on the table,' he says, putting an invisible gun on the table – 'Next thing the prick's shoutin, "Nae trouble, man!" Aye! Av picked the gun up n said, "Trouble?" He's on his feet now – "Trouble? Trou-ble? Al gie ye fuckin plenty, ya black bastard!"' he explains, pointing his cocked finger – 'That wis it, chalk fuckin white.'

Pat laughs – 'Pricks. Anyway, Derek, av been thinkin, time tae move abroad. Cut oot middle men aw thegither, know wit a mean?'

Derek's puzzled but listens – 'Derek, aw wi need is an openin tae bring the stuff in. An a think av got a way tae dae it – a mini-bus,' he states – 'A mini-bus.'

Derek sits staring at him – 'A bus? A fuckin bus?' he exclaims – 'N'widdy wi dae wi a bus?'

But Pat's been thinking ahead – 'A community bus, fur wee trips abroad, send aw the weans on a holiday,' he grins – 'False bottom on it, fulla kit.'

Derek doesn't know whether or not he's serious.

'Am serious. N'it'll work, Derek,' Pat smiles – 'Think aboot it. Customs urny gonny lookit weans. Wur fightin drugs.' Derek's mouth's open – 'A bus. Right, Pat a see wit ye mean. We send aw the weans oan holiday? Say it's tae fight drugs. Fuck me. Yer right, man.'

Pat smiles – 'We know the contacts, so fuck that mob doon the road. We don't need those people.'

Janis surprises them – 'Pat? S'that you? Naw s'awright, jist heard voices,' she says sleepily – 'Ye cummin tae bed?'

Pat gets up – 'Aye hen, comin the noo, anyway,' he says – 'Right, Derek. Al get a talk wi ye in the mornin. N'let Mick's wee gang loose. Thur daen a wee message fur us so mind they jellies n that money, okay?'

Derek slaps him on the back – 'Aye, Pat, nae problem. Al get a talk wi ye in the mornin. Aye, Mick, eh, wull get a laugh.' He winks as they part ways at the bottom of the stairs – 'Night, see ye in the mornin. Al jist get that money furst.'

Pat too tiptoes up to his bedroom – 'See ye in the mornin, night.'

Chapter Seven

NERDY AND GERRY are jellied out of their boxes as they march into the first garage about a week later – 'You the owner ey this pitch, Jimmy?' they ask a young mechanic bent over the engine of a car – 'Naw? Who's the owner then?'

Another, older mechanic slides out from under a car – 'S'me. Kin a help ye?' he asks.

Nerdy finally focuses on the source of the voice – 'Fucksake, man, thoat that motur wis talkin er,' he mutters – 'Aye, need a wee wurd wi ye, mate. Ye got an office?'

These are small-time businessmen; the fifty-five-year-old garage owner has never had offers for his premises, certainly never one like this – 'Sellin? This place?' he sighs – 'A didnae think it wis worth much tae be honest, but it's aw av got, am sorry.'

Gerry spins around in the swivel chair a few times before stopping; the 9mm's pointed directly at the owner – 'Listen. A don't think ye understaun. Wur noa askin ye tae sell it. Wur tellin ye. Noo here, sign that fuckin papur fore ye get plugged. Here, there's a tenner,' he says throwing a ten-pound note onto the table – 'Daen ye a fuckin favur, so am ur.'

Nerdy's sitting upright with his arms folded; the grin on his face could mean anything, but the pinned eyes are gleefully malignant – 'Don't get wide noo, pal, ur yer in trouble. Jist sign that thing n nuthins gonny happen,' he grins.

The owner doesn't believe this is happening; he can't take his eyes off the steel barrel of the gun, that black hole has his heart pounding. This is not a joke – 'Aww, wait a wee minut,' he wails – 'This is goat tae be some kinna joke. A own this place. Av worked aw ma days fur this. Fur Godsake. Av got a faimly tae feed. Ye'v got tae be jestin, eh lads?'

Gerry's leaning over the table; he's looking at his associate, smiling – 'Jimmy wur noa gettin through here. Widid a say tae him there?' he asks.

Nerdy shrugs – 'Said ye wur gonny plug um,' he replies.

The terrified owner flinches as the gun barrel is back-handed across his face.

'Wit's aw the jumpin fur ya fuckin bam?' demands Gerry – 'Fuckin told ye! Stop actin stupit an ye won't get hurt! Noo fuckin sign that!'

The man's looking desperately at the door; he's praying that a customer, his teenage apprentice, anyone, will walk in.

'Plug um,' giggles Nerdy – 'Wan in the heid an wull get tae fuck.' He gets up, and wrenches the gun away from his partner – 'Right, Gerry. Oot the road so ye don't get brains o'er ye. Hud enuff ey this prick,' he snaps – 'Get the door.'

The figure in the chair seizes up with fear as the gun is pushed into his face – 'Oh, no! Please, no!' Click; his face crumples as an empty chamber registers in his brain – 'Oh, no! Please! Nae mer! Al sign it! Al sign it!' he cries – 'Al sign it!'

Nerdy and Gerry look at each other; there's nothing like a vacant chamber to give that extra push – 'Right, then. Fuckin move.'

The owner collapses in tears as they walk out the door; he's signed his business over, for a tenner – 'Oh, Jesus. Jesus, oh, ohh,' he bubbles into his sleeve as the foul smell of his soiled trousers reaches his nostrils – 'Oh, Go-odd!'

Nerdy does a double-take on the way out; he picks up a packet from the table — 'Aww, fuckin magic man, wine gums,' he laughs — 'S'wee Jimmy's favourites. Thanks, pal! Hmmm. Black yins tae.'

Gerry rolls down the car window; the young mechanic looks up from the engine as he hears the two men call him over — 'Here, pal, don't open yer mooth, son. Ye wurk fur a new owner, okay?'

The young boy looks at the gun between the drivers legs — 'Eh? Wit? Naw, naw, goat nuthin tae dae wi me, mate,' he declares — 'M'only wurkin here.'

Nine days, twelve garages, and four hundred jellies later, Mick's wee gang meet some serious resistance; an owner who has himself had a taste of porridge, doesn't take too kindly to the threats and intimidation — 'Ye'll fuckin wi-it?' he roars — 'Get tae fuck oot ey here!'

Harry 'Basher' Galloway has recently completed a ten-year sentence and feels entitled to some respect; he considers himself a face having done heavy time, but jail is for all the bams, rockets and steamers — 'Who dae these pricks fink thur dealin wi?' he asks the small audience in his yard — 'Cunts widnae last two minutes in the jail.'

Big Basher's been living in another dimension; he's been existing in a hate factory, in a world of 'Us and Them'. He may physically be at liberty, but his thinking hasn't been stretched beyond the ancient mythology of Cons against Screws — 'Fuckin bams, eh boys?'

Maybe someone should have put him in the picture; him being a major face, but those pals don't seem to be saying too much — 'Aye, Basher. Wi gaun fur a pint Bashur?'

An hour later, Nerdy and Gerry are crashed-out on the sofa. They emerge from a two-week-old jellie haze with only vague memories of the events that have taken place.

'Bashur ur sumthin,' recalls Nerdy – 'Aye, Bashur, that wis it,' he muses, nursing a black eye – 'Thur wis a few urra guys there tae.'

Gerry confirms the recollection – 'Aye Basher, that wis it,' he nods – 'Wanney they big cunts, muscles on es foreheid. S'a squad ey thum when wi got there.'

The squad in the garage had been stunned when the two guys walked in that day.

'Here, who's the owner?' Nerdy had asked – 'Basher?'

Basher knocked the first one out, then he threw the other one out onto the main road, screaming – 'Ye'll fuckin wi-it?'

Mick knows him – 'Och, that big prick? Kin huv a go, but wull put a fuckin bullit in um, the prick. Wit happened wi the message? D'ye noa use at?'

Gerry laughs – 'He left it in the motur! Pull't oot a packet a fuckin wine gums. Nae wunner wi got battured.'

Nerdy smiles grotesquely – 'S'in the glove compartment. S'kerryin the sweeties in ma pockets fur days.' He grins sheepishly – 'Am gonny dae this cunt masel by the way,' he vows – 'Canny even eat a sweetie cosey that cunt.'

Mick picks up his 9mm – 'Think ye shood wi that fuckin coopin!' he says, stuffing the gun into a shoulder holster under his jacket – 'Right, c'mon en. Everycunt geared up? Right, let's go.'

The whole house is in hysterics with Nerdy – 'Aye, innit'l noa be fuckin wine gums iss time!' Everyone's geared up and ready to go – 'Aye, Mick, that's everycunt ready. Ye phonin Pat?' asks Gerry – 'Said tae remind ye.'

Pat's delighted to hear about the progress with the garages but is annoyed when told about Nerdy – 'Tell Nerdy tae lug that cunt.'

Nerdy's blootered as he squeezes himself into the back of the car – 'Move o'er you, ya cunt,' he growls – 'S'at a wee joint ye'v got there, Malky?'

Two joints fill the car with smoke – 'Right. Every cunt in? Let's go. Get a cuppla lines oot afore wi hit the traffic. Good Charlie, eh?' snorts Mick – 'Nerdy, hide that coopin man, frightenin they fuckin weans o'er there!'

Malky, the driver, snorts a line on the dash board – 'Mick? Wit's the address? Wer wi gaun?' he asks.

Mick spits out the passenger window – 'Maryhull. C'mon, get the boot doon. See wit this big prick's all about. Go doon Royston n up through Springburn.'

The carload of guys swerves about all over the road as they bear down on the garage; squibs and crackers explode all over the place as screeching heads poke out of the trail of smoke billowing from the windows – 'HA-UW YA FUCKERS!' BANG! BANG! BANG!

Basher's just leaving as the car comes hurtling towards him; he jumps as firecrackers explode around his feet – CRACK! POP! – 'Whauuugh! Wit the fuck?' CRACK! POP! Ping! He catches a distinctive ring whizzing past his ear as the first shot ricochets off an old car behind him.

'Ooops!' shouts Nerdy – 'A missed!'

His second shot smashes through cartilage and bone once called Basher – 'Ahyaaa!' he roars clutching his knee – 'Ma fuckin leg!'

Phut! Phut! Phut! The flat impotent sound of modern guns,

almost like toys, signals a direct hit; the caress as bone softly cracks open like an egg and six more bullets punch holes in the body – Thud! Thud! Thud! Thud! Thud! Thud! – 'Didnae miss at time!' shouts Nerdy.

Basher's screaming hysterically, laughing; blood's spurting all over him forming a blackening pool underneath his body. The stream fades as his heart pumps out its final beat in a burst of frothy blood. The last thing he sees is the big black hole down at the end of a Colt .45 – Nerdy's – 'Fuckin pricks!' he defiantly spits – 'Fuck you! Fuck you!'

Orange flame licks the side of his head before the pathetic look of the dead slips over his face like a mask; he falls silent, death's low key leaving only a sordid atmosphere.

They roar off in the car screaming and laughing; tree-top high on hash and coke, they head for the hills – 'Right! Back up the road! C'mon! Get the boot doon!'

People just walk past the body – 'Nuthin tae dae wi me.'

Chapter Eight

PAT AND JANIS watch the newsflash at home – 'Anurra shootin, eh. S'gettin like fuckin Dodge City,' Pat sniggers – 'Every time ye turn the telly oan thur's been a shootin. Thur wis mer shootins here last year than Northern Ireland. Amazin, eh?'

Janis nods – 'Aye, Pat. Shsht tae a hear the thing.'

Mark Geissler is standing in front of the garage – 'Yes, Shareen. I'm at the scene now. Police believe the killing may have been the result of a dispute between criminals. Mr Galloway is believed to have had links to the underworld. He had only recently completed a ten-year prison sentence for armed robbery.'

Shareen Nanjiani's face appears on the screen – 'Yes, Mark. Are the police following any definite leads?' she asks.

Pat shakes his head – 'The underworld?' he laughs – 'S'that Geissler. Am tellin ye. Coppers shood be watchin him. Es at every murder scene in Glesga.'

Mark Geissler glances to the side – 'Yes, Shareen. I have with me now Chief Inspector Ron McGhee. Chief Inspector, do the police have any leads? It's understood the victim may have had links to the underworld?'

Pat grins as the familiar fat face fills the screen.

'Well, Mark, Mr Galloway did have a connection with the criminal underworld, but we are treating this case as we would in any other circumstances, particularly an incident involving guns. We are determined to stamp out the growing gun culture.

We are going after them and they will be jailed, for a very, very long time,' he warns – 'We will pursue these people and put them away where they belong.'

Pat interrupts again – 'An incident? Some guy gets shot an it's an incident? That jist shows ye, eh. Lucky if a shootin gets page three these days.'

Janis agrees – 'A know. He looks a right bastard, dint ey?' she says.

Shareen Nanjiani smiles at them – 'Mark Geissler there, reporting. And now for other news,' she says, shuffling the papers on her desk – 'There was good news today for a family as they were reunited with a long lost friend. Rag Tag the cat disappeared on Guy Fawkes Night. Little Lorna Anderson had . . .'

Pat flicks off the television – 'Rag Tag the fuckin cat? S'it aw comin tae, eh. Anyway, ye up tae the day, hen?' he asks.

Janis looks in the mirror – 'Meetin that new accountant this efternin. Try'n shift some money through another account. S'gettin embarrassin, so it is. Thur's noa a hairstylist anywhere makin this kinna money. Vidal Sassoon disnae make five hunner grand a week cuttin hair, fur fucksake,' she says.

Pat picks up a newspaper – 'Oh, aye,' he replies – 'Al see if wi kin find a way a shiftin mer this week. Derek's meetin a guy, sum lifer in the Special Unit.'

Janis looks at his reflection in the mirror – 'The Special Unit? They're aw crackpots int they? A lassie that works fur me visits wanney thum up there. Says they kin thingmy, huv sex. A mean, in a jail?' she giggles – 'Sounds awright, eh.'

Pat laughs into his newspaper – 'Aye, sound. Naw this guy kin sell a paintin an en ey jist hauns the money intae the bank, nae questions asked,' he explains.

Janis has a final look at herself – 'Hmmm. Is ey an artist ur sumthin? Thur aw artists up there, int they?' she laughs – 'Him that dis es sculptures an that. Wit's es name? Es always in the newspapers? Och, thingmy. Widye ye call um? Ey wis torturin people n aw that.'

Pat continues studying the newspaper – 'Wullie Dempster,' he says.

She snaps her fingers – 'That's him! He noa write a book ur somethin? A story aboot the jail?' she asks – 'Es reformed noo ur somethin.'

Pat nods – 'Aye, Derek knows um fae the jail, sends um stuff in every week. Televisions an that. S'gaun tae wanney es exhibitions next week. Aye, s'in an art gallery. Ye wantey go?'

Janis shrieks – 'Wi-it? R'ye kiddin? A don't wantey meet him! Jesus! The guy's mad int ey? Wanney they fuckin sykapaths!' she shrieks – 'Ye kiddin!' She notices the newspaper shaking – 'You laughin at me? S'a funny?'

Pat looks up innocently – 'Witsat? Naw, naw. The guys awright, speaks aw polite an at. Honest! Es reformed, ye shood come doon n meet um fur a laugh. Wur gonny gie um a usin hen, es jist a bam,' he smiles – 'Humpty Dumpty.'

Janis looks at him – 'Humpty Dumpty?' she asks.

Pat sniggers – 'S'es nickname,' he says.

She doesn't believe him – 'Wi-it? Humpty . . . Aye, right. How d'ye get a name like that, Humpty Dumpty? Did ey faw aff the waw ur somethin?' she asks.

Pat folds away his paper – 'Aye, sound, hen, but yer gettin warm. S'a wee fat guy wi wanney they big giant heids,' he explains – 'N'every time es fell in the jail, screws put um back the gither again so . . .'

Janis laughs — 'Aye, well ey kin faw somewhere else. A don't wantey meet any these haufwits. A suppose es anurra wan sayin es innacent? That Woods wis in the papers again,' she remembers — 'Anurra hunger strike, claimin that thur innacent. That poor wean as well, deid.'

Pat cleans his spactacles — 'Well, funny enough, ey dis claim es innacent, but es oan es way oot noo, but es always said ey wis fitted up wi the coppers. Magine that, eh?' he smiles — 'Woods? Must be losin a lotta weight wi these hunger strikes. Anyway, d'ye noa fancy cummin tae this arty thing? S'in this pitch called The Third Eye Centre.'

Janis is adamant — 'Naw Pat, nae danjur. Av made ma mind up,' she states — 'S'*Angelena* Woods that's on the hunger strike, no him.'

Pat looks up — 'Es wife?' he asks — 'Es *wife* on a hunger strike?'

Janis nods — 'Aye, been forty days on it,' she replies.

Pat shrugs — 'Aw well, be daen ur model next. Anyway, wit aboot this art thing? D'ye noa fancy gaun? Be a laugh.'

'Pat! Naw! Av told ye. A don't wantey meet anya these fuckin haufwits n that's final.'

He picks up a book — 'Sound, hen, s'sound.'

The Third Eye Centre is packed; public figures, faces from the media, mingle with a selection of invited guests, including three warders heavily disguised in identical navy blue anoraks and representatives from the Scottish Office Prison Department.

Christopher Carel, the director of the art gallery, is into the final thread of a speech just as some new guests are arriving — 'And now! And with great pleasure! Indeed, first of all, let me express my most sincere gratitude to my next guest,' he beams – 'Without whom, I might add, none of this could have happened,' he gasps – 'Without his ceaseless work in the search for truth, his discoveries in bringing artists from all parts of the world, and illuminating the art world . . . it is with great pleasure that I present to you, our distinguished speaker, art entrepreneur, Mr Dicci Remarci!'

Champagne glasses ring amid the sound of applause as a small white-haired man in a dark suit appears on the podium. He's carrying a camera – 'Ladies. Gentlemen,' he gasps with arms open – 'Isn't this amazing?'

The general hum of agreement is hushed as he waves an arm – 'You know,' he smiles at the faces looking back – 'When Joseph Bueys and I first began our journey together some years ago, little did we know where that dialogue would eventually lead us.' He grins – 'The Special Unit at Barlinnie. The University of Life. You know, when we first walked through those gates, steel gates which could easily have inspired Piranesi, I was struck immediately by the space, the space occupied by one man. My friend, and artist, Billy Dempster.'

Dicci ackowledges the small eruption of applause – 'Thank you, thank you,' he smiles while taking a quick snap with the camera – 'Look around you. Look at this space. Is this not fantastic? That so many of us can occupy this space?' he asks, snapping all the while – 'Who could have believed that in one small space one man could produce such art?'

Janis shifts from one leg to the other – 'S'he gonny talk aw night?' she whispers – 'Av noa got a clue wit es oan aboot.'

Snap! Snap! Snap! – 'Isn't this wonderful?' asks the impresario – 'Friends, I give you . . . Billy Dempster!'

Wullie Dempster blushes as he takes the microphone –

'Well, what kin a say?' he grins awkwardly – 'Well, what am tryin tae do is eh, be creative. Ye know, when a wis furst haundid a lump a clay sumthin inside me jist exploded,' he explains – 'A mean, a hud never felt like this in ma life ye know. A hud been fightin the systum fur years. A hud been brutalised like an animal an suddenly aw these feelins happened.' He continues as memories flood back – 'Ye know, arty stuff wis fur sissies wer a came fae. A mean, we aw lived in the auld tinament hooses, ye know? Ye hud tae be hard but noo a look back an a think, God! Why?' He's wringing his hands – 'Why? So wit am daen is jist expressin ma feelins, am chann'llin ma energy intae sumthin posative, ye know? A mean, aw these powerful feelins,' he says, bowing – 'Well, thanks, but before a stop, a wid jist like tae say that av used auld tinament blocks because that's the wurld that av came fae.' He adds cheekily – 'So am gien thum a new life!'

Janis nudges Pat – 'S'at Humpty? Jesus, that's sum heid innit?' she giggles – 'Look at es wee bowley legs tae!'

Pat grins discreetly – 'Shsht, turn it up, you.'

Derek is watching other guests – 'Check that big fist, man,' he says, looking at a stone carving of a clenched fist – 'Brulliant, eh? Here,' he whispers – 'S'that Jack Lolly?'

Pat turns to look – 'Who?' he asks.

Derek nods in the direction of the balding gentleman with Dempster – 'The Provost. A think he's the Lord Provost,' he whispers – 'Try'n get an in wi him, eh, an wur laughin. Check aw they urra cunts, by the way, Scottish Office.'

Pat nods – 'Wit're they aw daen here?' he asks.

Derek shrugs – 'Fuck knows, cos es changed maybe.'

The Lord Provost is promoting the lifer's rehabilitation; the placement to art school is his baby – 'Yes, Billy is a changed man,' he's saying — 'Scotland has pioneered in the processes of rehabilitation, we are the model for the future.'

The experimental unit had brought interest from around the world as a new method in rehabilitation but had been controversial from the very beginning. It housed five of the country's most dangerous killers and the tabloid press had dug deep, probing for flaws in the new concept. The position just had to be a success — no two ways about it. Wullie Dempster had the weight of the world on his shoulders; one single mistake and it would spell the end of any future he might have had planned for himself — 'Wit? M'jist expressin ma feelins,' he could be heard saying — 'S'aw aboot resocializashun.'

Janis walks around the art gallery looking at the stone carvings — 'Wit dis that mean?' she asks looking at a sculpture — 'S'like a big prick on a dug's leash if ye ask me,' she concludes.

Derek eyes her with thinly disguised disgust — 'S'creative hen, creative. You widnae know wit that meant,' he snipes — 'Guy's daen es best, wurkin es ticket, an aw you kin see is big pricks.'

Pat senses an argument — 'Here, Derek, s'wit ye see innit? N'they dae look like pricks wi chains wrapped roon thum. You a fuckin art critic noo?'

Derek shrugs — 'Aw, here wi go,' he laughs — 'Aw, here. Wullie's cumin o'er so don't say anythin. Fucksake man, tryin tae dae a bitta fuckin graft, man.'

Wullie Dempster throws his arms around him — 'Derek! Thanks fur cumin. How ye doin, young yin?' he asks — 'Got that message, by the way, thanks.'

Derek hides his embarrassment; hugs are for sissies too — 'Wullie! Ach, nae problum. A like yer sculpures, by the way, fuckin brulliant,' he lies – 'Listen, S'Pat McGowan, an Janis, ma sister.'

Pat takes Wullie's hand – 'Aye, how ye doin?' he smiles – 'Like yer stuff. Ye learn that up in Bar L?'

Dempster beams – 'Janis? Pleased tae meet ye. N'your Pat? Pleased tae meet ye's. Barlinnie? Naw, Pat. S'aw negativity in that place. So widye think ey the exhibition?' he asks – 'M'jist expressin ma feelins, dae ye know wit a mean?'

Janis doesn't miss the gleam in his eye; she knows she looks good – 'S'awright. How dae ye dae it? V'ye got a wee tool?' she asks – 'Ad luv sumthin like that,' she smiles, pointing to what can only be a huge penis in a dog collar – 'Kinna wantey touch thum, dint ye.'

Dempster can't help himself; he's almost panting – 'Ye-aah? Well, why don't ye come up an visit?' he leers – 'A cood show ye how tae haunle a big wan.'

Pat doesn't bat an eyelid – 'Aye, Janis, Derek kin take ye up,' he grins – 'How d'ye visit? D'ye need a pass, Wullie?'

Oh, Wullie, Wullie, Wullie. Times have changed; this is evolution staring at you, this will eat you alive – 'Visit passes? Naw, thur's visits every day, an it's aw day,' he drools – 'Aw ye dae is gie yer name at the gate an a screw picks ye up an brings ye o'er. Janis kin phone in an let me know.'

Janis hooks him in – 'Oh, dae ye huv phones?' she asks – 'Home fae home, eh. N'wit's the visits like?'

Dempster cocks his head to the side; he senses the flesh below that black fabric; heat is flowing towards him – 'Well, hardly hame, but the visits? Lets jist say wur guaranteed privacy,' he winks.

Derek feels the connection's made – 'Right then, listen. How dae ye buy a sculpture? A mean, dae you get the money ur dae that mob put it in the bank?' he asks.

Dempster's ego is fully blown – 'That mob? Naw, av got an account. Witsat? Naw it usually comes in cash. A prefer cash, tae be honest, Derek. S'pecially if av sold wan in private, the buyers like anonymity,' he winks – 'Know wit a mean.'

Derek's amazed – 'So you jist haun a big chunka money intae the bank. Dae they noa asks questions?' he asks – 'S'amazin, man.'

Pat picks up the thread – 'So, if a gave you, say fifty grand, you cood jist take it intae the bank?' he asks – 'Ur a hunner grand? How's that?'

Dempster smiles smugly – 'Am an artist.'

Janis is relieved when he's grabbed by some other guests – 'Ugh. He's horrible. D'ye hear um tryin tae be wide there?' she shudders – 'Gie ye the creeps.'

Pat winks at her – 'S'got the hots fur you hen, eh?' he laughs – 'Anyway Derek'll be wi ye when ye go up.'

Janis draws him a look – 'See, you, by the way,' she purrs – 'Visitin that? Tries any es nonsense es in fur a shock. Am tellin ye, wit a shock al gie um.'

They wander around looking at the sculptures – 'Wull head off shortly. Go fur a meal. Fancy Janis, a wee curry?' asks Pat – 'Mani's ur sumthin?'

Janis peers at another phallic symbol – 'S'aff es heid int ey, Pat? Look at um. Who's that es wi?' she asks, looking over to the small gathering around yet another of those erections on the plinths – 'S'at no him fae the telly, Dave Thingmy? Oh look at thum!' she squeals – 'Thur kissin! Look at thum, thur sookin the face aff each urra!'

Pat looks – 'Headcases, bent shots the lottey thum, eh,' he

sniggers – 'Listen, thur aw startin tae get bevvied. Ye wantey head off?' he asks – 'Get Derek n wull leave. You see um anywhere, Janis?'

Janis sees him with a waitress – 'Mighta known,' she smirks – 'Al go an get um, Pat. Noise um up.'

Pat feels someone tugging at his sleeve – 'Amazing, isn't it?' says a voice.

'Wit-sat?' he asks staring down the lense of a camera.

'Isn't this wonderful?' the voice repeats. Snap! Snap! Snap! – 'All these people! In one small space! Amazing, isn't it?'

Pat tries to turn away – 'Listen, mate,' he's saying.

Snap! Snap! Snap – 'Isn't this fantastic?'

Pat turns – 'Get that thing oot ma fuckin face,' he hisses – 'Prick.'

The small clutch of television celebrities are oblivious to the other guests; the head at the centre of the group can't be seen but he's there – 'Am jist expressin ma powerful feelins. Who? Dustyovski? *Crime n Punishment*! Brulliant, so it is!'

Derek feels the hand on his arm – 'Wit?' he shouts above the din – 'A canny hear ye,' he shouts again – 'Witsat? Aw, right! Right, okay, noa be a minute!'

Janis pushes her way back through the packed huddle of guests – 'Am jist expressin ma feelins!' someone's shouting – 'S'resocializashun, so it is!'

Pat has someone up against the wall; there's a camera lying on the floor, broken, the film roll casing is empty – 'Were's the fuckin spool?' he's asking – 'The fuckin spool? Were is it?'

Derek and Janis pull him to the door – 'Space? Al put um in a six-feet-deep space, the prick.' He's grinning, but they see the look in his eyes.

'Right, Pat, c'mon, c'mon' Derek says – 'S'Dicci Remarci, Dempster's pal.'

Pat brushes them off – 'Right, s'sound. Wis jist that daft camera,' he grins – 'Did ye hear um? Anyway, c'mon. Mani's, fur a curry.' he concludes – 'V'hud anuff ey this shite. Phone that bampot an get a visit sortit oot, buy a cuppla they big boulders.'

Derek's nodding – 'Och, a noa. Thur aw headcases,' he laughs – 'Wis nippin that wee thing there tae. N'Morticia here put the fuckin brakes oan that, dint she, eh?'

Janis shrugs her shoulders – 'M'jist expressin ma feelins!'

They all burst out laughing – 'S'aw negativity!'

Part Two

Chapter Nine

BIG RON'S HAVING a tiresome day; the two files lying on his desktop pose a particularly perplexing problem; each file contains complaints against officers under his command. Who dreamt this one up? he wonders, looking at the two officers standing stiffly before him.

A Keystone Cops scenario lies before his eyes; thick hairy fingers drum the desktop as he ponders their histories with the police force. Intelligent enough, he thinks. No blemishes, or any unhealthy sick leave. Good, sound officers. So why? Why this stupidity?

William Brodie; Ron flat-footed the beat with this lad's father, what, twenty years ago? A good officer, indeed, a good friend; he'd known how to handle himself back then, in the old days. His commitment unquestionable and an absolute loyalty to the force. A chip off the old block? he asked himself. Did the boy have fibre, bottle? – 'Well, well, well. This is a serious complaint,' he mutters – 'Hmm. Very serious.'

Jackie Maloney; twelve years with us, he notes, and a Catholic – 'Any affiliations o'er the water, son?' he asks – 'None at aw? Hmm.'

Maloney looks stupid enough, but – 'Officur Brodie. Who had the bright idea a makin the arrest?' asks the inspector – 'S'it you?'

Officer Brodie stares straight ahead at the calendar on the wall behind the Inspector's head – 'Yes, sur!' he barks – 'Officur Maloney hud nuthin tae dae wi any this, sur! The decision wis mine, sur! N'a assaulted the suspect maself, sur!'

Yes; his father all over the back – 'Did you indeed? N'Maloney hud nae idea where aw that drink came fae? N'the cigarette cartons that wis discuvered in es house?' he grins – 'Oh, don't tell me. Ey jist fun thum. S'that right? Sounds like wan ey the tales ye'd expect fae the like'sa Barney Boone.'

Maloney shifts slightly; the trickle of sweat running all the way down from his neck to that forested valley between his cheeks feels like an army of red ants marching across a stretch of white, goose-pimpled terrain; the itching is relentless. He extends a desperate finger, but that darkest region on earth is beyond the long arm of the law – he bites his lip, wondering – 'Permission tae scratch ma arse, sur?'

No, better not.

The chief notices his discomfort – 'Problum, son?' he grins – 'Sit doon, the pairey ye.' he orders – 'Time wi sortit this oot.'

The two police officers glance at each other as they take a seat. What is he thinking? They wonder in silence. They had been expecting to lose their jobs; the theft of all the goods was in itself enough for automatic dismissal, but battering the suspect? Visions of prison loomed heavily in the air. Why? Why did they have to go after that little bastard? They had emptied the premises; they should have left it at that, another burglary, no big deal.

Maloney battered all his suspects; how were they to know that this one would be different? How were they to know that the shop belonged to the suspect's father? Fuckin Pakis. What was the suspect doing, anyway, sleeping on the fucking premises? How were they to know? They thought he was a burglar and now what . . . jail?

Chief Inspector McGhee leans his big, square jawbone on steepled fingers – 'Right. A want straight answers. Aff the record mind,' he grins – 'Long ye been at it? N'by the way, who put this character's name doon as Govan?'

Maloney and Brodie flinch; jail talk, this is fuckin jail talk – 'Ehm, am noa sure wit yer meanin, sur,' stammers Maloney – 'Long wi been at it?' he repeats – 'At wit, sur?' he asks – 'This wis the furst time wi—'

Big Ron interrupts his explanation – 'Listen, son. Don't waste ma time. Am tryin tae be fair. So am gonny ask ye wance mer. Noo. How long have you two hud yer hauns in the till?' he demands – 'N'don't insult ma intelligence noo.'

Brodie takes the dive – 'S'me, sur. Av been takin things fae burglaries fur awhile. Jist odds an ends. A regret it noo but thur's no much else a kin say sur, is thur?'

The Inspector looks to the partner – 'N'you?'

Maloney bows his head – 'Me tae, sur. N'the suspect did gie es name as Govan. Said es Da hud christened him Govan Bashir. Ey spoke in Scottish tae, sur. Said that it wis better than Elvis. That's when a hut um, sur.'

McGhee pushes the files into the drawer on his desk; he looks at them intently, firstly to demonstrate his power, and secondly to display grandfatherly fairness – 'Well, well, well. Wur finally progressin,' he smiles – 'They stay in ma desk. You'll baith remain suspended, full pay a course, jist fur the time bein. That shopkeeper's gonny huv tae be convinced that thur complaints huv been investigated and dealt wi thoroughly,' he continues – 'N'that's no gonny be easy, es boy's jaw's broke. Wance that's settled the pair ey ye kin return tae full duty. An fur your information. Halfey the black community have been born an bred in Glasgow. A don't want any racist complaints oan ma desk in the future. N'that better be clear tae you especially, Jack-o.'

Maloney and Brodie feel total relief; they can't believe their luck, their Chief is giving them a break.

'Ye'll be wurkin directly under ma supervision,' he's saying – 'Anurra thing. This whole matter remains wi me. Wan word fae eithery ye, an yer right doon that fuckin road. Understood?'

Maloney and Brodie are ecstatic, and are free, as they roar in unison – 'YESS, SURR! UNDERSTOOD, SURRR!'

Big Ron picks up the telephone as they leave his office – 'Hullo? Pat? Aye, s'me. An how's yerself? Good, good. Listen, think we shood maybe huv a drink? Aye, cuppla friendsa mine ye might be interested in. Aye, an a cuppla urra things tae.' He fingers the other report on his desk – 'S'Woods. Remember? Wo-ods, fae that kerry oan, mind a cuppla years ago. Angelena, s'right, that's hur. Well hunger strikes ur wan thing, but when it's a wumin, people start payin attention, know wit a mean?' he asks – 'S'Angelena, aye, fuckin pest. Oh, a know. She'd get parole if she wid jist play the game but aw this protest business? Right, okay. Friday? Usual place? Okay then, an by the way, av a wee message fur ye. Okay, bye,' he says hanging up. A hunger strike, he laughs to himself. Probably thinks they're trying to poison her.

Angelena lies prostrate on the old wooden board, covered only by a single army issue blanket, her thin frame, grinding with every movement against the harsh flat surface of the bed, is covered in sores, but never a whimper escapes her lips. The first three days had been the worst; hunger, though, had left her, leaving her blood to eat itself.

She had taught herself yoga; disciplining herself, practising the exercises every day, discovering new and inner strengths, until finally she overcame the loneliness of solitary confinement, refusing anything interpreted as a privilege, anything that could be taken away from her, anything the authorities could employ as punishment – even contact with other human beings.

'So? How are we today then?' a voice asks.

The prison doctor pauses before taking her pulse, knowing there would be no answer. This prisoner had been taken too far; beatings, food poisoning, and almost every other form of punishment imaginable, inflicted upon her person, and here he is, he thought, asking how she feels – 'Eaten anything today?' he asks.

The steel food tray lay on the floor in the corner of her cell – untouched – 'Well just be sure to keep taking liquids,' he nodded – 'See you again tomorrow.'

Somehow, she had reversed it all; prison warders tried to talk to her, prison governors tried to coax her, but silence reigned. He knew that her physiological state was sound, considering, but he felt deep concern for the woman, and regardless of what she may have done in the past, it was his duty as a doctor to relieve suffering, but how?

Three years; three long, lonely years of solitary confinement she had endured, but her determination hadn't deserted her; the fights with staff and inmates bore testament to her tenacity and ferocity – she was no 'beast'.

Divina, her sister, had needed something to create some kind of focus for Angelena's case, something to provoke the public. The hunger strike had been her only recourse, her only avenue of protest, much to the consternation of the prison management who were now begging her to eat, not for any altruistic interests but to ease the heat from the press.

She looked at the photograph of herself in the daily newspapers; the smiling face that looked back was from another time, a stranger from another life – she could no longer recognise herself. The world outside of her cell had changed so much in such a short space of time; her only connection, the daily newspapers, allowed her for an hour each day, a privilege she would accept for the time being, told her very little. Robert and John, they look so young in the photograph, she thought. She missed her man. Her heart had been wracked with pain in the beginning; the loss, gnawing into her in the night when unexpectedly she would awaken with the full realisation that they were separated – forever, for life.

But that was back then. Now she walked through walls, broke through the steel bars, travelled those long miles to find her man, to find him alone in a cell; transcendental meditation had released her, freed her spirit from the clay, the processes of memory, creating access into space.

Not a single teardrop fell upon her cheek. She had no tears left, only her memories, and determination to fight. Poor Robert, she smiles sadly, looking at his last letter as it sits neatly in the pile on the floor – 'My Darlin Angelena . . .'

Letters; precious pieces of paper, that's all she had left of her previous life, a few kind words here and there from friends, some too from people she hadn't known, the most touching of them a letter from their parish priest, Father Joseph Kennedy.

The letter from the priest had puzzled her. He believed in their innocence for some reason. He'd always seemed a nice man, she remembered, he always said hello in the street, always asked how her mother had been – 'How's the family, Angelena?' Most of the letters said that they couldn't believe her capable of anything like this, but the priest had been different, he'd said specifically that he had '*known*' that they were innocent. '*Known*' – not 'I think' but '*known.*'

Well, at least they had one person on their side; funny, he hadn't replied to her letter. Did he know something? Did someone confess to the murders? No, she thought, but he had said '*known*' in his letter – '*known*' definitely.

Who's that? she wonders as she flips through the pages. I know that face, she thinks, glimpsing a photograph – 'Sweeney?' she murmurs – 'S'that that Derek Sweeney? Aye, it is him,' she mutters – 'S'it sayin? ". . . recognition by the local authorities in the . . . FIGHTIN DRUGS?!"'

She browses through the feature – the war on drugs? – 'Th-at bastard? Rec-ogni-tion fur his tireless efforts wi deprived kids?' she sneers – 'S'aw his fuckin gear!'

She throws the paper aside and stares at the ceiling; the breakfast tray lies cold in the corner, but she can still smell the shrivelled slice of bacon. She smiles, thinking of the previous day. That screw asking if she had licked the bread, and then telling her that she wouldn't tell them. Tell who? she'd wondered; funny how they all think that they know how to handle her, that she'll speak to them and not the others – 'Leave this tae me. She knows me now. She'll speak tae me. I have a relationship with her, sir.'

Oh, Angelena knew them alright. She knew them by their sound, by their smells and by their very presence outside that fucking door; listening to them, listening to all the same stories night after night, listening to their gossip about each other, their deadly whispering, their affairs with other screws, their scams with canteens, wages, anything – a Biro pen, a sheet of shit paper.

Screws, she sniggers – fucking arseholes.

Divina's visit pass; had that bitch sent it out? Why had she asked if she had been due a visit? Had she licked the bread? Was she due a visit? Was that a warning? What made the bitch think that she would speak to her? Did *she* believe she was innocent? No, but that letter, he definitely meant '*known*' – definitely. He must know something. But then again, maybe not. He would have said something at the time, gone public or something. He was a priest; he would tell the truth, well, wouldn't he?

The door slams open – 'Dinner,' a voice says – 'Still nae eating, lass?'

She looked at the scratches on the wall; forty-five days she noted, forty-five days done without food. That's one-hundred-and-thirty-five meals. Oh, and plus forty-five buns at night; hardly likely to change her mind now at this stage, was she? Maybe this screw knew her better than the others.

'A dinny understaun ye, Woods. That's a braw pie n chips there. This'll get ye naewhere, lass.'

Angelena sneers as the door closes again. Bitch – 'S'a brrrrraw pie n chips there, lass!' she silently mimics. Why didn't she eat it then? Couldn't take her beady fucking eyes off the thing. A braw pie and chips. Fucking Highlanders – 'S'a braw moonlicht nicht the nicht!' The fuck are they all about? Fucking pies and chips. She better have put that visit pass out – 'Al take hur fuckin eye oot,' she silently vows.

Poor Robert, she thinks, picking up his last letter. Had he drawn these roses himself? Must have, she concludes, touching the tiny flowers drawn onto the paper – 'My Darlin

Angelena . . .' Must have drawn them himself. No one speaks to the 'beasts' in Perth Prison – 'Ma poor man,' she murmurs – 'Never hermed a soul.' Why couldn't he stand up for himself – be a man? Those bastards breaking his arm as he was being transferred. We're fair game for these people, but, she smiles, two can play at that game. Scalding that cow with boiling water had brought attacks on her to an end; that cow had no face left – no roses on her letters.

No one messed with Angelena; funny how they all respect violence. No matter what crime you are in for, if you can fight, no one says a thing. Any weakness and they'll eat you alive. The Cortonvale heavy team; lifers who think they're the fucking beez-neez, but she showed them. Boiling water and sugar wake-up call – 'S'yer tea, doll.'

The screams; fucking bitch – 'Fuckin Freddie Kruger,' she smirks.

A screw opens the door – 'A visitor fur you,' she says, kicking a pair of shoes into the cell – 'Get them on.'

Angelena feels light-headed as she climbs up from the board; the four screws keep an eye open as she pulls the laceless shoes onto her bare feet.

'Ye needin socks?' asks one, before noticing the looks of disapproval – 'Oh. Right then, lass, c'mon.'

Angelena's last pair of socks had been filled with a battery. A PP9 embedded in a lifer's cheekbone had been discovered one morning, just before breakfast – another of her 'scalps' who would remain rose-less.

The fluorescent lights in the visit room make her feel dirty; the rows of tables lie empty but she selects one furthest from the screws so that she can talk privately. Talk? Three months had passed since she last exercised her vocal chords;

twelve weeks, and not so much as a song in the night —
silence reigned.

Divina looks at her sister as she sits down — 'Ye awright,
hen?' she asks — 'Av brought ye . . . Witsat, hen?'

Angelena's eyes are shining — 'V'ye phoned um yet? Ey
knows sumthin. Am tellin ye. Ey said ey *knows*.' she croaks
— 'Ey definitely *knows*. Am tellin ye . . . ey *knows*.'

Divina drops her head — 'Aw, Angie, fucksake! Noa aw this
shite again!'

Chapter Ten

BIG RON ARRIVES early for the meeting; the bar is fairly quiet – 'A double son, nae ice.' he orders – 'S'quiet, eh?'

The barman glances around – 'S'early doors,' he replies – 'Be gled tae hear that last bell, tae be honest.'

Big Ron raises his glass to his lips – 'Oh? Been a long day?' he asks.

'Ach, well. Yer bored when it's like this,' replies the barman – 'Prefer it busy masel. Yer day aff?' he asks.

'Me? Yer never aff-duty in this game,' replies the cop – 'Stull, better than sittin aboot in a station aw day,' he winks – 'Same again son, nae ice.'

Pat appears by his side – 'Awright, big man,' he drawls – 'Sounded urgent? Bertie's conscience bothurin um again?'

Big Ron looks up – 'Aye, Pat, thought ad missed ye,' he replies – 'Bertie? Och, naw, es fine. Be in shortly.' He nods in the direction of a table in the corner – 'Naw, naw, wis jist a wee blether.' He winks – 'Might need a wee favour. Oh, here, afore a furget. Stick that in yer boot.'

Pat feels the package; powder, he smiles – 'Much?'

The chief shrugs – 'Cuppla ounce,' he says – 'D.S. took it aff that wee Rosinni. Turnt um o'er by mistake,' he continues – 'S'nuthin tae worry aboot. S'aw been sortit oot noo. Naw, thur's sumthin else. Cuppley ma young yins, made an arse ey a wee turn a while ago. V'got a fuckin Paki breathin doon ma neck noo.'

Pat twirls the ice around his glass – 'A Paki?' he laughs

– 'Pure trouble, that mob. Ye want sumthin done?' he asks.

'Naw, naw,' replies the cop – 'S'got tae be sumthin wi kin use against um, shut um up wi so thur's nae come back, police brutality ur any that kinna thing. D'ye know wit a mean?'

Pat nods – 'Aye. Wit aboot a burd, sexual harassment? People know wit thur like wi white wumin. A cood fire a wee burd in at um,' he suggests.

'Naw Pat, wid take too long,' replies the cop – 'Naw, sumthin mer immediate. Sumthin that kin shut um doon right away. Two good boys tae, the black bastard.'

Pat laughs – 'Rats. Wit aboot rats?' he asks.

'Here, Pat. That might jist be wit wur lookin fur,' agrees the cop – 'Rats. Aye, rats. But how wid ye get thum in? How wid ye get thum intae es shop?' he asks.

Pat twirls the ice around – 'Leave it tae me,' he smiles – 'Aw, here ey is,' he says as he glances up at the door – 'S'the bold yin. Look at um, hink ey wis on the fuckin run. Check um, Wee Shifty Spears.'

Bertie looks like a fugitive; the turned-up collar of his overcoat conceals the lower part of his unshaven face; two hunted eyes glance around the bar before he sneaks into the vacant seat at the table – 'Awright, Ron?' he asks – 'Pat, hullo, eh, eh, ye awright?' He grins as his colleague hits the bar – 'Aye, Ron, thanks. Double an a wee chaser tae, aye.'

Pat devours his soul; he looks at him for a moment, shaking his head – 'Trouble wee man, eh?' he says – 'A like yer disguise, by the way, the collar up an at, a wid nevera recognised ye wi the bunnit.'

Big Ron looks over from the bar; Bertie's terror is obvious

– 'S'up wi um noo?' he mutters irritably – 'Be Pat terrarisin the poor cunt again.'

Bertie's frozen; those bulging eyes, pleading Not Guilty – 'Trouble?' he almost squeals in response – 'Me-eee?'

Pat deadpans him – 'Noa seen the papurs the day?' he asks – 'M'surprised at ye, wee man. Thought ye'd a been Joe the Toff. London ur sumthin.'

Big Ron bangs the tumblers onto the table – 'S'the matter wi you noo?' he snaps – 'A canny leave ye fur five minutes! Noo nark it, am tellin ye, Bertie!'

Bertie's falsetto screech leaves his tormentor in stitches – 'But he's jist said! He's jist said am in trouble!' he squeals – 'Am in aw the papurs! Oh, Jesus Christ! A knew this wid happen! Oh, Jesus Christ! S'that bank, innit? S'that fuckin teller, innit?'

He yelps as the inspector's fingers dig into his arm – 'Sit n yer arse!' he growls – 'Pat, wull ye tell this bampot! Bertie! Sit n yer fuckin arse!' he repeats – 'Pat's kiddin ye. Listen tae me. Es kiddin ye. Thur's nuthin in the papurs. Pat?'

Pat twirls the rocks of ice – 'S'like Richard Kimble there wi that fuckin outfit. Look at um man,' he grins – 'Jist noisin um up. Yer like *The Fugitive* there, wee man.'

Bertie draws back his shoulders; he's looking at one and then the other – 'Kiddin me? Kiddin me?' he snarls – 'Eh? M'a a fuckin mug noo? Eh? Kiddin me? Eh? Eh? Aw right, a see noo. Eh? Wee Bert's a fuckin mug noo, eh?'

Big Ron's trying to keep a straight face; *The Fugitive?* Right enough, he thinks. Bertie does look like the profile of a wanted poster, but that puffed-up rib cage looks quite a sight – 'Bertie, listen. Pat didny mean tae bam ye up. Naw, naw, c'mon noo. Thur's nae need fur that kinna talk,' he warns – 'C'mon noo.'

Pat's humour has limits; he turns on the little runt of a man — 'Wit wis that?' he asks quietly — 'Did you threaten me there? Wit? Naw, Ron, fuckin shut it. Wit did you say there?'

Bertie's face is turning grey; tiny specks of spit fleck his skin but he doesn't make any move; remains like a stunned rabbit before those eyes — 'Don't you ever growl at me, Hectur. D'ye fuckin hear me?' they ask — 'Sort me oot? Al put ye in a bin bag, ya fuckin bampot.'

Bertie can't speak; terror has gripped his vocal chords.

'P-at, P-at, c'mon man. P-at c'mon noo, wur aw friends here,' soothes the Inspector — 'Pat, eh? C'mon Bert didny mean wit ey said. Eh, Bertie?'

Pat's contempt is obvious — 'Sound, Ron, sound,' he smiles — 'Here, Bertie. Stick that in ma motur,' he orders — 'M'needin a wurd wi the big yin — in private.'

Bertie picks up the package — heroin — but the brief interlude's preferable to the look in those eyes — 'The boot? Eh, right, right, nae bother,' he whimpers — 'Eh, wull a get in a round when am up?'

Big Ron pats him on the back — 'S'awright Bertie, s'awright. Al get thum in,' he sighs. Poor Bertie, he thinks — 'M'jist huvin a wee wurd aboot sumthin, a wee private thing,' he winks — 'Noa be long.'

Private? Bertie's head drops; he's out, he realises. Fuck. Why did he have to be so nervous? Panicking all the time. Almost twenty years, twenty years on the force. All those years, and what? A private talk? He looked at his big swanky car; was it worth all this? God, he thinks, what has he done? What has he let himself in for? McGowan's off his fucking head, a fucking psychopath. He frightened him; there was something really scary about him. Those fucking eyes, like a dead fish.

The Campsie Hills? Ron, Ron, Ron. What have you done? This guy's killing people; he's a fucking maniac, an animal.

He throws the package into the boot of the car – 'Heroin,' he mumbles – 'Wit the fuck am a daen?'

Should he take off? he wonders. The Campsie Hills loom before him. No, McGowan had people; bastards who would find him – 'Fuckin smack,' he wails silently – 'Weans ur dyin fae this stuff, s'like fuckin poison, fuckin killin innacent people.'

He slams the boot down and checks to make sure it's secure – 'Oh, God, wit've a dun?' he mumbles again – 'How um a gonny get ootey this mess?' Is there anyone he could talk to? Is there anyone who would believe him? He should never have taken the money; that fucking car. Why had he been so stupid?

Ron's looking across the table – 'Christsakes, Pat. Bertie's daen es best. Scarin um's jist makin um more nervous,' he says – 'S'no like you. S'the maitur wi ye?'

Pat shrugs his shoulders – 'Ach, dun fuck aw but moan, n the paw's oot every time ye see um,' he replies – 'Better start earnin es wages.'

Big Ron gulps his drink – 'Wit?' he exclaims – 'Paddy! Bertie binned that last kerry oan wi the garages. That Basher charactur as well. Jesus,' he laughs – 'Es earned a wage awright. Your jist n a bad mood, that's aw, m'surprised at ye.'

Pat laughs – 'Ach. S'sound, big yin, sound,' he replies – 'Aw here, look. Es peepin through the door. Bertie!' he shouts – 'Get a round, wee man! Aye! Coke fur me an the same fur yersels.'

Wee man? He's in; he leans on the bar – 'Gettin busy noo, eh, son?' he remarks.

'Aye mate,' replies the barman – 'Keeps ye on yer toes. Ice wi the Coke?'

Bertie looks over to the table — 'Pat! Ice?' he calls.

'Aye, wee man,' winks one of those terrible eyes — 'Plentya ice.'

His face is beaming as he joins the others at the table — 'Right, Ron, er ye go, big man.' he chirps — 'N'at wan's yours, Pat. Cheers, lads. S'at enuff ice, Pat?'

Stick it up ma arse Pat?

Pat punches him, almost affectionately, on the shoulder — 'Ach, Bertie boy. S'sound wee man, sound,' he grins — 'Need tae calm doon. S'only kiddin ye there.'

Big Ron's relieved — 'Aye yer a wee bit uptight, Bertie. Need tae take time oot noo an again,' he smiles — 'Yer an awful man, eh. Oh here, by the way,' he frowns — 'Bertie. V'you heard anathin aboot a priest? The Wulson case?'

Bertie scrutinises mid-air — 'The Wulson case? A priest?' he asks — 'A don't know wit ye mean. A priest? How, wit aboot um?'

Big Ron shakes his head — 'Ach, thur's been talk, probably the usual nonsense, but the priest wis there jist before the boy died,' he says — 'Jist wonderin if you mighta heard anathin.'

Pat leans forward — 'A priest? Furst av heard. Wee Davy, eh, shame. A hud um daen a wee bitta wurk tae, jist afore it happened. Where d'ye hear that anyway?' he asks.

Big Ron rolls his eyes — 'Aw, don't ask,' he replies — 'That Woods lassie's been daen a hunger strike. Been rantin n ravin aboot a confession. S'been in the papurs. A local priest, supposed tae a heard that boy's confession afore ey died.'

Bertie's keen to prove his value — 'Listen, al keep ma ears open,' he says — 'Noa know es name? The priest know sumthin?' he continues — 'Oot ey order, they two bastards killin that wee wean.'

Big Ron frowns – 'Nah, didny pay much attention tae it, tae tell ye the truth. But Jesus, that lassie. Furst wumin tae go on wanney these protests, so it's causin problems,' he explains – 'Ye know wit the press ur like, a wumin oan a hunger strike?'

Pat nods – 'Aye, s'unusual, innit?' he says – 'Aye, Bertie, put the feelurs oot. A widnae mind findin oot masel who shot um that night.'

Bertie's filled with self-importance again – 'Right, Pat, nae bother,' he says – 'Leave it wi me. You kin fill me in later, big man, details an at.'

Glasses chink as they agree – 'Ye-es, Bertie boy. Sound, wee man, sound. S'mer like it, eh,' smiles Pat – 'Need tae stop worryin, nuthin's gonny happen, n'remember – yev got me at yer back.'

Big Ron's signalling the barman – 'Pat? Naw? Okay, Bertie? Same again? Oh, ye headin off, Pat?' he asks – 'Ach, wan fur the road. Aye, Woods, the fullah. That time a interviewed um up the road,' he winks – 'Wulson's murdur wis doon tae him. Mer ur less admitted it. Eh? Oh, aye. Ey laughed when a asked um tae come clean. Said ey hoped the wee yin rottit in hell. Aye, they wur es exact wurds,' he grins – 'A contract definitely, but a wid jist like tae know wit wis said at the scene, the priest, know wit a mean?'

Pat stretches his arms – 'Aw, well,' he yawns – 'See wit happens. Right, listen, al huv tae head off, n jist leave that urra thing. Al get sumthin sortit oot. Shut this cunt up n see wit the score is. Hamilton Ackies, eh?'

Big Ron raises his glass – 'S'ppreciatit, Paddy. Boab Brodie's boy. Minda Auld Boab, Bertie?' he asks – 'Wurked up n the Northern?' – 'Auld Boab?' exclaims Bertie – 'Ach, Ron, ye kiddin man? Fucksake, Boab put me through the ropes when a wis a boy. Ey wis desk sergeant then. S'a shame fur um. Wit's es boy daen?' he asks.

Pat throws a bundle onto the table – 'S'ten there. S'Bertie's n yours. Right, then,' he says – 'Witsat? Aye, bring thum doon n al huv a blethur wi thum. S'thur names?'

Big Ron palms the banknotes without a word – 'Jack Maloney, Billy Brodie; two good yins. Right, al let ye get away n al fix up a meetin, sweatin thum oot the noo so thur's nae misunderstandins. Anyway. Aw the best, Pat.'

'Aye Pat, see ye later,' echoes Bertie – 'N'thanks, Pat. Nae mer nonsense, a swear.'

Pat pays for another round before leaving – 'Right! See ye later,' he calls – 'S'sound, boys, sound.'

He slips into his car – *'N'thanks, Pat. Nae mer nonsense, a swear.'* Click – 'S'sound, eh, sound,' he mutters, swinging the car out into the night – 'Right, head up the road. See wit this big yin's been up tae. The priest, eh?'

Big Ron and Bertie remain behind to have a few more drinks; the big man looks at his partner through watery eyes – 'Bertie, Bertie, Bertie,' he sighs – 'Wit wi gonny dae wi ye, eh? Here. There ye go,' he says, passing him his cut of the money – 'S'five grand there, n it's your round, by the way.'

Bertie fingers the thick pile before pocketing it – 'Aye, well, eh. Nearly bloomered there, eh?' he cackles nervously – 'But a telt um, dint a? A telt that cunt that time, dint a, big man? Aye, eh, the Campsies?'

Big Ron laughs – 'Aye, Bertie,' he chuckles – 'Jist don't get kerried away wi yersel. Eh, s'your round, son, c'mon en.'

Bertie peels twenty off at the bar – 'Aye son, two doubles,' he grins crookedly – 'Aye-a herm, herm, herm,' he splutters – 'Cuppla cigars tae, son.'

Big Ron looks up – 'A ceegar?' he grins – 'Cheers, Bertie. Cheers.'

'Cheers' echoes Bertie – 'Needed that. So,' he says, smacking his lips – 'S'Boab Brodie's boy like?'

Big Ron clenches his teeth as he downs his double – 'Whooya!' he exclaims – 'Tastes better in wur ain company, eh? Brodie? S'faithur, right doon the back,' he replies.

He puts his glass down – 'Am bringin thum in. Maloney's thick. A Paddy, but the two ey thum ur good boys. Wull gie thum a wee break. N'you kin keep an eye oan thum. Same again?' he asks getting up to go to the bar.

Bertie downs the double before the big man sits down – 'Aye. Al look efter thum, Ron. Whooya! Aye. Dis taste better in yer ain company, right anuff,' he agrees.

Big Ron's having double vision – 'Aye, Bertie. Don't be too forward wi that yin. Aye, n never underestimate these people,' he says – 'Oh, don't o'erestimate um either. Thur dope dealers, that's aw, low life. But there tae be used,' he grins – 'N'remember, they wurk fur us, ma auld son. Look at me. Dae ye think ad a got ma chief chasin low life? An inspector?' he asks – 'Naw Bertie, thiefs ur different fae this lot. These people wid murder thur grannies.'

Bertie's nodding – 'Aye. Anurra double, big man?' he asks – 'Aye, Ron, a know wit yer sayin but a hud tae say sumthin there,' he says before going to the bar.

Big Ron's still talking as another glass is set down – 'Cheers, Bertie,' he smiles – 'Aye. N'they wurk fur us. But yer criminal?'

Bertie's nodding – 'Aye. But that bastard hud tae be

told there,' he says — 'S'me he's tryin tae make a cunt ey.'

Big Ron smacks his lips — 'Whoooyacuntye!' he exclaims, banging the glass down on the table — 'Naw, yer criminal's different. He'll take a heavy sentence 'fore grassin, but these people?' he sneers, looking over to the bar — 'Scum. Right! Aye! Two doubles, son!' he calls to the barman — 'Aye, Bertie. Scum. Noa like the auld team, at least they hud bottle.'

Bertie thanks the barman — 'Hanks, son.' he says — 'Jist geez anurra two doubles o'er. Aye. A hud tae tell um there. Am noa fuckin mug.'

Big Ron nods to the barman — 'Cheers, son,' he says — 'Ay-e. Aw that auld-fashioned pride. Thur codes a honour, but dope?' he smiles — 'Oh, but they're above aw that, int they? Fuckin snobs, n that's the paradox, ye know. Stull. Ye hud tae admire some ey they auld yins, they hud a bitta style aboot thum. D'ye mind auld Barney Boone?' he asks — 'Auld Bernard, eh.'

Bertie's nodding — 'Aye. Al Campsies um, the cunt,' he sneers — 'Who dis ey think ey is? Al Cafuckinpone?'

Big Ron agrees — 'Aye. Like dinosaurs, so they ur,' he laughs — 'Fuckin dinosaurs. An believe you me, thull noa last, be extinct, but these people. Auld Bernard Boone, eh? An auld rogue if ever thur wis wan. Poor auld cunt copped it tae. That McGinty done um. M'sure ey it. Cood never prove it but a know ey wis involved.'

Bertie signals the barman — 'Aye. Telt that cunt, so a did,' he says — 'Noa be sa keen n future. A mean, a am the polis, fur fucksake. Me, a am the fuckin polis.'

Big Ron thanks the barman — 'Cheers, son. Aye, extinct. But us?' he sniggers — 'They need us. The landscape's changin, 'fore ye know it, we're redundant, eh. That's were thur wrang. Take heroin oot the picture an that mob's finished tae.'

Bertie's nodding – 'Aye. See me, by the way. Ad leathur that yin. The Campsies? Am a supposed tae be scared ur sumthin?' he asks – 'A mean. See me? Av been at this gem aw ma life. A dealt wi Arthur Thomson, an there wis a real gangster.'

Big Ron's staring into space – 'Aye, extinct,' he mutters – 'But always remember. You an me ma auld son, s'you n me son. Here! Cheers!' he exclaims – 'You n me son, eh! Numero Uno!'

Bertie raises his glass – 'Aye! Me n you, big yin!' he cries – 'Cheers, big man! Hic! Aw fuck, the hic-uups! Whuuup!'

Big Ron slaps him on the back – 'Aye Bertie, yer a good yin, son. N'don't you worry wi him. Toe-rag son, s'aw he is, a toe-rag,' he says affectionately – 'Yer a good yin, son. Ye wur always a good yin,' he adds – 'Pat the rat, aye, eh.'

Bertie's eyes are burning with pride; pity his wife hadn't lived to benefit from his new-found wealth, he thinks – 'Ma Margaret, eh.'

Margaret; that cancer had eaten away at her. He hated even thinking about it, but the booze always brought back the memories. Really, this was why he had hit the bottle so hard in the first place – 'Aye, Ron, s'noa like the auld days, is it?'

Big Ron's face creases with amusement – 'The auld days, eh,' he smiles – 'Aye, Bertie. A stull mind aw the good times wi hud, d'ye mind?'

Bertie remembers alright – 'Aye, Ron. Oor Margaret liked you. N'Jeanie, best a pals so they wur. How's she keepin anyway?' he asks – 'V'noa seen ur since . . . the . . . eh.'

Big Ron laughs – 'Ma Jean? Ach, ye know wit she's like.

Aye, they wur good pals the two ey thum. Margaret n Jean, eh. Lovely lookin lassies, wint they? Christ knows wit they saw in us, eh, cuppla rogues.'

Bertie's remembering — 'Aye. Ma Margaret wis a good lassie. S'never been any urra wumin in ma life, ye know,' he says — 'S'never interestit. Margaret wis . . .'

Big Ron interrupts — 'Aye. Wull, right then, ma auld son. Time tae hit the road. Wan an wull get hame.'

Bertie's nodding. Home? he thinks. Margaret was home. He has no home; four walls, and sticks of furniture isn't a home — 'Witsat? Aye, Ron, hame, aye,' he replies — 'You head off. Am gonny huv a cuppla drinks 'fore a head up the road.'

Big Ron doesn't notice his partner's mood change — 'Aye! Two doubles, son!' he calls to the barman — 'Cheers, son.'

Bertie thanks the barman — 'Cheers, son,' he says, looking down at the glass — 'Cheers, son,' Margaret and him; they had never drank, they couldn't afford to really, but they had been too happy to care about that kind of thing. She would have hated this; this dope business — 'Eh? Witsat?' he asks looking up — 'Ye off then?'

Big Ron's on his feet — 'Aye. You awright there?' he asks — 'Listen don't let that punk bother ye. That's a toe-rag, a watur-rat. D'ye hear me noo?'

Bertie takes his hand — 'Wit? Ach, don't be daft. S'thinkin aboot sumthin else there so don't worry. Al sort that cunt oot, big man.'

Big Ron hugs him to his huge barrel-chest — 'Aye, Bertie! Yer the best, ma auld son. A world champion!'

Bertie watches him lumber to the door, and disappear into the night; the big man was his only friend — 'Cheerio Ron, cheerio,' he mumbles — 'Aye. See me? M'the wurld's champion. Wurld's champion so am ur. Aye, Margaret, me n you, hen.'

Pat finds Derek in the house when he returns home.

'Awright, Pat. How'd it go? D'they want this time? Mer fuckin muney?'

Pat throws his jacket over a seat — 'Ach, the usual,' he replies — 'Janis up the stairs? Need tae get a wee talk wi ye,' he winks — 'Cuppla things.'

Janis looks round the door — 'Thought that wis you. Ye hungry?' she asks — 'Av kept yer tea.'

Pat shrugs — 'Naw, s'okay, hen, am no that hungry,' he replies — 'The weans up in thur room?' he asks — 'Al nip up n see thum fore they got tae bed.'

Janis smiles — 'Aye, been waitin aw night,' she says — 'Right then, listen, am gonny be huvin a good long bath so ye sure yer no hungry?'

Pat lights a cigarette — 'Naw, naw, on ye go. We're needin tae get a wee blether tae sort a few things oot so jist huv yer bath, hen,' he says taking a deep drag — 'Ach, jist a thing wi some Paki shop. Anyway, al be up in a minute.'

Derek flips off the television — 'A Paki?' he asks, puzzled — 'Sellin turbans, ur wit?' he laughs — 'Ye wanta coffee? A Coke ur sumthin? Naw? Right, okay, s'the score? Wid Boris Karloff want ye fur?'

Pat sits down — 'Al go n see the weans furst Derek. Ye watchin by the way?' he asks, nodding at the television — 'The Borgia's?' he laughs — 'S'it like?'

Derek laughs — 'Fuckin brulliant, Pat. Honest, man. S'fuckin brulliant. Cesare Borgia, he's a fuckin machine, man. Kills every cunt, man. Humps es fuckin sistur. Aw heavy man. Fuckin heavy.'

Janis draws him a look – 'Right, Pat. Al leave ye's tae it,' she says – 'Al only be in an hoor ur that. Al tell the weans yer cummin up.'

Pat nods – 'Be up the noo, hen.'

Derek returns to the programme – 'See ye when ye come back doon,' he laughs – 'Al be watchin this. S'fuckin brulliant, so it is.'

Pat shakes his head – 'Sound, big yin, sound. Be back doon shortly,' he smiles – 'Al tell ye the end if ye want. See that guy there . . .'

Derek throws a newspaper at him – 'Naw! Naw! C'mon, Pat. Don't spoil it,' he howls at him – 'Aye, right. Okay, al see ye when ye'v seen the weans. Think thur wantey ask ye sumthin anyway.'

Laura's face lights up as her father peeps round the door – 'You's two no sleepin yet? S'twelve a'clock, man,' he jokes – 'Nah, miss me en?'

Zoe turns her nose up – 'Tch. You're always late,' she says petulantly – 'Where have ye been, Daddy?' she asks, as he sits down on her bed.

Laura climbs onto her sister's bed and cuddles her father – 'Yes, we missed you, didn't we, Zoe?' she smiles – 'Zoe! Didn't we?'

Pat smells a ruse – 'Right, wit ye's efter? Ma noa gettin any cuddles?' he asks with mock tears – 'Nah, been busy at wurk, darlin. Anyway, c'mon tell me, wit ye's efter? A need tae get tae bed. Uncle Derek wants tae see me tae. Guess wit es daen? S'doon there watchin cartoons. Aye! Mickey Mouse! S'daft tae, int ey? Jist like Daddy.'

The girls giggle, knowing they've been rumbled – 'Och, Daddy. S'nothing, honest. We wanted to ask if we could go and see Scheme?'

Pat's hackles rise slightly. Scheme, he thinks. A brilliant band, but he's afraid they'd be exposed to drugs – his drugs. Scheme, he smiles. Best band ever to emerge from Glasgow. Their junk reputation had fucked any possibilities of a record contract. The band had emerged from poverty to produce the best sounds around for a long time but – 'Right, listen, let me think aboot it,' he decides – 'F'a let ye go, wull ye let sumdae watch ye's? Uncle Derek ur sumdae like that?'

They squeal with sheer delight – 'Ye-eees, Daddy! She fancies the lead singer, Daddy!' Laura giggles – 'She does, Daddy! Honest! She fancies him!'

Zoe pouts her pretty lips, blushing – 'Tch. No I don't. S'Laura, Daddy. S'her, so it is. I think he's ugly.'

Pat pokes her gently in the ribs – 'S'that right? Magine that, eh,' he sighs – 'Wisnae that long ago a wis readin you two bedtime stories n noo it's boyfriends an Scheme?'

Zoe snuggles into his arms – 'But Daddy, can we go, please?' she asks – 'Mummy was wanting to go too. She could take us.'

Pat grins wryly – 'Mummy, eh?' he says – 'Mummy thinks she's a young yin, dint she? N'wit aboot me? Ma no invited?'

'Ye-es, Daddy!'

Pat smiles – 'Nah, av got too much wurk tae dae, darlin. Ad luv tae a went tae but av too much tae dae, honest,' he says – 'Scheme, eh. Great band, int they? Wit aboot The Beatles? Noa like The Beatles?'

Zoe throws her hair back – 'Och Daddy! They're old!' she exclaims – 'But can we go then?'

Pat throws his arms up in defeat — 'Ach, a suppose so. But right noo, it's bedtime. A promise, but let me talk tae Mummy,' he smiles — 'She kin take ye an make sure thur's nae boyfriends!' He hugs them both before turning the bedside lamps out — 'Night en darlins,' he whispers — 'Don't let the bed bugs bite.'

He feels the thrill of fatherhood as they pull the bed quilts around themselves — 'Night, Daddy. Love you,' they whisper.

He slips down the stairs — 'Ma wee darlins,' he mutters, closing the dining-room door behind him — 'Derek, turn that doon a bit, weans ur sleepin.'

Derek stretches his arms, yawning — 'Whoof. Nearly conked oot there,' he sighs — 'Av noa tae say, but a take it am gaun tae see Scheme?'

Pat laughs — 'Paira real yins, int they?' he replies — 'Janis'll take thum. Run amok wi you, ya cunt.'

Derek pours a coffee while they settle down in the dim light of a lamp — 'So wit's been happenin en?' he asks — 'The Hammer gie ye that gear back? Wee Mick wis rajin but kept es mooth shut. Coppers shot the dug, by the way.'

Pat frowns — 'Aye, cuppla ounce. A didny even know they wur bustit. Disnae matter anyway. Naw, es got anurra cuppla coppurs ey wants tae bring in. Cuppla real yins a think, but usable,' he says — 'Auld Tyson? That big prick never mentioned. Ach, well, it need puttin doon anyway.'

Derek smiles — 'Aye. Wee Mick'll probably want a big funeral an aw that. Bury um oot in the back. D'ye get they cunts taped?' he asks — 'Great, Pat. A hate that big prick. Ye'd think ey wis made up wi deid bodies, wint ye? Erms doon tae es knees. An that big stupit fuckin heid. Cood land a fuckin space ship oan it.'

Pat throws the tape onto the sofa – 'Aye, sound. But thur's a Paki causin bother. Ach, these two bampots chased a boy ootey a pitch n en battured um. They thought ey wis tannin the place. Turns oot the shop wis es auld man's so the da's kickin up fuck.'

Derek laughs – 'Fuckin Pakis, man. M'tellin ye. Thur pure trouble that mob. They get brulliant hash tae. Noa sort sumthin oot wi thum?' he asks – 'Wid the boy dae?'

Pat shakes his head – 'Fuck knows. Pumpin a wee burd. Get Nerdy an es wee mob in, full it wi rats. Fuck the place up.' he says – 'Shut this Paki up.'

Derek's amazed – 'Rats? The fuck ur they gonny dae?' he asks – 'Tan the cheese ur sumthin?'

Pat grins – 'N-aw. That health mob'll be there. They kin shut the shop doon on the spot. They're fuckin heavy, kin shut ye doon like that,' he explains, snapping his fingers – 'Sumthin else that big yin mentioned. Mind that priest?'

Derek's puzzled – 'Priest?' he asks.

Pat begins to fill him in – 'Aye, mind that kerry oan wi wee Wulson?'

Derek slaps his knee – 'Right! V'got ye. Kennedy ur sumthin. Aye anyway, wit aboot um?' he asks.

Pat shrugs – 'Well, thur's talk that the wee yin made sum kinna confession n that daft cow's makin noises. Woods's missus, that Angelena,' he says – 'That big yin seemed a wee bit worried. She's oan a hunger strike tae, by the way.'

Derek laughs – 'A hunger strike? Ach, yer kiddin me on. A wumin on a hunger strike? Stupit cow. A hunger strike?' he sneers – 'Mattress'll be fulla fuckin Mars Bars.'

Pat laughs too – 'Aye. Anyway. Gie McGinty a wee phone aboot the priest. See wit this prick's all about. Find oot if ey dis know anythin. McGinty kin huv a wee wurd wi um.'

Derek nods – 'Oh here, by the way. V'got anurra driver fur the bus. The press ur right behind us tae. D'ye read that wee bit the urra day? Aye, big local hero here, eh. Am organisin the next trip fur the weans. V'already contacted yer man so the next batch's ready. This daft Paki'd be handy if we cood get um graftin fur us. S'drivurs wi need n a Paki wid be handy, ye no think so, Pat?'

Pat shakes his head – 'N-aw. S'gaun awright the noo so jist leave it. S'sound wi locals daen the drivin an aw that. Naw, Nerdy kin dae the business. We want these two daft coppers tied up anyway. N'mind McGinty. That Woods cunt better noa gie us a sore heid wi aw this pish aboot priests n that.'

Chapter Eleven

THE GARNGAD SHOPS could hardly be described as a shopping centre, but it was where all the local population happened to meet occasionally, particularly the women of the area. Especially those women who rose early; early enough to catch those fortnightly brown envelopes coming through the door from the social security.

This is where information filtered out into the wider community; the place where gossip festered like poison in scabby mouths. It's where heads were chopped off. Cashing that giro could be dangerous.

'Durty wee slag, so she is.'

Wee Ina McGuire flinches; her pinched, featureless face turns scarlet-red as the queue shifts uneasily behind her. She tries to shrink from the hatred burning her back, but it is impossible to avoid the eyes upon her. Wee Ina knows who is behind her. They all know, but no one will say anything. No one will intervene. Not so much as a whisper will escape regardless of what anyone might want to say. Well, at least not until backs are turned – 'A cheek she's got wi that fuckin sister ey hurs.'

Divina O'Kane is a big woman; battered a few men in her day too. This seven-stone drug addict in front of her has to be punished. Divina's family has suffered. Someone has to pay for that; for the pain inflicted upon her mother – 'Al see you n a minute, ya wee slag,' she spits, pushing aside her husband – 'Am gonny be ootside – waitin!'

Daft Tony knows not to try to stop her. He hunches inside his combat jacket, trying to look diplomatic, but fearful too that his wife might notice. A clenched jawbone does the trick. He'll look angry and serious grinding his teeth – 'Right, Divina! Am wi you! Look at that jawbone, hen!'

Wee Ina's hands are trembling as she signs her giro; having her period isn't helping either. The thick wad of toilet roll packed down her knickers is doing little to dampen the reek of fish, but that last bag of powder had wiped her out. She hadn't eaten food since the day before, but she'll be fine. As soon she gets a bag, she'll be fine – that is if she can survive the next few minutes – 'Thanks, mister,' she whispers, grabbing the bank notes. She stuffs the money into the pocket of her skin-tight jeans, and puts her head down as she walks to the door. She'll be fine now. A tenner-bag and she'll be fine. Wee Mick Rosinni's got good kit. A tenner-bag and—

'Here you, ya wee slag!' a voice roars – 'A wanta fuckin wurd wi you.'

Divina's waiting for her, right enough – 'Lookit ye. Ya wee junky bastard. D'you know ma Maw's in Woodilee?' she sneers, poking the pile of bones – 'Aye! Cosey you n yer fuckin man!'

Tony's finally at the counter. He can hear his wife shouting outside in the street. Che Guevara's face is peeping out from the inside of his combat jacket as he slips his giro through the metal grill – 'Right, thanks, mate. Nae borra. Ta,' he grins nervously from behind his flimsy 'see through' beard. He considers buying the bread and things – but no. He'd better get out there. She'll think he's taking a back seat. Sounds as if things are getting heavy – 'Right. See ye in anurra fortnight en, comrade!'

The Pakistani shopkeeper shakes his head – 'Jesus,' he smiles – 'Dun es nut that wee guy. Next, please. Aye, Mrs Murray, how ye doin, hen? Gettin cauld, eh, doll?'

Ina's becoming desperate; the finger prodding her broken, fragile frame hurts – 'Look Divina,' she groans – 'Wis nuthin tae dae wi me, man. Gonny let me go. Please, man, please, am aw sore, man,' she continues as nerve endings explode – 'Aw please, man.' Divina, though, is taking revenge – 'Aw sore? Ma Maw's fuckin sore cosey yous junky bastards!' she shouts – 'Ma Maw's hud a breakdoon cosey you people an ma sistur's lyin the fuckin jail fur nuthin!'

Ina's breaking down – 'Divina, please, man. Lookit the statey me,' she wails – 'Wit ur ye gien me a hard time fur? Av noa dun anathun, man. S'Davy telt they lies, noa me, it wisnae me,' she moans – 'Ye kin ask that priest, man. He wis there. Go an ask the fuckin guy yersel.'

Divina's taken aback – 'Wi-it?' she asks, startled – 'The priest wis there? Where? Wit ye talkin aboot?' she demands – 'The priest wis where?'

Ina's trying to break free – 'Aw look, please,' she cries – 'When Davy got shot, man. A priest gave um they last rites. Noo let me go, man. A need a fuckin hit, man.'

Divina's stunned. He was there? Angelena's been tellin the truth all along? She lets Ina loose but warns her – 'Right, you. Listen. Your comin doon ey that lawyers wi me the morra ur am tellin ye. Al battur your fuckin cunt in.'

Ina's nodding – 'Cool, man, cool. Al be there. A swear. Noo gonny leave's alane. Am jist needin a hit furst.'

Divina's right in her face – 'Noo, Ina. Am warnin ye. See if av got tae come lookin fur you the morra. A swear al fuckin dae you in. Noo, meet me here the morra at wanna clock. Right? Ye got that? Wanna fuckin clock.'

Divina and Tony look at each other as she staggers off down the street.

'Noo Divina,' he says — 'S'the lawyurs furst. Am tellin ye. Don't go marchin intae ey that chapel the day,' he continues — 'That mob don't huv tae answer any questions. But they lawyurs kin hit um wi a citation. Noo this is important, hen. A know yer rajin but . . .'

Divina's staring at him. Disbelief is written all over her face. Poor Angelena. All this time, trying to get someone to believe her. And all this time, too, that bastard had never said a word — 'Right, Tony, right. Naw, yer right,' she says, shaking — 'That auld bastard. But the lawyers furst. Naw, yer right. This is important. But jist you wait tae a see that bastard when am dun wi aw this,' she hisses — 'Ma sistur lyin there tae. Aw they fuckin years in solatary kinfinement? An he's doon there takin holidays tae fuckin Lourdes?'

Tony takes her by the arm — 'C'mon. Up the road, hen,' he says soothingly — 'Yer rajin, hen, an anger's a wasta time wi these people. N'don't you worry, hen. Angelena'll be delighted,' he continues — 'This'll cheer ur up. Gie ur mer strength. Aye, hen. N'don't you worry. Wull fight these people tae the end. S'capitalism so it is. Fed up tryin tae tell aw these fuckin dumplins. N'don't you worry. When the revalution happens, they priests ur furst oan the list.'

Divina lets him steer her up the road — 'Aye, Tony. Yer dead right. Wull get up tae the hoose an phone ur lawyer right away. Get um tae see us the morra. Wit wis it ey wis called again?'

Tony has it in a flash — 'Dunbar. Good lawyer tae, but ey

wis right up against it. They coppers knew it wis a fit-up as well,' he states – 'Hmm. Might be ontae ma hole here,' he thinks to himself – 'Aye, Divina. Wull fight this mob. Am right behind ye,' he leers behind her back – 'Right behind ye, hen.'

Tony puts the kettle on while his wife calls the lawyer's office – 'Wanta Jaffa Cake, hen, wi yer tea?' he asks – 'S'two left. N'tell him it's urgent, by the way. N'don't let um put ye aff. Cunts ur aw the same. Palmin ye aff wi sum understudy.'

Divina's furiously nodding into the telephone – 'Yes. That's right, dear. Mrs Angelena Woods. Eh? Naw, ur sistur, am the big sistur,' she says. Then, covering the receiver – 'Aye, Tony. Mer Jaffas n the fridge,' she whispers – 'Pardun? Yes, that's right. Mr Dunbar dealt wi the case. Pardun? Three o'clock? That's fine. Thank you. Cheerio.'

Tony looks up – 'D'they say?' he asks.

Divina swallows a biscuit whole – 'Morra, three a'clock,' she gulps – 'That wis jist thur secratury. Sounded awright.'

Tony puts down his tea cup – 'Aye. S'the best way, hen. Cood see ye wur rajin o'er at the shops. S'how a pull't ye away. Ye'd a jist battured hur an then wi wid nevera fun oot. N'don't worry aboot the lawyer. A know how tae talk tae these cunts.'

Divina rolls her eyes – 'Oh, a know. S'gettin aw wurked up there,' she says – 'A widda battured hur there. Jist as well you came oot. M'stull tremblin. Lookit ma hauns.'

Tony gives her a knowing look – 'Aye. Kin see yer up tae high dough,' he agrees – 'It might be a thingmy. A good idea tae, eh, know wit a mean?'

Divina picks up the two cups – 'Right. Al jist wash these

furst an you get yersel ready. Been a cuppla days anyway,' she smiles – 'Noa be a minute.'

Tony is a runt but hung like a donkey. He strips down to expose his rakish, hairy body and that 'tackle' hanging down there like a bunch of bananas – 'Check this hing,' he sighs when she returns – 'S'fuckin rampant, hen.'

He's stroking the huge purple head as it jerks and throbs in his hands – 'Fuck me,' he groans, watching his wife tear her clothes off.

'Am fuckin chokin fur it tae, so am ur.' she moans – 'Right. Doon on that fler! C'mon, move!'

Divina throws him on his back and mounts him like a horse – 'Ohyafuckerye. Auwww. Auwww,' she groans, flipping the huge head up and down her lips a few times before sinking down onto the pole – 'Right up me,' she groans – 'That's it. Auwww. Stick it right up ma hole. Sling that fuckin thing right intae me. Auwww, ya bastard. Auwww. Hardur!' she growls, grinding him into the floor – 'That's it. Auwww. Shuv it right up ma hole!'

Tony grunts every time her huge arse slaps down on his thighs.

'Hardur! C'mon noo, son. That's it. Hardur! Oh ya bastard, ye. That's it. Auwww. That's it. Auwww. Shuv it right up me!' she pants – 'Hardur! Oh, ya! Oofff! Hardur!'

She's wailing now, relentlessly pounding his body – 'S'it! Keep gaun! Hardur! Stick it right up me! S'it! Hardur! Fastur! Fastur! Auwww, yesss! That's it. Fastur! Right up me. Yesss! Hardur! Fuck me! S'it! Fastur! Fastur! Fastur! Oh, ya fucker, ye. S'it! Don't stop! Don't stop!'

Tony's buttocks are rubbing against the carpet, crushed into the texture, as she finally hits her peak.

'Oooo. Keep gaun! M'nearly there,' she gasps – 'That's it. Hump me, son. Hump the fuckin arse aff me, son. That's it. Auwwwya! Auwwwya!' she screams before collapsing on top of him – 'Auwww, Tony,' she whimpers – 'Auwww, baby. Wis fuckin brulliant. Auwww. Jesus. Auwww. Whoof.'

Tony lies there, fucked, flattened by her huge tits – 'Let is oot! C'mon. Divina. C'mon. A canny breathe, hen,' he gasps – 'Aw. Magic, eh?' he grins, slapping her arse – 'Fuck. Am knackured, man,' he gasps – 'Makin a wee cuppa tea? Any Jaffas left ben there? L'need a cuppla biscuits tae get iss thing back up again.'

Mr Dunbar looks up from his desk – 'Good afternoon. Mrs Morrison? I see, Angelena's your sister,' he smiles, as she introduces the others – 'Nice to meet you,' he continues – 'Do have a seat. A coffee? Tea?' he asks – 'No? Fine then. Now, I understand that you have some new information concerning the case involving Mr and Mrs Woods?'

Divina is looking at him – 'S'right, Mr Dunbar. S'ma husband, Tony. And,' she smiles nervously – 'Ina Wulson,' she says – 'David Wulson's wife.'

Tony detects some confusion – 'Wulson wis the main witness at thur trial, if ye recall,' he explains – 'N'Ina knows sumthin. A priest took a confession. S'a conspiracy, if ye ask me but . . .'

Mr Dunbar pulls a notepad from a drawer and begins taking notes – 'So, let me get all this straight. You are married to Mr Wilson?' he asks glancing up from the pad – 'I'm not sure I follow. He's dead? Oh, I see now.'

Ina fidgets in the chair – 'Davy telt me that ey lied. A don't know how, but he did lie. Maybe sumdae piyed um money. A don't know. Ey jist telt me it wis aw shite, es evidence in court n at, ye know wit a mean. But the priest heard um as well, so he knows the truth,' she says – 'S'names' Kennedy. Ye know, like Presadint Kennedy? Aye, man. Wull, ye shood go n see um an al back ye up this time.'

Tony chirps in – 'Wee Wulson wis shot jist efter the trial. An this priest fullah gave um the last rites,' he sniggers, recognising mutual intelligence as the lawyer frowns – 'Oh, a know. Opium ey the masses. But anyway. Ey telt this priest that ey lied durin Rab's n Angelena's trial. S'right Ina, innit? Jist when ey wis dyin?'

Mr Dunbar puts down his pen and leans back in his chair – 'So let me get this straight. Father Kennedy took a confession on the night your husband was killed?' he asks – 'I see now. But why have you waited until now to come forward with this information? I only ask because it will be one of the things you will be asked, Mrs Wilson. That is, if we can even get it into an appeal court,' he explains.

Ina begins to rock to and fro slightly on the chair – 'S'daen ma heid in, man. At wis aw, but a mean. Am wullin tae go intae a court, man, an tell thum,' she says – 'Ma man wis oan smack as well, ye know wit a mean? A mean, ey telt me wan night, telt me ey wis gonny be makin a lotta muney as soon as the trial wis finished.'

The lawyer leans on his elbows – 'And did he tell you where or why he would get that money, or who from?' he asks.

Ina looks at the others – 'S'ey talkin aboot, man? V'jist telt um the score, man. A don't know wit es talkin aboot,' she slurs – 'Where ur wit ur, eh? S'ey talkin aboot man? Ye know wit a mean? S'ey talkin aboot? V'jist telt um the score hint a? A don't know wit es fuckin talkin aboot, man.'

Divina's glaring at her. Smack. This stupid cow, she thinks — 'Naw, listen. Mr Dunbar is askin how ey wis gonny get this muney. Your Davy. How wis ey gonny get aw this muney. That's wit ey means, innit?' she asks, turning to the lawyer — 'S'at wit ye wur meanin?'

Tony unfolds his arms to reveal the freshly washed face of Che Guevara — 'Right, look, Mr Dunbar. Ina's been takin heroin. Divina's a bit embarrassed here. But the priest's yer main man. We're against aw iss stuff, heroin,' he explains — 'But ye need tae try an understaun sumthin. We're the wurkin class, dae ye know wit a mean? Wee Ina's jist anurra example. A symptum ey the capitalist systum. A mean. Yer no gonny find any stockhaudurs up the Garngad. Giro's urny divadens, if ye know wit a mean.'

Mr Dunbar is fascinated — 'Yes, Mr Morrison, I do understand. Hmm, it's interesting,' he says — 'I gather you take an interest in the political affairs of this country?'

Tony turns bashful — 'Witsat? Well, a mean. Take the coal industry. Decimated under this capitalist government. Any bampot kin see that. Capital's creatit through labour but the laboururs' share is wages. But tae the boss class it's dividens, shares, stocks n aw that.'

Divina's watching Ina — 'Look, wit aboot this priest. Shood wi noa be talkin aboot him ur a statement ur sumthin?' she asks, nodding in the direction of Ina — 'A mean. She said that he knows the truth. Wid it no be better tae send sumdae up tae see um, ur a letter?'

Mr Dunbar nods — 'Yes, sure. Sorry, Mrs Morrison. What is the address?' he asks — 'I'll have my secretary arrange a visit and I'll go out there personally,' he says — 'And then I'll be in touch. And don't worry. We deal with heroin users regularly, no need to feel any embarrassment on my behalf.'

He shakes their hands as they leave his office – 'I'm quite sure we may find this piece of information invaluable. But, it's always best not to build up too much hope. It will be a long battle proving your sister's innocence. How is her health, by the way?'

Tony slaps him on the shoulder – 'Thanks, Mr Dunbar. Oh, Angelena? Well the hunger strike's caused a lotta publicity. But she's noa too bad, int she? Divina visits ur aw the time. Wull tell her the news,' he smiles.

'Aye, Mr Dunbar, thanks,' says Divina – 'Am drappin ur a wee letter the night. Keep ur cheered up. Poor Robert. Wi Angelena on this hunger strike,' she continues – 'S'heid's dun in. Anyway Mr Dunbar, thanks.'

Ina shrinks from the traffic and pedestrians as they spill onto Sauchiehall Street.

'See you, by the way. Yer a fuckin haufwit, so ye ur,' growls Divina – 'Kin you noa keep yer heid thegither fur five minutes? D'ye see ur there Tony? Nearly fell aff the chair. Ina, the fuck ur ye daen oan that shite anyway?'

Ina's blinded by the daylight. She screws her eyes up – 'Wit? Wit've a dun noo? How ma supposed tae know wit ey wis talkin aboot?' she whinges – 'V'dun ma best, man. Canny dae mer than that, man, kin a? Anyway. Wid ey say, the guy?' she asks – 'Disey think thull get oot noo ur wit? A mean a telt the guy the truth there, Divina.'

Divina pushes her into a taxi – 'Och, get in n shut up, Ina,' she sighs – 'Ye coodny take you anywhere.'

Tony climbs in after them – 'The Garngad, mate,' he tells the driver – 'Jist drap us aff it the shops.'

Divina takes up half the seat – 'Wid ye think, Tony? You understaun these things. Wit wis aw that aboot urra appeals n aw that?' she asks – 'S'a nice man, wint ey? A lottey thum think thur above ye, dint they?'

Tony leans back – 'Ach thur aw the same, hen. S'jist a job. Don't be kiddid cos thuv a posh accent n aw that. They wurk fur the people. They get a wage so thur nae bettur than us,' he explains – 'Anurra appeal means we might get anurra trial. An at's when they kin get released. Called a stated case, like bail. But, naw. Ye cood tell ey knew. A wis watchin um takin notes aw the time, specially when wi mentioned the priest. A cood see es eyes lightin up right away n at's a good sign. That's wit thur like, these people. Better waken hur up,' he nods.

Divina swings round – 'Och, Jesus Christ. Ina!' she hisses – 'Ina! Sit up right wull ye!? Fucksake, man!'

Ina comes roaring back to reality – 'M'gouchin, man. Fucksake, man. Am noa sleepin. Am listenin, honest, am listenin,' she mumbles as her head sags again – 'Five minutes. A jist need five minutes n al be bran new. Listen. Gonny drap me fore the shops? Up at wee Mick Rosinni's. V'a wee message fur um,' she asks, as the last jag wears off – 'A jist need tae see um aboot a wee message, man.'

Divina shakes her head – 'No real, int she?' she says – 'Rosinni? Wit ye gaun up there fur? Mer smack?' she sneers – 'Rosinni? Thinks es a wee gangster. Him an aw they daft wee pals.'

Tony just grins – 'Ach, jist leave ur, Divina. S'hur choice, innit? Canny force people tae dae sumthin they don't wantey,' he states – 'S'aw part ey the problum, ye know. Thur shood be mer dun fur people like hur. S'a fuckin illness that stuff. S'like smokin fags. People get addicted n aw the big manufacturers make aw the pay. Goverment disnae gie a fuck. S'aw big business, hen, big business.' He continues – 'Naw. He knew, that lawyer. A wis watchin um when she wis talkin tae um. Kept takin notes, an honest ey widny waste es time if ey thought thur wisnae a case. That's the way they wurk. Time's muney tae these people. So a think es got a case wi the priest.'

Divina looks at him – 'Oh, Tony, a hope so. Poor Angelena. Aw that time n me tellin ur tae pull urself thegither. That priest. Oh, am tellin ye. He's gonny get it fae me. Wait tae a see him. Am tellin ye,' she warns – 'Oh, don't worry. Al wait tae the lawyers hud a talk wi um furst but jist wait tae a get a haudey um. Ma Maw lyin in Woodilee. Here, that's right!' she exclaims – 'Ey actually asked me how she wis daen? Aye. Up at the shops a few weeks ago. Aye, ey asked me how she wis gettin on, an wit a shame it wis an aw that. Wit an arsehole, eh?'

Tony looks ahead – 'Well. Av telt ye afore. That's the strength ey these people. They terrarise the wurkin classes. Tellin thum thur's a place called hell. Aye, an en they tell the upper classes they kin dae witever they want. S'the upper classes that gie thum a wage. Jist look at sojurs. Gettin killed aw o'er the place. Telt tae go an fight fur thur country. Then these priests, blessin thum. Tellin thum it's okay tae kill sum urra poor cunt in the same boat,' he sneers – 'Naw. Invaluable, hen. That's wit that lawyer said there. An invaluable means it means sumthin important. Naw, he knows thur's a case. Ey widny waste es time, cos at means muney. Invaluable hen, invaluable. N'don't you worry aboot the medicine man. Lawyers kin make thum talk in a court. Al read up on it the night again jist tae make sure, but don't you worry aboot that bead rattler.'

Divina's wringing her hands – 'Oh, Tony a hope so. Al

write ur a wee note the night so she'll be gled tae see me oan the next visit. A feel terrible efter that last visit. Telt ur she wis gaun aff ur heid wi aw this kerry oan aboot the priest,' she sobs — 'Oh, Tony, a hope so.'

Ina bounces forward as the taxi pulls to a halt at the shops.

'Much?' asks Tony — 'Av nae change so jist make it the two quid, comrade.'

The driver looks in the mirror as they all climb out — 'Comrade?' he thinks — 'Miserable wee cunt. S'ey want? Five pence change? Probably fuckin dope dealurs tae.'

Tony and Divina watch Ina as she makes a beeline for a bag — 'Ach, jist leave ur. She won't get faur,' he says — 'The priest's the main man anyway. Right, ye want a cuppla packets a crisps fur the night, hen? Might as well get thum the noo. Save us huvin tae go doon tae the van when it comes roon the night. Better get a cuppla stamps tae fur letters. Al write a wee note as well tae Rab,' he promises — 'Sounded depressed that last time ey wrote. Said thur wis a visit pass but the envalope wis empty. Ach, well, so ye wanta cuppla sweeties en?'

Divina checks her purse — 'Aye, might as well. Cuppla films oan the night tae so get me a cuppla sweeties an en al write the letters when wur in bed,' she agrees — 'Aye, poor Rab. Nae faimily either. Aye, Tony, dae a wee letter tae um. Guy's heid must be dun in. N'oor Angelena bein oan that hunger strike. S'got Rab's heid right up es arse so it hus. S'a fuckin liberty.'

Tony's nodding — 'Aye, hen. Ootey fuckin order,' he agrees — 'Listen. Wull a get a big box a Jaffas? Ye stull seem up tae high dough, know wit a mean, hen? We kin dae a cuppla letters an en maybe huv a wee thingmy n the kip this time?'

Chapter Twelve

MR BASHIR LOOKS up at the round, bevelled mirror in the corner of his premises – 'What are those two up to?' he wonders, watching two girls – 'D'better keep an eye on them,' he decides, as another shriek errupts from their direction – 'Whughhh!'

Other shoppers, too, have begun jumping back from the food tins and shelves of bread at the different locations in the shop – 'Whughhh!' they're squealing – 'Whughhh! Oh, Jesus! Look! Er anurra wan! Look!' shrieks another – 'D'ye see that there? Sumthin moved there. Am tellin ye! Thur's sumthin . . . Whughhh!'

Mr Bashir smells a rat – 'What the bludee hell?' he exclaims as two shoppers rush out past the till – 'Oi! You bludee pay!' he roars after them, wagging his head – 'You pay! You bludee thieves, so you are!'

He locks the till. That bloody son of mine, the thinks. He should be here to help run the bloody shop instead of playing those bloody fruit machines. A short spell back home, he thinks. That would sort him out. Maybe learn bloody values, instead of stealing all the time – 'Bludee sort im out,' he mutters – 'A bludee thief, so he is.'

He tiptoes down the aisles. Bloody shoplifters, that's what this is. They think he is stupid. But he knows all the moves. Twenty bloody years he's had his shop – 'Yes, a spell back home. Sort that little bludee thief out.'

Govan, his son, is conspicuously absent. Saturday. The

busiest day of the week, but after he'd stocked the shelves he'd disappeared.

'S'rats in er, Bash,' says one of his customers.

'What?' he cries – 'Bludee rats? In my shop?'

A small crowd has gathered by the bread – 'Look! In there,' says one.

'Thur's wan in there tae,' says another, pointing to the deep-freezer, while her pal fills a pram with a load of tinned ham.

'Look, Bash! There's wan! Behind the breed!'

Mr Bashir is having difficulty keeping his eye on all the sticky fingers manoeuvring his goods behind his back – 'Where?' he snaps, wheeling round again – 'I no see it. S'no bludee rats in my shop!'

Two young girls disagree – 'Thur everyfuckinwhere! F'ma wean catches anathin fae this place you're for it, so ye ur!' hisses one.

'Aye! N'am phonin the health board! The place's fuckin manky, so it is!' threatens the other, pushing back a stiff clump of bleached-blonde hair 'S'like a fuckin rats flittin, so it is!'

Mr Bashir's catching brief glimpses of tails disappearing down through the alleyways of tinned foods. He tries to belt one with a sweeping broom as the tail flees among the bread stacks – 'The bludee hell?' he cries as more rats come scrambling out from cover to dodge the broom – 'Bludee ra-ats! Bludee ra-ats!' he's screeching, whacking into shelves as rodents scurry around or stand still from sheer fright – 'Bludee ra-ats!'

He tries to prevent people leaving the shop – 'Please! Please! he begs – 'Please help to catch the bludee buggars!' he pleads – 'I give you free loaf, missus!'

Rena, the bleached blonde looks at him – 'S'got a cheek,

hint ey?' she sneers – 'S'noa that when es makin complaints aboot urra people is it?' she continues – 'Eh? N'makin complaints aboot white peepul tae? S'got a fuckin cheek, hint ey, Alice?'

Alice, her friend, draws him a look. And if looks could kill, he'd be in trouble – 'Aye, a know Rena,' she smirks – 'Thur aw the same, so they ur. Thur always gaun oan aboot sumthin n blamin ordinury white people tae.'

Rena laughs – 'L'take mer than a loaf a breed tae shut me up,' she sniggers, nodding in the direction of the door – 'Think you better calm doon n get yer story right fore the polis start askin questions.'

Alice agrees entirely – 'Aye. M'sure a saw two wee boys messin aboot when a came in. Aye, they hud a bag, looked like thur wis sumthin innit, sumthin movin, alive,' she reveals – 'Aye, twoey thum. Boot fourteen. Weans, wi rats.'

Mr Bashir swivels round – 'The policemen?' He gasps, seeing those two very familiar figures standing outside on the pavement – 'Bludee fuck!' he wails – 'The bludee fuck, no! No, please! Not those two bludee bastards!'

PC Brodie and PC Maloney are taking down statements. They're peering through the steel-grilled mesh of the window every now and again before returning their attention to the crowd – 'So it wis in the food?' one is asking – 'Definitely inside the packets? Right, fine, dear.'

Rena takes the panic-stricken shopkeeper by the elbow – 'Listen, Bash,' she whispers, quickly – 'You dae us a wee bitta good n we'll dae you a wee bitta good.'

Alice agrees – 'Aye. Two boys, boot fourteen,' she grins, glancing at the door – 'Sure a heard wanney thum sayin sumthin aboot rats n laughin.'

Mr Bashir gets the message – 'Right then, right, right,' he blubbers – 'Hurry. S'bludee bastards are coming in shop.'

Rena steers him round behind a stack of cereal boxes as the two policemen push open the door to look for the proprietor – 'Right, Bash,' she whispers – 'S'twenty-five quid ur it's a written complaint. Twenty-five – each. S'up tae yersel.'

Mr Bashir is still nodding furiously as the two policemen peep round the boxes – 'Wee wurd wi ye, Mr Bashir,' requests PC Maloney – 'V'hud a wee complaint aboot the durt in yer shop.'

The proprietor throws his hands in the air – 'Atil be bludee right!' he shouts, wagging his head – 'My shop is no dirty! No bludee dirt in my wee shop!'

PC Brodie tries to slow him down as he fills his notebook – 'Haud oan! Haud oan a wee minute, wull ye,' he frowns – 'Right, that's better. Take yer time n jist answer aw the questions.'

Mr Bashir, however, is having none of it – 'Bludee questions?' he storms – 'No bludee questions. Tis two bludee bastards harrassing me, so it is!'

PC Maloney feels his hackles rising but holds his temper – 'S'urra people s'makin the complaints, sir. S'yer customurs in fact,' he replies – 'Am jist tryin tae ask ye a cuppla questions. N'fact we might be better in yer office.'

Rena and Alice make their presence felt as the two cops try to lead the shopkeeper to his back office – 'Eh, a wee minute,' huffs the blonde – 'We wur here furst.'

PC Brodie looks suspiciously at the pair – 'We'll take it fae here,' he grins – 'M'sure we kin sort it aw oot wi Mr Bashir.'

Mr Bashir senses haggling – 'Bludee sortit oot?' he exclaims – 'S'twenty-five bludee quids sortit oot?'

PC Maloney looks up from his notebook – 'S'that a bribe there?' he asks – 'Did ye try tae bribe us there?' he repeats, looking to his colleague – 'Tried tae bribe us there, dint ey?' he asks.

PC Brodie, too, begins taking notes – 'S'a bribe awright,' he replies – 'A heard um clear as day. Twenty-five quid, eh,' he laughs – 'Suppose that wid be each?'

Mr Bashir explodes – 'Ye-es! That bludee right! Twenty-bludee-five each! The bludee hell. You people!' he's roaring – 'Now you want fifty bludee quids. Right! I'll give you fifty bludee quids!' he continues, throwing down the banknotes – 'Now all of you get out! Get bludee out of my wee shop!'

Rena and Alice make a sharp exit – 'Ye'v noa heard the lasta this!' shouts Alice – 'Am gonny write tae ma MP!'

Rena holds the door open while her friend guides the pram, packed to the gunnels, out onto the pavement – 'Aye! That's right! F'ma wean's goat any fleas ur anathin your in serious trouble you, ya black bastard!' she calls back as a car slows down to let them cross the road – 'S'got a cheek, hint ey?'

Mr Bashir is still throwing money down as the police panda car arrives to take him to the station – 'Bludee fucking harassment!' he's screaming – 'You people! The bludee quids you are after! What about my shop? Who will look after my wee shop? The bludee quids you are after! What about bludee wee shop?'

Some rats remain behind, hidden amongst the tinned foods and stacks of bread, while others explore cracks in the floor. They creep in and out of the building, and into the rubbish spill out back. They hunch and cower, twitching, and sniffing as the crashing steel shutters echo around the premises.

'And who be looking after my wee shop?' cries a voice in the distance.

Some rats return to the fresh foods, while most slip along the walls, and creep into old boarded-up houses.

'Mind yer heid,' someone replies.

Chapter Thirteen

RAB WOODS SITS naked in the corner staring into space. The scabs at the corner of his mouth have festered again. The habitual relentless picking brings him comfort while he stares at nothing. A dirty fingernail flicks back and forth across the ragged edges; the rough, dry and hard skin begins to leak – 'A wunder wit she's gonny think?' he asks himself – 'Probably take it bad,' he sighs again.

When he first began talking to himself he felt self-conscious. Could they hear him? he had often wondered. He had been convinced that they had been listening outside the door all the time way back then, but now? How long had it been? Three, maybe four years? He couldn't remember. Now they didn't even look at him, didn't even answer any questions either. No, they had stopped that about a year ago, or was it two? Not that it mattered now anyway. No, when he became aware that he had been talking to himself he had thought about them first, but really it had nothing to do with anyone at all. No. It had more to do with himself, his own feelings about the talking. But really there had been nothing at all for him to feel embarrassed about. The talking; his self-consciousness about it. It had been quite silly, almost childish. He had felt the same awkwardness talking into a telephone, or tape-recorders – 'Testing. Testing. Testing. One. Two. Three.' Then the stuttering, and stammering. Trying to string a sentence together, and worse still was hearing your own voice on playback – 'Fuck. S'that me er? S'that the way a talk?'

No, it was nothing. Some days, or nights. He could never tell the time down here in his dungeon. He knew that he was underneath C/Hall in Perth Prison. That was about as much as he knew. The blanket they had thrown over his head during and after the trial lay there on the floor still. Filthy now, but warm in the winter. No, it was nothing. Some days, or nights, he whispered – 'Angelena. Angelena. Angelena.'

And if no one else was listening to him then she might just hear him in the night. No, it was nothing. Some days, or nights, he listened, just in case she too was whispering from some other cell. Other times he wept until nothing at all could be heard, and at last they were together again in some other part of his mind that remained alert while his body lay still, worn and exhausted from the weeping – it was nothing at all, not really.

He looks down at the piece of blue-lined paper lying on the floor at his feet; the prison's standard weekly issue – one sheet only. The plastic Biro pen he had been allowed to keep in his dungeon since coming off 'suicide observation' but nothing else; trousers, shirt and shoes lay outside the door. Category A. Rule 36.

He no longer bothered to wear clothes, except during the cold winter months. He just wasn't here anymore. They never looked at him. When he asked for something it was ignored or, like the food, kicked in his direction. No, it was nothing – not anymore.

He looks down at the paper again; the rose in the right-hand corner of the sheet, he'll do that first, he decides. That will give him time to gather and assemble his thoughts before attempting to articulate them on paper – 'Never much cop at this lark, Rab,' he smiles – 'Shooda stuck in mer at school, son.' The dagger plunging through a broken heart he always left to the very end of the letter. He'd draw them later.

My Darling Angelena . . .

I love and miss you as always my darling and I hope you are fine. I got the last letter you sent me and it was great and it was great heering from you again.

well my darling how are things with you? I am still missing you in heer. same as always. ha. ha. did you get they other letter I sent you? when I read your letter it reely cheered me up ha ha.

well my darling I am looking forward to a visit. Tony said they wer coming up to see me but the visit pass never got ther so it was tore up again. as usual ha ha. so I hope they get the next visit pass so I can find out what you hav been up to. they hav told me you are okay so I feel better but you must hav lost a lot of weight so you will be ded slim again. not to worry my darling coz I will always love you with all my heart for ever so never ever forget my darling that I will always love you

PTO

He picks at a fresh scab, reading the letter over again before trying to continue on the other side of the page – 'Fucksake, Rab. This is murdur, man, innit?'

He looks at the walls. They're moaning tonight. He can feel the mood of the cell. Its different atmospheres. Sometimes the dungeon feels flat, bland and almost calm. At other times it's absolutely jumping. Especially if insects from the cold earth below the dungeon discover a source of heat above. They come crawling up through the cracks in the foundations, slithering through the seams to settle on the surface of the ancient wooden floorboards until daylight. He feels the space within the container expand as the tiny insects and other small creatures excite the air and create rhythms, scuttling across the broken terrain below his feet, or scaling the sweating walls to hang on the ceiling indefinitely – 'Cauld the night, eh?' he'll say – 'Lookin fur heat, eh?'

His life, he feels, like theirs, in the end, has no end. Only the beginnings of other new angles. His eye moves along the lines of smaller horizons – a crust of bread lying on the floor, a hair on his head, a Biro pen. But tonight the walls are mournful – 'Aye, eh. Ye'v no dun me eny herm,' he whispers, while a cockroach shelters quietly alone in a corner – 'Kept us aw warm when it wis cauld.'

He hears their steel-studded boots crunching down the stairs just as he slips the letter into the envelope. No one looks at him as he lays the letter on top of the desk. They never do. There's another letter lying there too, the one from Tony – 'S'thur nae mail fur me boss?' he asks. No, they never answered any questions either – 'Mind n post that wan. S'tae ma wife.' he says.

No, he just isn't here anymore.

Father Kennedy quietly hums to himself while preparing the sacraments of the altar; a task normally performed by his altar boys, but not today. This is a special day. He has relieved them of their duties to attend the 'Old Firm' match at 'Paradise' – Parkhead. He glances at the clock on the wall for the hundredth time. No, he daren't think of the result; he'll only jinx them. A Hail Mary or two is alright, but don't push it. Anyway he had agreed to see the solicitor today; he'd be calling in at some point. I should have gone with the boys, he thinks.

'Bloody solicitors. You'd think they'd be at the game,' he mutters, only to bless himself yet again for cursing – 'Forgive me, Father in Heaven.'

Still, this was indeed an important matter; those two poor, unfortunate people, he thinks. What must it be like? he wonders. To be in prison. Prison is one thing but to be incarcerated for life? And for a crime you did not commit? He shakes his head, whispering – 'Dear God. Let the truth be my path.'

The letters from the girl; begging him to speak with their lawyer. What if he is wrong? What if his assumption has been nothing more than that, an assumption? God only knows, hadn't he heard enough stories in the confessional box? Hadn't he spent half his life as a priest listening to tales of passion and betrayal? But, there had been something, something different that night when he'd had to administer the last rites – and there had been the trial.

Or had his thinking simply been influenced by the reports in the press days later? He just can't be sure anymore, it all seems so long ago now.

Dear God, please, please – 'Let the truth be my path.'

Let the lawyer decide whether or not the information held any significance. That was their job, establishing the relevant facts. They have the expertise in such areas; after all it was not within his charge to investigate criminal matters. As the parish priest, he could only listen and pray; pray for the poor, unfortunate lives of his parishioners; lives disfigured by poverty, by their lonely grief-stricken existence upon this earth.

What did he as a priest have to offer the congregation? he often asked himself. What did he have to give? Forgiveness? Jesus commanded – 'Feed my lambs.' What arrogance to forgive the poor for their lives while the few are praised for their vulgarity, their greed, their very obscenity. Would forgiveness put food on the table, or in the mouths of the lambs?

He felt at times a deep sense of shame at the mockery of the Church in the face of these people's lives; lives devastated by the terrible scourge of heroin, by their desperation to escape the harsher reality of poverty.

He looks up at the clock yet again. No, he dare not. Ten minutes to go! To jinx them now would be unpardonable, a mortal sin. Oh well, he thinks, looking around. There had to be something needing doing, anything at all to keep his mind off the game and of course this other business.

Another Hail Mary wouldn't do any harm would it? After all, a good result would mean full capacity at tomorrow's service. No, he'd better not; not again. Why had he agreed to meet that solicitor, and today of all days? He could have been at the game instead of footering around here all afternoon, folding and refolding the vestments for tomorrow's service.

Mr Roy Dunbar is getting more and more annoyed. He looks at his watch again – 'I'll definitely be late now,' he mutters – 'Be as well to make another appointment. Never make it in this bloody traffic.'

He has been stuck in a traffic jam for ages due to the 'Old Firm' match between Celtic and Rangers – 'The Gers,' he smirks, confidently – 'I wonder how they're getting on?' Difficult to guess, looking at the hordes of fans blocking all the traffic. Chants could mean anything really. He tries the car radio again – static. He curses his secretary again. She should have known better than to have arranged the appointment for today. He might just have decided to go and see the game after all. The others at the office had season tickets and had offered him a seat. A Rangers scarf among that sea of emerald green? Hardly bloody likely, he laughs, looking at his watch. Missing the game didn't bother him that much. Still, a good result would wipe the smirks off their faces – 'Wonder if I should ask someone?' he wonders – 'No. They react badly if they lose,' he decides, listening to the chanting hordes heading home for the sectarian tea.

WE ARE! WE ARE! WE ARE THE BILLY BOYS!
WULL FUCK THE FENIANS OOT THE CUP
AS SURE AS WE'RE ALIVE!
COS WE! ARE! THE BRIGTON BILLY BOYS!
GOD BLESS THE QUEEN!

What is the point? the priest asks himself yet again. It isn't as if he had concrete evidence.

He had made an assumption, is all. O-h, God! Why, why, why had he been so stupid? He had merely written to the girl out of compassion. To try to offer her moral support; to give her courage, nothing more.

He could always say that he could not break his vows, but then again, what if they are innocent? What if they are the victims of a terrible miscarriage of justice? And, what if the people who are responsible—

Click. Click. Click. Click.

Father Kennedy hears the sound; he stops polishing the

chalice for a moment to make sure; he listens again for the footsteps in the main chapel. The leather shoes echo on the marble floor — 'Fathur Kennedy?' a voice calls — 'Fathur Kennedy?'

Father Kennedy fastens his dog-collar. 'At long last,' he murmurs, glancing up again at the wall clock. No, no, no, he decides, not with only two minutes to go. He'll hear the result of the game soon enough. He'll see the solicitor first and then maybe he'll have something to celebrate, maybe even a pint of Guinness. Who knows?

The thought puts a smile on his round ruddy-complexioned face as he opens the door to check who is outside — 'Mr Dunbar, is it?' he asks the smartly dressed gentleman at the front pews — 'Would you like to come inside? We won't be disturbed in here.'

My, my, he thinks, taking in the beautifully cut crombie coat, and the double-breasted suit. Expensive, no doubt. Must earn a fortune, he decides, as the young man wafts past him. Brut aftershave, he guesses, as the vestry fills with the strong, pungent aroma.

'S'it Fathur Kennedy?' asks the gentleman, reaching inside his coat.

'Ye-es. S'Father Kennedy,' replies the priest — 'A cup of tea?' he asks, turning to fill the kettle up at the sink — 'I'm not at all sure how I can be of help, Mr Dunbar.'

YEESSSSSSSSSSSSSSSS!

Father Kennedy hears the roar go up outside in the streets. The whistle has gone; but his cheers can't be heard; the scream in his throat is drowned out as the final result is relayed by those fans who can no longer afford to buy their season ticket.

YE-ES! TWO NUTHIN! YE-ESS! FOLLOW,
FOLLOW! WE WILL FOLLOW CELTIC!
UP TAE WUR KNEES IN ORANGE BLOOD
BUT WE WULL FOLLOW ON!
COS WE ARE THE GLASGOW TIMALOYS!
HALAUW! HALAUW!'

Roy Dunbar drums his fingers impatiently on the steering-wheel — 'O-oh, c'mon. What are they waiting for now? Bloody policemen,' he curses again — 'I'm never going to make it now. That bloody idiot of a woman! I should have gone to the game! Sitting here all bloody day!'

He tries the radio once more and catches the late results — 'Aberdeen, one. Hearts, two,' drones the commentator — 'Celtic, two. Rangers, nil.'

Roy balks, flipping off his car radio, already dreading the smirks come Monday — 'O-hhh, well,' he sighs — 'Thank God I didn't go after all.'

Someone who should have gone to the game was old Father Kennedy. With God on his side, the football match might just have saved his life. God was on someone's side that afternoon. He always is and usually it's the winner. God never backs a loser. But most certainly He wasn't on the side of His faithful messenger on earth either. No. He's been turning colder by the minute, lying below the small vestry altar in a pool of thick, dark life-blood. The cosmic 'Old Firm Final'.

The tiny atoms and particles of dark matter which give us

the illusion of solidity have begun disintegrating at sub-atomic level as death greets life once more in the endless cycle.

'Let the truth be his path.'

The Wee Glen regular crowd are momentarily stunned into absolute silence; the shock registering on their faces, however, has nothing to do with football results.

'Shsht, fur fucksake, tryin tae hear the fuckin thing,' someone snaps — 'Sharrup, you — dafty!'

The glare from the coloured television screen casts an orange glow upon the crowd of crooked countenances; broken faces stare and scrawny necks strain to catch all the gory details of yet another murder in their district —

'S'like Dodge City, innit?' mutters a voice.

'S'it a priest, right enough?' asks another — 'Unbelievable, man.'

The television presenter confirms that it is indeed a priest — 'Father Kennedy had no known living relatives. Police described the killing of the sixty-five-year-old priest as a particularly brutal murder. The police also wish to interview a man as part of their enquiries. The smartly dressed man with distinctive cropped red hair was seen leaving the chapel earlier today. This has been Shareen Nanjiani.'

A plethora of theories erupt around the bar; the motive behind the slaying provides an unexpected diversion from the evening's sports. Primitive fascination with death brings out the most morbid aspects of human nature.

'S'at anurra murdur? Fuckinhell, eh? A priest? Think it wis a robbery?' someone asks.

'Naw. Be wanney they nutcases al bet,' another replies.

'Ginger hair? Be a bonkers case. They red-heidid cunts ur

aw the same. Be wanney they ubsessive cunts. Fun um jist aboot an hoor ago tae. Jist shows ye, dinnit? Kin never tell when it's gonny happen.'

The debates rage on – 'Be boys ur sumthin. Aw the same that mob. You wait an see. Be boys, weans ur sumthin. Aw they cunts ur intae it. You wait an see. Be tamperin ur sumthin like that.'

The bar's professional experts know what really happened – 'Nae danjur. UVF. Been that mob,' voices one – 'S'been wanney that urra mob. Been watchin um. Parkheid every week. Brigton mob, al bet. Aye, ey. Cos es a Pape. L'no cum in here the bastards – pickin a daft auld priest – a Pape.'

A Pape indeed. Johnny McGinty checks his arms for any powder burns. They come no more Papish than his old mob – the Real Shamrock.

Jesus commanded – 'Feed my lambs.'

Well, Father Kennedy could rest in the knowledge that one lamb in particular had been fed today – 'Dae a wanta cuppa tea?' smiles Johnny – 'Aye, two sugars.' Phut! Phut! Phut! Phut! Four in the back – 'Nae mulk, Fathur.' Phut! Phut! Two in the head – 'A like it strong.'

He's annoyed that he'd had to miss the cup final. Sunday would have been preferable he thinks, throwing the bin-liners into the boot. But, then again. That place would have been packed out for the day with that dedicated flock – looking down their noses: the tragically scarred knees and curved spines of 'sinners' seeking solace from the debts terrorising their souls, searching for that final sign saying – Going Up.

Chapels, defaulted debts and rent arrears. The blood and guts. The foundations of faith. No, it wasn't for him. He'd seen the light. Religion is for the spiritually blind, he decides. People like his long-dead mother – 'Auld Mary McGinty, eh,' he mutters – 'Terrarised the wumin, so they did.'

He sparks a cigarette – 'Vengeance is Mine sayeth the Lord,' he grins, dragging smoke deep down into his lungs – 'S'at right?' he puffs, blowing through his nostrils – 'Well. S'noa the day.' Whoooosh! The old banger bursts into flames as he flicks the match inside – 'Definitely noa the day.'

Angelena has two letters today. One from Divina and the other from Rab. She reads her sister's letter first – 'Ye-ess!' she croaks excitedly as she reads it through – 'A told thum ey knew! A told thum the priest knew!'

The priest is going to come forward – at last. She can't believe the news. Now Divina knows the truth. She sighs in relief. At long last. She picks up the letter again. Great. Their lawyer is going to talk to him personally. At long last. Brilliant, she thinks. The priest will talk to the lawyer. She had been right; right all along. The priest did know something. But what is all this about the lies? she asks herself. Ina told the lawyer about the lies? What did her sister mean? she wondered – 'Ina told the lawyer aboot the lies,' she'd written.

What lies did she mean? She scrutinises the letter again. Lies, she nods. What lies? Davy Wilson had lied at the trial; they knew that, but did she mean him or were these to do with something else? Other lies maybe? No, it had to be to do with the trial. It had to be. She picks up the letter again. Lies, definitely. There could be no mistake. Ina told the lawyer, she's written here. Ina – told – the – lawyer – about – the – lies. No, it has to be to do with the trial. It can't be anything else, she laughs – 'God. Thank God they know am innacent.'

She fishes out the priest's letter from the bundle in the corner – just to make sure. No, he definitely meant 'known', definitely. But what was it? she asked herself. What did he know? Divina doesn't mention. Only that the lawyer will speak to him, but she doesn't elaborate. What had they discovered? Fucksake, Divina, she thinks. What are the lies? Is it the trial?

The years in solitary confinement had taken their toll on her brain. She had nowhere to run when the horrors crushed reality into a spot on the endless wall around her. A dimension of 'if only' and 'might have been'; had their taxi been late that night, had her mother not come, had they had the baby that would now never be born.

Life in solitary could expand this wonderscape into a reality, but once down that path there was no return. She knew of prisoners who had become lost, trapped between a reality and fantasy. Pale blue paint designed to have a calming effect lacerating their brains until they shrank and shrivelled. Their lives dehydrated and disintegrated, like dried wells. Dying of thirst, alone in empty cells.

Angelena picks up the other letter. She relishes these moments. She lies back on the bed – 'Poor Robert,' she thinks – 'Hates writin letters jist cos ey canny spell. Aw, look at that. S'mā wee rose. Aw jist wait tae ey hears the news.'

She snatches her sister's letter up again – 'Naw. It means lies,' she laughs, nervously, dropping it again to the floor – 'My Darling Angelena . . .' she whispers.

Did Ina know something then? The thought hits her like a thunderbolt. Ina – told – the lawyer – aboot – the – lies. Ina knew? Does this mean that she knew at the time of the trial? she asks herself. There is something she isn't getting, she thinks, trying to read between the lines. There's something –

'Och, stop worryin. Divina knows the truth so stop worryin. Ma man, wit a shame,' she sighs as she turns the page – 'Sounds a wee bit down,' she murmurs, looking at the drawing – 'Gettin noa bad. Aw, listen tae um,' she laughs, fingering the heart drawn at the bottom of the page – 'Aye, noa bad, Rab.'

Me again ha ha. as I was saying I will never ever forget you so dont worry about me in heer coz I think of you all the time and I no you do as well. but not to worry ha ha.

Anyway I must go now. slop out again ha ha. but seeriusly you no that I love you. learning big words now ha ha. I hope this is cheering you up coz I dont want you to worry about me coz ther is no point. I no I dont deserv you. but I will always love you so always remember that I love you my darling. anyway I heer the screws back so it must be is slop out in a minut. well that is the screws down heer now so I better sign off now. But I will still be thinking of you in my hed so dont worry my darling. and dont worry about me okay. take care my darling. and look after your wee self for me coz I will always love you forever. I am thinking of you.

From your loving husband Rab.

PS. Tony is a good guy. tell them I was asking for them and to take care. fingers crossed fur Celtic on Saturday. Angelena you tell them it was me and get out parole.

Angelena holds the letter to her breast – 'Aw, wait tae ey hears the news.' She almost weeps, looking again at the sheet of paper. Celtic, eh. She doesn't know how he does it but somehow he knows the football results. Must be the screws talking, she thinks. Parole? Tell them it was me and get out on parole? – 'Tell thum it wis me an get oot oan parole? Wi-itsat? Parole? S'at a sick joke, Rab?'

Tell who? And tell them what? she asks herself – 'S'ey talkin aboot?'

She's still reading the letter aloud when the cell door opens. A governor walks in with four screws – 'Your husband's dead. He was found dead in his cell last night,' states the governor – 'Do you want to see a doctor?'

Angelena remains silent, numb as she receives the news. She holds Rab's letter tightly to her breast, staring ahead at nothing. The governor is talking, but Angelena can't hear her.

'Keep an eye on her,' instructs the governor, leaving the cell – 'She'll come round. I don't want any suicides in my prison.'

Angelena doesn't hear them leave. She can't hear anything, only whispering as night stars shine upon cold steel bars – 'Angelena. Angelena. Angelena.'

Chapter Fourteen

BIG RON'S BAR is heaving. The pastel jumpers are absent today as the thug element occupies the premises for the football. But the television is knackered.

'Fucksake, man! Kinna fuckin place is iss?' ask disgruntled fans – 'A final n thur's nae fuckin telly?'

The barman holds up his hands – 'M'sorry, boys. Gen up,' he explains – 'A wantit tae see it as well. Thing jist conked oot. Gen up, supposed tae be a guy comin oot tae fix it iss efternin so wull see wit happens.'

Big Ron's having a pow-wow with his introductions – Maloney and Brodie.

'They two wee burds wur a laugh,' chuckles Maloney – 'Got twenty-five quid aff um. An then ey tries tae bribe us as well?'

Big Ron's pleased – 'Did ye know thum?' he asks – 'Aw a see, a cuppla chancurs. We won't be hearin fae him fur a wee while.' He signals the barman – 'Av written tae the bugger masel,' he continues – 'Disnae mean any herm. Jist gets kerried away, an this boya his. Trouble, that yin. Right, Maloney. S'your round, son.'

Big Jack Maloney sets down the drinks – 'S'your double, sur, n at wan Wullie's. S'Bert bringin this guy in tae meet us, sur?' he asks – 'V'ye known um long, sur?'

Big Ron smiles – 'Naw. Pat'll be here shortly, n listen, son. Cut oot the "sur" business wull ye,' he says – 'Wur aff duty. It's Ron ur big man, okay?'

Maloney grins like a big daft boy — 'Nae borra, big man!' he says raising his pint glass in a toast — 'Cheers, big man.'

Wullie Brodie returns from the toilet. His fairish complexion belies the toughness and venom lying beneath the surface — 'Thanks, Jack,' he says, taking his seat — 'S'a helluva noisy place, innit?' he adds, eyeing the neds hogging the bar — 'Ye awright then?'

Jack nods — 'Aye, cheers, mate,' he smiles — 'Aye, s'mobbed, noisy right anuff.'

Big Ron clocks Bertie — 'Maloney. There's Bertie. Gie um a shout,' he orders — 'Cood get lost o'er there wi that young team.'

Wullie Brodie gets up and waves — 'Bertie! Bertie!' he calls — 'O'er here, mate. Here, a seat, auld yin. Take that yin,' he continues, pushing a chair under the older cop — 'N'a heavy d'ye say? Right, pinta heavy an a chaser.'

Bertie's bemused by the fussing over him — 'S'Brodie's boy, innit?' he smiles, watching as the young cop pushes his way through the crowd to the bar — 'Da's double, int ey?' he asks — 'Eh, Ron? Da's double.'

Big Ron nods — 'Aye Bert. Faithur right doon the back,' he smiles — 'Jack Maloney, an this is Bertie.'

Jack and Bertie shake hands over the table.

'How'd ye do?' grins the young cop.

'A dae okay,' smiles the older cop — 'Pleased tae meet ye, son,' he chuckles.

'Right, noo. Bert's gonny be keepin an eye oan you two,' continues Big Ron — 'Noo. F'thur's a problum, ye see Bert. Sumthin ye need tae know, see Bert. Under nae circumstances dae ye contact me. Clear?' he asks — 'Ye don't talk tae me tae a talk tae you. S'that clear?' he repeats — 'S'fine then.

Bertie'll huv yer wages but ye dae wit he says. Nae question asked, okay?'

Wullie Brodie picks up when he returns to the table – 'Jack'll fill me in later, boss,' he says – 'Everybody got thur drinks?'

Bertie's shaking his head – 'Unbelievable, innit?' he says – 'Yer jist like yer Da. Voice's the same as well. Eh, Ron?'

Big Ron's nodding – 'Aye, son. Yer faithur wis a good yin,' he agrees – 'Aye, Wullie, ye even walk like yer faithur. S'a hard man, yer Da. Fair but hard. Knew the score tae.'

Bertie's floating down memory lane as he looks up – 'Aw, shite,' he groans – 'Here it's comin – King Rat McGowan.'

Pat acknowledges the four heads turned in his direction – 'Nae scores yet?' he asks, taking a seat from another table – 'How ye doin, big man?'

Big Ron beams – 'Hullawrer, Pat!' he exclaims – 'A wee Coke? Maloney, Coke, son.' he orders – 'Right, Pat. Aye, things are noa too bad. Jist been hearin aboot the rats n that,' he adds, winking – 'Clamped up. Complaints drapped. Oh, here. Pat. Wullie Brodie. Urra yin's Maloney.'

Pat reaches across the table – 'How ye doin?' he smiles.

'Bran new,' replies the cop as they shake hands – 'Pleased tae meet ye.'

Jack nods as he returns to his seat – 'Aye, how ye doin? Pleased tae meet ye. A Coke, winnit?' he asks – 'Ye noa drink beer?'

Big Ron's looking at him – Aherm!' he coughs – 'Right, Pat. The lads here know the score. Bertie'll be keepin an eye oan thum tae they find thur feet.'

Pat lights a cigarette – 'N'who's keepin an eye oan him?' he sniggers – 'S'sound, big man, sound.'

Bertie flinches, but ignores the remark – 'Aye, thull be

wurkin wi me tae they know the score. Wullie's Da wurked wi me years ago. S'aw different then but . . .'

Pat butts in – 'Aye, that's fine. Don't want the full life story, Bert. Know wit a mean?' he asks – 'Less said the better.'

Big Ron rolls his eyes. Jesus. A daft snide remark and he's crushed. Look at him, he thinks – 'So, Pat. How'd ye manage to get that place fulla rats?'

Bertie chances his arm – 'Phoned es cousins, dint ye?' he splutters – 'Eh, Pat, phoned yer . . . Ach, nevermind.'

Pat looks over the top of his spectacles – 'Ma cousins?' he frowns – 'Oh, right. A see wit ye mean,' he continues – 'The rats? Wee Govan dumped thum there that mornin. Aye, there's wan fur the books, eh. Wee Govan, sound, man, sound.'

'Govan?' blurts out Big Ron – 'N'who's he?' he asks – 'Govan? Kinna bloody name's that?'

Pat's smiling – 'Govan? S'Nerdy's wee pal.' he says – 'That Paki punter's boy, it's es son.'

Govan Bashir? Big Ron's looking at him in disbelief – 'Govan?' he exclaims – 'That's the boy's real name? A thought they two wur at the kiddin wi the charge sheet.'

Pat laughs – 'Said it wis better than Elvis,' he sniggers.

Bertie, too, laughs – 'Govan, eh?' he chortles – 'Jesus. V'heard it aw noo. S'ey got a wee sistur – Maryhull?'

Pat for once relents – 'Sound Bertie, sound,' he chuckles – 'Maryhull Bashur, eh,' he adds – 'Anyway. Better get the wages oot the road, eh. M'meetin a guy later so al be headin off shortly.'

Maloney looks at the five grand in his hands – 'Wit dae a dae fur this? he asks – 'S'it fur?'

Pat looks him straight in the eye – 'Jist dae wit yer telt,' he says – 'N'don't ask fuckin questions.'

Big Ron's raging. This fucking halfwit, he thinks – 'Nae scores in yet wi the Gers?' he asks – 'Thur's a wireless o'er there but . . .'

The roar drowns him out as the results finally do come over on the radio – 'Celtic, two. Rangers, nil.'

YEESSSSSSSSSSSSSSSSSS!
YEESSSSSSSSSSSSSSSSSS!

Ron's head drops. Fenian bastards, he thinks – 'Wit wis that? Two nuthin?' he asks through gritted teeth – 'Ach, well, eh. Canny win thum aw. Anyway. Muloney, s'your round,' he snaps.

Big Jack's banging the table – 'Ye-s! Ya beauty!' he's roaring – 'Ye-es! Ye-es! Ye-es! Ya beauty! Right, Wullie! Tenner, son. C'mon, cough it up.'

The Hammer frowns – 'A thought you wurny interestit in aw that business fae o'er the water then? Thought you wur a Prod?' he sneers – 'L'need tae keep an eye oan you. Right. C'mon then,' he barks – 'S'your fuckin round. Ye waitin oan, son.'

Big Jack can't keep the smile off his face – 'A Prod? Naw, but am noa interestit in they urra cunts either,' he declares – 'But am a fuckin Tim!'

Big Ron's having a difficult time with the punters shouting at the bar, one in particular is irritating him—

'Mervelous! Ebsolutely mervelous!'

Pat looks across at the character with the accent – 'Who is that?' he asks – 'S'dun es fuckin nut, hint ey?' he laughs – 'S'in here aw the time. S'ey got shares in the place?' he asks – 'Merveluss?'

Big Ron rolls his eyes – 'Aw, a know,' he groans – 'An alky. In here everyday. Anyway how's that brother n law ey yours these days?' he asks – 'Goan you three, o'er tae the bar a minut tae we get a wee blether.'

Pat shrugs – 'Derek? Es away the noo. Istanbul,' he says – 'S'daen the usual wurk wi the bus,' he adds – 'S'got a big squada weans wi um. Nae danjur a gettin a pull at customs wi weans, been a pure fuckin cakewalk fae day wan.'

Big Ron laughs, watching the other three standing at the bar – 'W'dye think?' he asks, nodding in their direction – 'Here, by the way. S'this av been hearin. You up seein an auld frienda mine – Dempster.'

Pat laughs – 'We're usin um the noo. Changin a lotta muney. We buy the sculptures an he puts it straight back in a dummy account wi Janis,' he explains – 'How? S'at a problum?'

Big Ron doesn't look happy at all – 'Muney? Pat. A put that bastard away, ye know,' he crows – 'Canny be trusted, that yin. Up there sayin es changed. Well. S'up tae you wit ye dae, but watch that cunt.'

Pat pats him on the shoulder – 'S'a prick, big man. S'the mattur wi ye? Cos Rangurs got beat? Auld heid nippin?' he taunts – 'S'big Jack bothurin ye? S'sound. Long as ey dis es wurk s'sound, innit?'

Big Ron shrugs – 'Aye. Right, anyway. Al huv a wurd wi um aboot the questions. You headin off then?' he asks – 'Better say cheerio.'

Pat agrees, walking with him to the bar – 'Wee Bertie,' he chuckles – 'D'ye hear um there? The wee dig at me n the rats?' he chuckles – 'Some man, int ey? Be o'er there the noo, tellin they two am an arsehole.'

Bertie looks up as they reach the bar – 'Thought you two

wur talkin,' he says – 'V'telt the boys ye like a wee bitta privacy sometimes, eh Pat?'

Pat laughs – 'Aye, good yin. Right, listen, am off. Al be in touch, okay?' he says – 'He'll tell ye the score, but if ye wanty make serious muney s'up tae yerself.'

Wullie grips his hand – 'Nae bother,' he smiles – 'Good meetin ye by the way. N'don't worry aboot the big yin,' he adds nodding to his colleague – 'S'brand new. Talks too much but es solid so nae problum, okay.'

Pat nods – 'Sound, Wullie, sound. Anyway keep yer eye on the bold yin,' he sniggers at Bertie – 'Canny take a joke. Gets aw uptight. Okay, al see ye's,' he waves, making his way to the door – 'Okay, Bertie Boy!'

Bertie mutters under his breath – 'Aye, fuck you. Fuckin bam. Al Campsies the cunt,' he grumbles, but no one is listening to him.

'Mervelous! Ebsolutely mervelous!' that voice roars again – 'Ebsolutely mervelous! C'mon Glesgow Celtic! Mervelous!'

Janis is watching the television when her man gets home – 'V'ye seen the news?' she asks – 'That Rab Woods is deid.'

Pat is genuinely surprised – 'Woods? Ye kiddin?' he laughs – 'Thought aw that mob wur fightin thur case? Happened anyway? Top eself?'

Janis nods her head – 'Aye. Coodnya been much ey a man,' she says – 'That's that lassie left tae take the blame noo. Sounded like a fuckin real yin anyway.'

Pat hangs his jacket in the hall – 'Rab Woods,' he grins, coming back into the dining-room – 'The big shot, eh. Suicide?' he sneers – 'Derek'll kill es sel laughin when a tell um.'

The tape had been a waste of time. There was too much noise, he thinks. There will be other opportunities. He had them by the balls. That was enough — 'S'ey phoned? Naw? Aw well. Heid'll be nippen as usual,' he smiles — 'Aw, they weans.'

Janis raises her eyebrows — 'M'fraid Derek laughs at any rotten news,' she says — 'The man's sick, if ye ask me. Naw, es noa phoned,' she adds — 'Ye hungry?'

Pat shakes his head — 'Naw, hen. S'the weans?' he asks — 'They noa in?'

Janis detects the slight alarm in his voice — 'S'the school party. S'adults there as well. Al pick thum up maself,' she says, reassuring him — 'Ye been anyway?' she asks — 'A thought ye wur coming hame early?'

Pat nods — 'Aye. S'right,' he replies — 'Ach wis jist tae talk tae thum. Watched some ey the game as well,' he explains — 'Didny notice the time.'

Janis looks at him — 'The game?' she asks — 'S'that right? Who won then? Oh? S'at right? Celtic wis it?'

Pat senses suspicion in the air — 'S'this? A fuckin quiz?' he asks — 'Who won? Who scored? Many wur thur? Fucksake, Janis, ye dun yer nut?'

Janis draws him a look — 'Aye, right. When did you become interestit in fitbaw? Right then, who scored the two goals?' she laughs — 'C'mon, en. S'the players names?' she taunts — 'C'mon Pat. Ye'r face is turnin red. Wit ye gettin embarrassed fur?'

Pat dumps the newspaper — 'Wit? Ye think av got some wee burd?' he laughs — 'Aw. A see noo. D'ye want me up the stairs? S'at wit this is aw aboot? Ye want fucked?' he leers — 'Whose face is red noo, eh? Ye wantey?' he prods, getting up — 'C'mon. Ye wantey head up the stairs ur wit?'

Janis is mortified — 'Wi-it? Jesus!' she squeals — 'See you!' she giggles, pushing him away — 'Naw, Pat. Naw. We canny. The weans. C'mon, noo,' she protests — 'Na-aw! Chuck it!' she screams, as she sees his prick — 'Get that thing away fae me!' She fights, but he's pinning her to the floor.

'Eh?' he's panting — 'Ye want this hing? Eh?' he snarls, pulling down her skin-tight jeans — 'C'mon. Up n yer knees. That's it. That's i-it.'

Janis stretches her knees apart and arches her back — 'Ohh. Ye-es,' she grunts — 'S'it Pat. Slow doon. Slow doon. That's it. Nice n easy, oofff. Ye-esss.'

Pat feels her pushing her thighs back against him as he rams his prick into her — 'Aw, ye-es,' he groans — 'Wiggle it. S'it, wiggle it, hen,' he moans slapping her cheeks — 'A luv fuckin ye. Auwww ya fucker, ye.'

'Ye-es, baby. S'it,' she moans — 'S'it, hardur. Oh, fuck! Ye-es! Harder!' she wails — 'S'it, Pat! C'mon! Hardur! Right up! S'it!'

Pat feels his legs straining as he batters his prick into her hole — 'Auwww. Ye-es! Ye like that?' he pants, fingering her arse — 'D'ye like that? D'ye like it up yer arsehole? Eh? S'at good?' he continues as he speeds up — 'Eh? Auwww! Wiggle it! C'mon ya big fuckin hump, ye! Wiggle it! Fastur! S'it! Fastur!' he gasps — 'Fastur!'

Janis feels his prick swell — 'Ye-es!' she grunts, tightening her cunt muscles — 'Ye-es. Fastur! Fast-ur! Fastur! S'it!' she screams, twisting and rotating her cheeks — 'Ye-es. S'it! Hardur! Ram it right up me!' she cries, dragging her long fingernails along the floor like talons — 'Auwww, Pat! Auwww! Auwww!'

Pat's labouring his lungs — 'Auwww! Auwwww! Don't stop!

Keep wigglin! Auwww! Auwww! Am cumin! Auwww! Am cumin! Am cumin!' he roars — 'Awya! Auwwwya fucker, ye! Auwww!'

Janis feels his sperm soak her insides — 'Auwww! Me tae, doll! Me tae, darlin! Auww! Auww! Auww!' she grunts — 'Auww! Auww! Auww!'

Pat lights a cigarette while Janis fixes her hair in the mirror — 'S'aw right fur you, innit?' she smiles at the reflection — 'Av got the weans tae pick up. Ach. It wis jist a party fur the weans an thur pals,' she adds — 'Laura wantit tae go as well, so. Oh. See thur wis a priest shot the day. Aye, thur wis a newsflash this efternin. Shame, innit?'

Pat takes a deep drag on his cigarette — 'Magine that, eh?'

Janis stands up to admire herself — 'S'a guy wi red hair.'

Chapter Fifteen

BIG RON IS under terrible pressure, there have been too many killings and now a priest lies dead on a slab – 'Pat. We need a body fur this an fast. A priest? Ye seen any ey the papurs the day?'

Pat's looking at the two cops – 'S'this wit you've phoned me fur? This daft priest?' he asks in mock amazement – 'S'the mattur wi ye? Yer fuckin chalk-white man?'

Big Ron bangs his drink down onto the table – 'V'ye seen these headlines?' he rasps, demonstrating the earnest nature of his mood – 'Thur sayin that a shood resign! Aye! Every single fuckin papur! Resign! N'fur a fuckin priest?' he snarls – 'A priest? The press ur camped ootside the fuckin station! Wid ye believe it? Resign?'

Oh, so that's it, thinks Pat – 'So wit ye gonny dae?' he drawls – 'V'they noa captured this punter wi the red hair?'

Big Ron scowls into his drink – 'Red hair?' he sneers – 'Many cunts dae ye see walkin aboot the streets wi red hair? We gonny pull thum aw in?' he snaps – 'Naw, Pat. Am under real pressure here. A need a name n fast.'

Pat sips his Coke, completely unfazed – 'Sound, big man, sound. Take McGinty. Got red hair, hint ey?' he laughs – 'Ye want him?'

Big Ron looks at him, a look filled with hope – 'McGinty? Ye serious?' he asks – 'Wis it him? Thought he wis in Manchestur.'

Pat twirls the ice around his glass – 'Wis it wit? S'it make any difference? S'a name, innit?' he grins – 'Calm doon, man. Al line um up fur ye,' he adds – 'Ye panickin fur? You're the polis, int ye? S'your script, innit, so wit ye worryin fur? S'they urra two, by the way? Fled the country ur wit?' he sniggers – 'Ron, stop worryin. S'sound, big man, sound.'

Maloney and Brodie are absent. This is private, but the older policeman doesn't feel privileged by the invitation. Bertie's barely said a word. He's just staring blankly at the table top – 'The fuck you starin at, Bertie?' scowls Pat.

Bertie flinches, but he remains silent. Ron knows, he thinks. He's pretending that he doesn't know who is behind this. He has to. A blind man could see it. Jesus, he thinks. A priest. He's a Prod. But that sort of thing only happened in Northern Ireland. Didn't it? This is Glasgow. Those kind of things didn't happen here, surely?

Big Ron signals the barman – 'A double, Bertie?' he asks – 'Bertie?' he repeats – 'Fur fucksake,' he sighs – 'Bertie!'

The policeman has the horrors – 'Eh? Aw, sorry. Wis miles away there,' he stammers as empty eyes wheel round on him again – 'Sorry. Aye, a double.'

It's him.

'Ye feelin awright Bertie?' asks Pat – 'Don't look too good fae here. Sure a that? Yer awright?'

It's definitely him – 'Sumthin oan ma mind. At's aw,' snaps the old cop – 'Kinna noa think noo withoot explainin maself?'

Big Ron interrupts but Bertie doesn't catch what he says. Bertie keeps staring down at the table. He tries to call up events in his drink-sodden brain. He's certain that somebody mentioned the priest the last time they all had a drink. What had it been about again? He tries hard to remember, but his memory is gone. Big Ron knows though. He must know. All these wee private talks. He must know. Every time a name comes up they end up in a box. It's definitely him. Big Ron knows, definitely. Who's next? Jesus. The cold chill of the Campsie Hills descends upon him like a veil. A priest? he thinks. Dear God. How could anyone do that? It's fucking him alright.

Big Ron's nodding – 'Aye, right, right,' he's saying – 'Ye'll huv um where? W-it? Your jokin, int ye? Dempster as well?'

Bertie doesn't hear the reply. He doesn't want to hear their plans. He doesn't want to hear who's to be killed next – 'Listen, Ron. Am gonny head off,' he says – 'Think that last pint wis aff.' He can't look at those eyes.

'Aye, Bertie. Told ye wurny lookin too clever there. Here, ye wanta cuppla quid?' asks Pat – 'Naw? Must be noa well, eh? Knockin back muney noo?'

Bertie feigns a smile – 'Naw. Honest, am fine. V'stull got a cuppla grand left,' he says excusing himself – 'Al catch ye later. Think it's time tae go hame. Margaret's waitin,' he mutters – 'See ye, then.'

Big Ron barely notices him leave – 'S'Bert away?' he asks – 'A never heard um. When did ey go?'

Pat smiles – 'Here. S'a cuppla grand. Bertie left es wages. Think your needin a wee vacation, big yin,' he says – 'Too much pressure. Aye, Dempstur, eh. Ach, tried tae get wide wi money, the cunt. Anyway, stop panickin.'

Bertie staggers down lane after lane until finally he emerges from his thoughts down by the river – 'Scum. The twoey thum,' he mutters, throwing bank notes into the dark, murky waters – 'Ron. Ye wur ma best pal. But yer jist like the rest ey thum.'

Dear God. His Margaret? What would she think of him? Heroin? Corruption? Bank robberies? What next? They killed that priest. He feels it in his bones. He knew. But Big Ron? Why, Ron? Why? All that shite. Things have changed? Sure, but does that mean we become like them? Drug dealers and murderers? He stares down into that black water. Oh, Margaret, he thinks. Please forgive me, please forgive me – 'Scum,' he mutters to himself – 'Fuckin sc-um. Al show the cunts,' he adds staggering into a telephone kiosk – 'Fuckin show thum. Hullo!' he shouts down the receiver – 'S'Bert Spears here, put me straight through tae the duty Inspectur.'

Big Ron signals the barman – 'Right, then. Al leave it wi you then,' he says – 'Be nice tae say hullo tae that bastard,' he adds – 'Sure ye don't want a Coke?'

Pat shakes his head – 'Na. Better head up the road. V'hardly seen the two weans these last few weeks,' he says – 'So jist leave it wi me, okay. Sit things oot ur take a vacation. Ye'll be famous again anyway in a cuppla days.'

Big Ron finally smiles – 'Well. A hope so,' he beams – 'Be seein ye, okay. N'keep me up tae date. N'al get that date fur ye. M'dyin tae see that yin's face,' he laughs – 'The hard man, eh.'

Pat feels the cold night bite into him as he jumps into his car – *'Think it's time tae go hame. Margaret's waitin.'* Click. He pushes the tape-recorder aside and switches on the engine – 'Aye, Bertie. Me tae, son. McGinty. A better phone him the night. Good grafter tae, but that's the way it goes,' he chuckles – 'Dempstur, eh. The hard man, right enuff.'

Chapter Sixteen

WULLIE DEMPSTER IS preparing for his first day at the Glasgow Art School – 'Hammer an chisels, n'muney,' he mutters, checking his things. He looks around the cell, taking a deep breath – 'Jesus. Butterflies,' he laughs – 'Right. Wallet, right v'got that.'

He takes another look at himself again in the full-length mirror. He zips the expensive leather jerkin to the neck. Turns around and unzips it again. No, I'll leave it open he decides. Don't want to look too formal, he thinks. Makes me look uptight. Are these denims too tight? he wonders – 'Aherm. Eh,' he coughs – 'Wullie Dempstur. Special Unit. Hullo. How'd ye do. Na-ah.'

He tilts his head to the side, leans slightly back. The image staring back looks hard as nails – 'Hi there. Willie Dempstur. I dae sculptures. Fuck!' he snaps, making another attempt at his introduction – 'Aherm. Eh. Ma name's. Aw, fuck it.'

He pats the back pocket of his jeans – 'Bank book. S'everythin. Let's go en,' he grins, taking the stairs two at a time – 'Hope this guy's got the car ready.'

The screws are all reading newspapers as he walks into the staff room – 'S'me, Gerry. Is there somebody tae take me down tae the gate?' he asks – 'M'ready tae go.'

Gerry looks up as a chorus of good cheer erupts.

'Mornin, Wullie.' 'Right, Wullie.' 'Okay, Wullie.'

Wullie bounces through the main gate. His first day of freedom, he thinks. And without a prison escort. Two years.

Two years, and they will let him out. They can't keep him in any longer. He has demonstrated that human beings can change. Two years, and it will be over. Surprised the press aren't here, he thinks, looking around – 'Where is this fuckin guy?' he asks himself as a car crawls up the drive.

McGinty leans out the driver's window – 'Wullie Dempstur?' he asks – 'Am McGinty.' he smiles – 'Sorry am late. Pat phoned last night,' he adds – 'S'short notice but nae problem. Where dae ye wantey go?'

Wullie rolls down the passenger window as he makes himself comfortable – 'Straight doon tae the art school, kid,' he replies – 'You've tae drive me back? Right. Be there fur five a'clock. Am due back at six,' he adds – 'So don't be late. Right, son?'

McGinty nods as the jail fades in his rear-view mirror – 'Eh? Oh, aye,' he says – 'Five on the dot. Right, nae problum.'

Wullie leans out of the window – 'S'yer name again, son?' he asks – 'McGinty? Rings a bell. Ye been up in Peterheid?'

Johnny stares straight ahead watching the traffic – 'Me? Naw,' he replies – 'Av dun a few jakeys. Sixty days an at. Nae big sentences.'

Wullie frowns for a moment – 'McGinty?' he repeats – 'Definitely know the name but a canny place yer face. By the way. Did Pat gie ye money fur me?'

Johnny smiles in the mirror – 'Got pull't fur a murdur years ago,' he says – 'Nuthin tae dae wi me, know wit a mean,' he adds – 'Barney Boone? Ye heard ey um? Guy dun um in. N'that mob tried tae dae me wi it. But eh, money? Nah, Pat never said.'

Wullie's looking at him – 'Barney Boone?' he exclaims – 'Auld Barney? Thief? Ochh, fur fucksake, man,' he laughs

– 'Auld Barney? McGinty? S'right. Fucksake, that must be a good few year ago, eh?'

Johnny nods – 'A wis only a boy then,' he shrugs – 'Aye, it wis a long time ago. Long've ye dun yerself noo?'

Wullie leans back – 'Thirteen years,' he says – 'Flies in. A mean, don't get me wrang, son. S'a long time but ye kin haunle it. God!' he exclaims suddenly – 'Smell that, eh. Freshly cut grass! Amazin, man,' he adds – 'Pat no mention money at aw then?'

Johnny looks at his face in the mirror – 'Aye. Must be heavy. S'this you gettin oot fur the day then?' he asks – 'Pat said yer good at that arty stuff. V'ye used that tae wurk yer ticket?' he asks – 'Wur ye expectin money?'

Wullie ignores the question. He knows this bampot wouldn't understand – 'Aye, aye.' he sighs – 'N'wit you intae?' he asks – 'Ye makin a few quid fur yerself, kid?'

Johnny lights a cigarette – 'Aye, aye,' he replies through a cloud of smoke.

'Aw here, son!' exclaims Wullie – 'C'mon noo. Get that fuckin thing oot man,' he orders – 'D'ye huv tae smoke, son? Fucksake. A young guy like you. Ye shood be trainin. Gettin up every mornin an joggin.'

Johnny doesn't believe this.

'Fucksake, son. Lookit me,' continues Wullie – 'Nuthin kin control me. Ad never let anathin control me. Smokin?'

Johnny pulls the car over – 'S'us. Ye want me tae wit fur ye?' he asks – 'A kin take ye wherever ye want.'

Wullie slams the car door behind him – 'Naw. Listen,' he says – 'Jist be here at five on the dot, okay.'

Johnny watches him look up at the sky again. Fresh-cut grass up there? he wonders. Must be heavy in that place with him running around, he thinks. Oh, Jesus. Check the denims, he smiles, looking out the window. They must be cutting right into the cheeks of his arse. Where has this guy been? He pulls off the hand-brake and calls out – 'Okay. Five on the dot. L'get ye here?' he asks.

Wullie's already mincing up the front steps – 'Aye, son. Catch ye later,' he calls back, pushing through the swing doors of the entrance.

'Nae problum. See ye later oan. An don't worry. Al be there on the dot,' shouts Johnny. Son? He drives off smiling – 'Al be there awright. That Pat bastard didny mention ey wis nuts.'

Johnny had taken the telephone call the night before. He was having his jag – 'Pat? How ye doin,' he'd said – 'Who? Aye, sure. S'nae bother. Much?' he'd added – 'Ten grand? Magic. Jist make sure es late gettin back the jail?'

Ten grand? he thought, tying the belt around his arm. Ten grand for a drive? Not too bad, he smiled, gripping the strap in his teeth. He flicked the needle before plunging a vein – 'Noa bad at aw-w – ye-esss.'

Wullie blunders through a few doors before finally finding the sculpture department in the building opposite the old school – 'Eh. Wullie Dempstur. Special Unit,' he blurts out, noticing an absence of students – 'Naib'dy here yet?'

Cliff Bowen, the tutor, looks at him – 'Who?' he asks timidly – 'Oh, sorry. Right. Sorry. Bit early in the morning.' he adds – 'Well. Eh. What would you like to do?'

Wullie dumps his tools on a bench – 'Wull, eh. Right, then. Av tae go an see the Lord Provost,' he explains – 'Wur havin lunch down the toon. Al be back here fur three ur, say, four.' He adds – 'That okay with yerself?'

Cliff Bowen looks at the floor – 'Eh. Fine, then,' he smiles, almost apologetically – 'I'll be, eh, down the pub around noon. Four o'clock you say? Fine, fine. I hope you enjoy your lunch. Would you like to look around before you go? I'll be acting as your supervisor while you're here, but feel free. And do take advantage of the facilities.'

Wullie lifts the toolbag and then decides to leave it under a bench – 'Yeah, sure. Cliff's your name. S'at right?' he asks – 'Yeah, Cliff, fine. So how did you get intae sculpture then? Ye from Glesgow?'

Cliff looks down at the floor – 'Ehm,' he smiles nervously – 'I've been teaching mostly these past years. Left Liverpool, eh. Oh, I'm not sure. But tell me,' he smiles – 'How did the prison, the authorities, eh . . .'

Wullie feels the guy's nervousness – 'Me? How did a get intae it?' he asks – 'Well. A wis jist a young guy caught up in vialence n at,' he explains – 'But the furst time they haundit me a hammer n chisel . . .' He pauses – 'It wis like a discovery inside me. That's wit it wis like. The endey a voyage. D'ye know wit a mean, Cliff?' he asks – 'A fell tae the grun, Cliff. Fell tae ma knees. They powerful feelins a felt. D'ye know wit a mean, Cliff?'

Cliff notices a crack in the floor, but he is listening.

'Ma wurk hus attracted the attention of lot'sa urra artists. But don't get me wrang, Cliff. A mean art?' laughs Wullie – 'That wis fur poofs n sissies at school. Hard men urny interestit in art. But human beins kin change,' he continues – 'A poured these really powerful feelins intae stane. Sometimes it tore ma insides apart. But expressin masel is mer important than stabbin people. D'ye know wit a mean, Cliff?'

Cliff's nodding – 'Eh, yeah, sure, sure,' he smiles, opening the swing doors – 'This is the Mackintosh Building,' he adds, sweeping an arm around the foyer. An old plaster cast model looks down upon them as they pass.

'God, man!' exclaims Wullie – 'They Michelangelos ur brulliant, int they?'

Cliff frowns, slightly confused – 'Oh, these?' he titters – 'Sorry. Eh, are you interested in Classical Greek?'

Wullie is overawed by the scale of the plaster models – 'Lookit thum! A feel inspired already,' he replies without answering the question – 'Lookit aw they details in that wan. Look, Cliff. Veins. Aw, God. S'unbelievable, so it is.'

Cliff's nodding – 'Eh, yeah, sure,' he says – 'Um, Richard Serra's fascinating I think. It has to be the use of space, um, and of course the form. The students are mostly keen on Donald Judd. I'm sure they would enjoy discussing his use of space and scale. Or do you prefer Caro?'

Wullie tugs at the seams of his jeans – 'Carol? Who's she again?' he asks – 'Naw. Av been too busy graftin masel,' he adds – 'A mean. Am up every mornin at six, an efter a wurk oot am straight oot there.'

Cliff's looking at the floor still – 'Oh, sorry,' he says – 'Um. Well, then. S'almost eleven. So if you want to have your lunch?'

Wullie looks at his watch – 'God! So it is,' he exclaims – 'Right. Well al be back here fur four,' he says – 'Al look in at the studio furst. Make sure ma tools ur okay.'

Cliff watches him strut down the steps – 'Um, yes, sure,' he smiles – 'Four. Fine. You should find me in the, in the pub.' He adds – 'I'll see you, then.' Where did he get those jeans? he wonders.

Wullie briefly pops back into the sculpture department. The toolbag is safe. What are these things? he wonders, looking at the small maquettes lying around the studio. He doesn't understand. Are there no real sculptures – stones? Where are they all? He should have had the prison deliver one of his carvings to the school. The 'feet' might have given the students an idea of what he was doing. Where are they? he wonders. They had been told he was coming, surely?

Sauchiehall Street. Wullie can't believe it. He's on the street. He is actually walking along the street – alone. He's nodding to everyone who passes. They'll recognise his face from the press, he thinks – 'Hi there, missus.'

Jesus. They know him alright. He feels their glances. Well, he thinks. This is what it is going to be like when I'm released. Might as well get used to it, he grins. A press conference. Yeah, that might be a good idea. A press conference on his release. Or, a documentary. Yeah, and more elocution lessons. Yeah, then they would realise he really was serious – 'Hi there, missus.' he chuckles – 'Hullo there.'

George Square. God. The last time he walked through here. Sheriff Court. Yeah, so long ago. Yeah, breach of the peace, that's right – 'Well. Here we ur,' he mutters, as he walks into the City Chambers – 'Ehm. Hullo there,' he smiles at the usher – 'Wullie Dempstur. Special Unit. Kin ye tell the . . . Witsat?' he asks – 'Dempstur. That's right. Willie Dempstur. Special Unit.'

There appears to be some confusion – 'Barlinnie. Eh, pardon?' he asks – 'It is the jail. That's right. Dempstur. Av tae meet the Lord Provost. Witsat?'

The Lord Provost's not in? No, there has to be a mistake – 'Eh, no, no,' he grins – 'Am meetin um here. That's right. Pardon?' he asks, astounded – 'The polis? Wit? Naw, naw. Am leavin. S'awright. Am leavin.'

What's happened? he wonders. The Lord Provost knew he was coming. Twelve, he'd said. He looks at his watch again. Half past eleven. Oh, well. There's been a mistake. Might as well head back to the art school. Yeah, do some carving. The governor can phone the Lord Provost — 'That cheeky cunt there,' he mutters — 'Hi there, missus.'

Sauchiehall Street again. God, he just can't take this in. He's actually walking up the street — alone! Jesus, he exclaims. Lauder's Bar. He's tempted but his face is too well-known. One journalist. That's all it would take. One reporter and it would be all over the national news.

'Hi Wullie,' mutters a voice.

'Wi-it! Who? Ehm, who are?' Wullie asks the woman — 'Do I . . . Have we met? Is it? Is it really you?' he gasps, recognising a familiar face from the past — 'God! Is it? Is it really?'

The face looking at him frowns — 'Eh? Ye talkin like that fur?' she asks — 'S'me. Anne McLaughlin,' she adds — 'Och. Stop actin aw stupit. Yev noa been away that long, fur Christsakes.'

Wullie's face is scarlet — 'Eh. Thingmy. Listen, eh. Am in a hurry,' he smiles — 'S'nice seein ye again. Aye, fine. Right. Cheerio.'

See. She might just have seen him look into Lauder's. And then what? Yeah, sure — 'Hullo there, missus.'

Wullie Brodie and Maloney are by the bar. The Irish man drinks almost three quarters of his beer in one gulp — 'Ye-es!' he burps — 'Needid that, al tell ye. Same again, mate. N'kin ye turn the telly oan?' he adds — 'S'it been fixed? Wantey catch the news.'

Brodie's drink is barely touched as the barman pours two

more pints – 'Terrible news eh?' he says apologetically – 'Came in quite a lot, tae. How's the big man takin it?' he asks – 'Quiet wee guy as well.'

Brodie shrugs – 'Aye, well. A suppose so,' he says – 'Widny be me anyway. Al tell ye that.'

Maloney's downing another pint – 'S'better noo,' he says, wiping the back of a huge hand across his pinched mouth – 'Aye, pal,' he replies, casting a sly glance in the direction of his partner – 'It is a shame, so it is,' he adds – 'S'terrible the things people huv tae face in this business. People don't really understaun. They think it's aw car chases. Cops n robbers, but thur's terrible stress involved.'

A hush descends upon the bar – 'S'the news oan noo,' someone says – 'Shsht, tae wi hear wit's happened.'

Shareen Nanjiani's familiar face beams into the daily lives of the customers in the bar like clockwork – 'Christ. S'that the time already?' someone mutters – 'Wee darlin, int she?'

People feel they've known her all their lives. And why not? She keeps them informed of events outside those half-filled tumblers and other midday aperitifs – 'Ray Davies is intae ur,' smirks a voice in the 'know' – 'The Kinks. S'right. The lead singer. Fancies ur, so ey dis.' How else could they find out what was happening in the world beyond their bleary-eyed horizons?

'Shsht. S'hear s'happenin, wull ye?' repeats a voice.

'And today's other news,' smiles the television presenter, appropriating the required tone – 'Strathclyde police today launched an investigation into the death of a police officer found dead in the early hours of this morning. Sergeant Robert Spears who had been with the police force for eighteen years, was discovered by a member of the public who had been walking his dog by the banks of the River Clyde. Mark Geissler is there now. Mark?'

A handsome young face appears on the television screen – 'Yes, Shareen,' he blusters as high winds threaten to blow him off the bridge – 'I'm here now near the spot where the body of the man was discovered. Sergeant 'Bertie' Spears as he was known, was due to retire. It is believed he had been depressed due to the death of his wife but the police believe the man may simply have fallen from the bridge. The police are expected to issue a statement to that effect later today.' He adds – 'Back to you at the studio, Shareen.'

Shareen looks down as she returns to the screen – 'Mark Geissler there reporting. We will have more news on that matter later today,' she says, pausing – 'There was good news today for a family in Fife,' she smiles – 'Little Emily Watson . . .'

Brodie shakes his head – 'Wee Bertie, eh,' he snorts – 'Sad wee man. A sad, sad wee man. Livin in the past. The auld days, eh.'

Oh, things had definitely changed – 'Ach. Guy jist wanted a quiet life. S'a shame fur guys like that. A quiet life. That wis aw,' says Maloney – 'Jist a quiet life.'

Brodie leans on the bar – 'Aye, well,' he sniggers – 'S'made a splash noo.'

Jackie draws him a look – 'S'that supposed tae be funny?' he asks – 'A don't find that funny, Wullie.'

Wullie leans across the bar – 'Gie it time,' he smirks – 'L'sink in inna minut. Splash? D'ye get it noo? Splash – water?'

Maloney turns away – 'Ach, fuck off,' he snaps – 'Canny make you oot sometimes. Ey wis a pal ey yer Da's.'

Brodie looks at his partner – 'Ma Da?' he smiles – 'Ma Da died like a dog. Skint n noa even an insurance policy tae cover es funeral. Ma poor Maw hud tae go n tap a fuckin money-lender tae bury that bastard so don't you talk tae me aboot es pals. Where wur aw the pals then?' he demands – 'Wee Bertie? Fuck um.'

Jackie can't find an answer – 'Right, right. Fair enough. Am jist sayin it wis a shame. That's aw. A thought ye liked Bertie?'

Wullie shakes his head – 'Jack, listen. Av nuthin against the guy,' he explains – 'Sure. Ey wis a nice wee guy. Sure. Ey wis a cop, but so what?' he asks, holding up a hand to prevent his partner answering the question – 'Look, Jack. Ma Da wurked aw es days wi the force,' he continues – 'N'wit did they dae fur him? Nuthin. Ey died penniless n spittin blood. Twenty-five year n wit? Nuthin. Ma Maw wis left wi a uniform n a paira boots. Big Bad Boab Brodie eh, the best desk sergeant in the city.'

Jack's stunned – 'Wullie.' he says – 'A don't believe this. Eh? Bertie wis wanney us. N'noo your sayin so what?'

Brodie shakes his head again – 'Jack, look,' he sighs – 'Bertie wis okay. A told ye that a liked um. But am noa gonny get aw sentamental cos es jumped affey a bridge. D'ye noa see wit a mean?' he asks – 'S'his problem,' he adds – 'Es makin mer money than es ever hud in es life. N'noo av tae feel sorry fur um cos ey tops es self? Fuck.'

Jack nods – 'Aw, a see. Money,' he smirks – 'That's wit it's aw aboot, money.'

Wullie's bewildered – 'Wit's that?' he asks – 'W-ell. D'you wantey spend aw yer days listenin tae Pakis' complaints an stealin crates a beer? Fine. You go right ahead. But don't expect me tae start greetin jist because some poor sad wee man coodny take the pressure. Me? Am lookin efter number wan. Cos nae other cunt is.'

Jack looks down at the bar — 'Ye've changed, Wullie,' he says — 'Ye wur never like this before,' he adds — 'A don't know wit it is. But yer noa the same guy a knew. Am bein straight wi ye. Yer noa the same guy, an that's the truth, Wullie. Ye've changed, mate.'

Wullie corrects him — 'Naw, Jack,' he says — 'Av jist woke up.'

Shareen Nanjiani breaks the brooding mood — 'We'll be back at six,' she smiles — 'But before then, here's Helen with the weather.'

A tall, tartan-jacketed girl appears at the left of the screen — 'Yes, Shareen,' she smiles cheerily — 'Weather troubling most of us this morning it seems,' she adds, pointing to the weather map — 'The north-east will become fairly cold as gusty winds and showers falling overnight come in from Argyll. And here looking at the satellite images we can see that snow as it freezes on the hills, bringing bitterly cold temperatures much later in the evening so wrap up warm.'

Leather jerkins aren't exactly the appropriate garb for outdoor conditions. Then again Wullie Dempster hadn't been planning on any trips to the Campsie Hills — 'Ha-ud oan.' he exclaims — 'Where wi gaun? This isnae the way tae the jail.'

Johnny looks in the rear-view mirror — 'Drapin aff a wee message,' he smiles — 'Thur's plentya time. Anyway, thought ye liked the smella grass?'

Wullie looks out the window, slightly confused — 'A wee message?' he asks — 'Hope it isnae dope, pal?'

Pal? Johnny glances across at the passenger – 'Dope?' ask pinned pupils – 'Noo, dae a look like a dope fiend? Naw. S'jist a message. N'don't worry. Al be back in plentya time. S'only ten past five man, bagsa time.'

Wullie's still not happy, but – 'S'okay, then. Long as wur back up the road in time,' he says – 'V'ye been anyway?'

Johnny shrugs – 'Ach,' he sighs – 'Jist drove aboot the toon.'

Wullie shakes his head – 'Drove aboot?' he exclaims – 'Honest. Yous young yins. Al be locked in a cell at nine. Locked i-nn. D'ye know wit that feels like, son? Eh? Locked up like an animal?'

Johnny shrugs – 'V'never dun a big yin,' he replies – 'Told ye that the day. V'telt ye a canny imagine wit it's like in there.'

Never done a big sentence? Wullie smirks. Humphh. This guy's life is just one long sentence. Young people, he thinks. Just what are they doing with their lives? he has to ask himself – 'Oh. Drivin aboot the toon,' he mimics.

And those art students too with their 'forms'. Where were all the sculptures? The real sculptures, the stone carvings – 'V'ye got a burd?' he asks – 'S'that were wur gaun?'

Johnny keeps his eye on the road – 'Witsat?' he asks over his shoulder. A girlfriend? Hypodermic needles could hardly be described as sleeping companions. However, they did provide the pleasure he craved. It was an unusual relationship and one without complication. They made love three times a day – foreplay consisted of a teaspoon and a burner. Satisfaction guaranteed – 'Eh, naw. Got wan yerself?'

Dempster looks ahead. People, he thinks, watching as pedestrians whizz past the car in a blur. He stares; his focus fixed to the flashing stream of images zooming behind them as they race towards the future. God, if they only knew what he had to suffer as a human being – locked up – behind a steel door – 'Seven,' he replies – 'Wan burd's too dangerous in ma position. Naw, son,' he adds – 'N'ma position yev got tae spread oot yer emotions. Ye canny afford tae get involved cos these things jist don't last. Noa in the jail.'

Johnny looks straight ahead – 'Aw ri-ght,' he replies, watching the roads begin to bend and narrow – 'A see wit ye mean,' he agrees, adding – 'But ur you noa due oot? Guy in your pasition man. Thought ye wid wantey settle doon n gettin a flat n that. M'sure ye like wanney yer burds.'

Wullie shakes his head – 'A flat?' he sniggers – 'Ye don't know much aboot me dae ye, son?' he asks – 'Naw. Av got ma ain burd,' he explains – 'She's a professional. Da's loaded,' he smirks – 'Loaded.'

Johnny frowns – 'S'at the sweetie mob?' he asks – 'Must be loaded, eh,' he nods – 'Ye ridin this wee thing?'

Wullie flinches. Riding this wee thing? He leans toward the driver's ear – 'Ye see, son. This is wit happens,' he snaps – 'Ye talk tae people. N'then wit happens?' he sneers – 'Familiarity. Jist canny help thurselves,' he adds – 'Familiarity, son. Breeds contempt.'

Johnny takes the bend ahead without warning – 'Oops,' he grins apologetically as the passenger slams against the door – 'Ye awright there?' he asks, as small, gritty stones crash and rattle around the chassis – 'S'durt roads, man. Menace wi moturs.'

Wullie's trying to hold himself down in the seat – 'Je-sus!' he roars – 'Wi gaun campin ur wit? R'the fuck ur ye gaun?'

Johnny hugs the steering-wheel – 'Sorry,' he shouts – 'S'a

wee short cut. S'noa that faur noo,' he adds, as the car rocks and bounces along the unused dirt path – 'Road's five minutes away.'

The car crunches to a halt as he slams on the brakes – 'S'a wee village,' he explains getting out of the car – 'S'jist up the road a bit. Al nip up masel n be back inna cuppla minutes. S'at okay?' he asks, adding – 'Kin ye geez a haun a wee minute? S'jist tae get sumthin ootey the boot.'

Dempster doesn't believe this. Where did they dig this bampot up from? he wonders, getting out of the car – 'The bo-ot?' he asks sarcastically – 'Listen. You be back here in five minutes pronto, right? S'gettin like a fuckin pantomime here,' he adds, pulling his leather jerkin higher to hide from the vicious wind whipping mercilessly at his ears as it screeches across the barren landscape – 'Noo. C'mon,' he chatters – 'Feel that wind, man.'

Johnny's bending over the boot – 'Canny see it,' he mutters, fumbling among the old oil rags and leather bags – 'S'funny,' he continues – 'Canny see it.'

Wullie's patience is reaching an end. He leans over, trying to look inside – 'Right noo, c'mon,' he huffs – 'Hurry up,' he puffs – 'Might help f'ye opened the fuckin thing,' he adds, pushing at the hood.

Bang! The blow twists his head, almost wrenching it from his shoulders – 'Nggnnn!' he spits as teeth crunch and break in his skull – 'Nggnnn!'

A forlorn, grey sky spins above as ringing sounds erupt in his ears – 'Yer bran new,' whispers a voice – 'Be bran new inna minut,' the voice continues, rolling up a sleeve of the leather jerkin – 'Be bran new inna wee minut,' it repeats – 'S'it noo, e-asy.'

Wullie's head lolls loosely on his chest as he lies slumped against the car bumper. A slight pin-prick on his inner left forearm spreads into warm numbness as a tourniquet restricts the flow of blood to his fingers – 'Nggnnn,' he rumbles from behind a broken jaw – 'Nggnnn,' he breathes – 'Nggnnn.'

Johnny flicks the plastic tube of the hypodermic – 'Hmmm,' he grins, watching a tiny bubble squirt from the needle – 'S'it ready,' he murmurs, adding – 'Check they pipes, man.' He crouches over the unconscious body – 'Hmmm,' he thinks, tapping the tracks with a fingertip as a particularly thick throbbing vein screams at him – 'Me! Me! Me!'

Wullie rouses slightly as a strange, warm sensation erupts around the soles of his feet like embers from a fire. He stirs as a steady warm glow reaches the virgin territory of his vascular system – 'Nggnnn,' he cries as a gentle tap knocks upon the doors to the sanctum of the pineal gland – 'Ngg-mmmm,' he whimpers as nerve ends melt, suffuse in an orgiastic mass of flesh on the cold, rocky earth – 'Ngg-mmmm.'

Johnny fires up a joint – 'Head off inna minut,' he decides, watching the figure on the ground – 'A pure waste,' he mutters, stuffing some bags into leather pockets – 'Good kit tae,' he adds, poking one of the bags to make sure the powder falls into the lining of the pockets – 'Pure fuckin waste.'

His thoughts are suddenly disturbed as two pinned pupils piercing him with pure hate and panic – 'Nggnnn!' they rage – 'Nggnnn!' they cry as heroin paralyses any notions of movement – 'Nggnnn!'

Johnny takes a deep drag – 'Wee draw?' he asks as his head disappears in a cloud of smoke – 'Nice wi a smoke,' he continues as he reappears again – 'Nice stone, eh?' he asks – 'Furst hit? S'the best wan, so it is.'

Wullie lies limp like a bundle of crumpled rags – 'Nggmmm,' he whimpers as the flush of heroin submerges him in a warmth. His eyelids feel like huge, heavy shutters as they try to blink – boing – boing – boing – 'Nggmmm.'

Johnny drags deeply on the joint – 'So? R'you a right hard man, en?' he asks – 'Well, that's wit the papurs say innit?' he continues, blowing smoke rings into the face of the prostrate figure by the car – 'Scotland's toughest an aw that. Anyway, listen. Wance a finish this al head off,' he adds – 'Take it ye loss yer date fur bein late?'

He offers the joint – 'Sure ye don't want a wee draw?' he asks, getting up – 'Oh, well,' he smiles, stubbing out the roach – 'Right. Am off-ski. S'nice meetin ye, by the way.'

Johnny hears the police helicopter before he sees it hovering above the car. He's no more than a few yards from the spot where he's left Dempster – 'S'that fuckin noise?' he wonders, sticking his head out of the window – 'Fuck,' he sighs, peering through a tomado of dust and twigs – 'Fuckin coppers.'

Big Ron bursts from the first of the four police cars to come screeching to a halt on all sides of the vehicle – 'Right, McGinty,' he sneers, snatching the ignition key from the driver – 'Oot the car. Move!'

Johnny's grinning as he's slammed face first across the bonnet of the car. There's no resistance as his legs are kicked apart and handcuffs are slapped onto his wrists from behind – 'Watch the suit,' he smirks.

'John McGinty,' snaps Big Ron – 'Am charging you wi the murdura Father Joseph Kennedy! Anythin you have to say now may be used against you at a later date in a court of law! D'you have anythin tae say tae the charges brought against you?'

The momentum of the arrest is lost when a faint whimpering sound, carried on the wind, reaches their ears — 'Nggmmm.'

Big Ron laughs knowingly — 'Oh. That'll be Wullie,' he can't resist saying — 'Wondered where ye'd left him. Right. Get this thing doon tae the station,' he adds — 'Noa be walkin this time, McGinty.'

That'll be Wullie? How did he know it would be him? Johnny spits a goggle straight in his face — 'You jist telt me who yer grass is, ya fat prick.'

Wullie Brodie's jaw drops as he catches the headlines on *Scotland Today* — 'Wit? Shsht.' he gasps — 'Wissat McGinty they said there?'

Maloney looks up at the television, slightly puzzled — 'Wit? Who?' he asks.

'Shsht.' replies his partner — 'McGinty. M'sure that's wit she said there.'

Maloney's still confused — 'Who?' he repeats.

'McGinty,' replies Brodie — 'McGinty. Am posative that wis es name there on the news.'

Shareen Nanjiani confirms that it was indeed the name mentioned — 'Police have today arrested a Glasgow man in connection with the murder of a Catholic priest, Father Joseph Kennedy.'

Brodie slams the bar — 'Ye-s!' he roars while the presenter continues.

'John McGinty, who was arrested during an unrelated incident involving assault and kidnapping, is to appear in court tomorrow.'

The Hammer's face fills the screen but his glory is drowned

out by cheers – 'Ye-s! Ya fuckin beauty!' roars Brodie, hugging Maloney – 'See? See wit a mean noo?'

Big headlines and media worship would moderate the moodiness of their chief but the big Irish man is still baffled – 'Who is ey, fur fucksake?' he exclaims – 'Who is ey?'

Brodie's grinning from ear to ear – 'McGinty!' he laughs – 'McGinty, Jack! S'John McGinty! Wis him that fucked up ma Da!'

Maloney's looking at him – 'Yer Da?' he asks, bemused – 'S'he got tae dae wi yer old boy?'

Brodie pulls himself together – 'Es retirement,' he explains – 'Ma Da hud tae retire cos ey him!'

The penny begins to drop – 'A see,' nods Maloney – 'A thought it wis ill-health? Wit's this guy got tae dae wi it?'

Brodie leads him across to the table – 'Naw Jack. That wis the official line. Auld Boab hud smothered up fur a death in the cells wan night,' he whispers – 'Some Paki died in a cell. Ma Da dummied things up.'

Maloney's listening to the account – 'S'an accident, Jack,' continues Brodie – 'These things happen. But McGinty'd battered the guy. A think ey wis charged, but because that slag walked, oor guys wur done.'

Maloney's nodding, listening.

'S'a long time ago but it jist shows ye, eh. The big yin finally nipped um,' smiles Brodie – 'The long arm ey the law, eh?'

Brodie signals the barman – 'Who dun the Paki then?' persists Maloney.

'Wit? Who dun um?' exclaims Brodie – 'A jist told ye wit happened. Jesus are ye no listenin? A Paki died – choked on es ain vomit. N'McGinty hud battered . . . Och, nevermind. R'you Sherlock fuckin Holmes noo ur sumthin?'

Maloney shrugs – 'Sorry, Wullie,' he grins apologetically – 'S'jist that, we-ll. S'jist the joab,' he laughs – 'M'turnin intae a big bizzie, eh?'

Brodie punches him affectionately – 'Jackie, Jackie, Jackie,' he sighs – 'Wit we gonny dae wi ye, big man? Noo look, seriously. Ye know yer ma best mate, eh? Dint ye? Eh, big man?'

Maloney blushes slightly – 'Ye wantey haud ma haun?' he chuckles – 'Naw Wullie, am only kiddin. A know wit ye mean.'

Wullie laughs too – 'Aw, tryin tae be wide noo, eh?' he grins – 'Naw, naw, but seriously, we need tae huv a wee talk. A know yer no happy, an well, we need tae sort it oot coz a don't wantey faw oot wi ye, big man.'

Jack's startled for a moment – 'Fall oot wi me?' he asks – 'Wid'ye mean, Wullie? Ur ye jokin? Yer ma best mate, man.'

Wullie bows his head – 'A know aw that,' he replies – 'S'jist that, well ye know wit am sayin.'

Jack's taken aback; his partner and friend, he really is serious – 'Na Wullie, naw man. Naw, look, mate,' he says – 'McGowan disnae bother me, honest.'

Wullie looks up at him.

'Naw, Wullie, honest,' continues the big man – 'A don't like the guy, sure. But thur's a lotta people a don't like. But thur's nae problum, gen up.'

Wullie needs more – 'Well, wit aboot aw that shite at the bar?' he asks – 'Wee Bertie n aw that?'

Jack shakes his head – 'Bert? Och, Wullie, fur fucksake. A jist felt sorry fur the guy. A mean, ey wis hermless. A jist felt sorry fur um, that's aw,' he says – 'You said it yerself, dint ye?'

Wullie agrees – 'A-ye, a kn-ow th-at,' he replies – 'But dae ye think he widda felt any sympathy fur you if you'd topped yerself?' he asks, holding up a hand – 'Naw, naw . . . let me finish. Bertie wis jist a sad wee man riddled wi guilt aboot es wife. Sure a felt sorry fur um. A mean, am noa monstur, um a?'

Jack shrugs into his beer glass.

'An the fact is. Ey widda dun it anyway,' continues Wullie – 'That guy gave um a wage, so ye canny blame him.'

Jack looks up – 'McGowan? Av never said it wis him, Wullie,' he exclaims.

'Naw . . . but that's wit ye meant, wint it?' replies Wullie – 'Lo-ok. Bertie's been bent fur years, so ey wis, whole career probably, so naibody turned um intae anathin. Ey wis already in fur a long time so don't try n make oot that it wis Pat.'

Jack shakes his head – 'Na, Wullie, yer wrang,' he states – 'Av never said it wis him. A jist said a didny like the guy, that wis aw.'

Wullie shrugs – 'Right, en,' he says – 'So the guy geez you ten grand, an you don't like um? How dae ye wurk that wan oot?'

Jack doesn't have an answer.

'Listen,' continues Wullie – 'Yer jist gonny huv tae get it intae yer heid that things've changed. Look,' he says with growing impatience – 'Av told ye before. F'we want promotion, scalps ur anathin at aw like that – we get it. Big McGhee's jist dun that bampot efter years a waitin. N'check yer pockets, big yin. How much ye got?' he asks – 'Eh? Two grand? Three? When did you ever huv that much money? That's only the beginnin but if your gonny piss aboot moanin an askin stupit questions aw the time then yer oan yer todd.'

Jack's injured by the ultimatum – 'Wullie, fur fucksake,' he moans – 'Av always asked lotsa daft questions, man, ye know that. A know wur ontae a good thing here. N'am no moanin aboot anathin – make a change if a wis, ya cunt.'

Wullie smiles – 'Jackie, fur fucksake, big man,' he chuckles – 'Am jist tryin tae look oot fur ye, man. Yer ma best mate but am jist bein straight wi ye before wur in too deep, an by the way – when've a ever moaned aboot anathin, ya big real yin, ye?'

Jack plants a huge palm on the table, rattling the glasses – 'Wit?' he exclaims – 'Yer a moany-face cunt! Moaned the face affey me the furst day we wur oan duty!'

Wullie's affronted – 'Me?' he laughs – 'That's no true! S'you, ya cunt! F'it wisnae fur me ye widda been stuck behind a desk in some wee poxy station!'

Jack pans it – 'A-way ye go, Brodie,' he laughs – 'A de-sk? Wi these fuckin legs? No fucking danger!'

Wullie looks at his watch – 'S'the backey seven,' he says – 'Fancy Victoria's? Fancy? Pat's telt thum the score. Fancy? Noise up the gangsturs?' he persists – 'Big Ron'll be in shortly n we don't want landit wi him aw night. Disnae like you, by the way.'

Jack looks at him – 'Aye? How's that? S'ey said sumthin tae ye?' he asks.

'Aye. Said that big yin's a moany-face cunt, Brodie!' he laughs – 'See? Even he's sayin it!'

Jack pushes him away – 'Ach fuck you, Brodie!'

The barman nods as they're leaving – 'Night en, lads!' he calls after them.

'Night then, pal!' they reply.

'Any messages fur the big man?' the barman calls as they reach the door.

'Aye,' shouts Brodie – 'Tell um that wis a good result wi the priest murdur! Am coverin the drinks fur the night, okay! Square it the morra!'

The barman smiles – 'Cheers, men!'

'Cheers!'

Chapter Seventeen

ANGELENA IS DEVASTATED by the news of the priest's death. Poor Father Kennedy, her one hope, gone.

'That priest knew sumthin. He knew sumthin. Thuv dun um in. Dun um in,' she mutters to herself.

Why did she get up from the bed, she wonders? The three steps back are exhausting – 'Oh, God help me,' she prays – 'God help me.'

Angelena's back in the middle of the floor, frowning. Why did she get up from the bed, she asks herself? Was it to look out of the window? She looks back again at the steel tubular bed, trying to retrace her steps back to the point of thought. Fuck, she thinks. Why did she get up? The three steps back to the bed are exhausting.

'*S'a braw pie there, lass!*'

What? Was that the food tray being dumped outside the door there? Was it to take a piss? Did she get up to take a piss? She can't remember. It's not that important, but still. She hovers on the edge of the bed, uncertain, unable to lie back down again, just in case it comes back, and she has to go through the process all over again.

'*S'a braw pie there, lass!*'

She fixes her gaze on the familiar patterns in the paint cracks on the wall opposite as she rocks gently back and forth. The motion brings her comfort, gently rocking while she stares at the wall. The wall is hers now – hers for natural life.

'*A frightnur. That's right, sur!*'

Angelena finally lies back down. Her skeletal frame settling into the faint impressions moulded into the thick, black foam mattress. She stares through the ceiling, her frame burnt out like a dry twig. Cold water, she thinks. Yes, that was it. A nice cold glass of clean fresh water. That would be wonderful, a glass of cold water to whet her palate and broken lips.

'*S'a braw pie there, lass!*'

And Jesus commanded – '*Feed my lambs.*'

Yes, a nice cold glass of clean fresh water . . .

Her body groans as she rises. The rubber-covered mattress sucks the skin away from her bones as she pulls herself up to the edge of the bed. She steadies herself until all the dizziness passes and scuffs across greyish-green linoleum in her plastic slippers. One two three steps she takes, before stopping.

Why did she get up from the bed, she asks herself? Was it to look out of the window? She looks back at the bed, trying to retrace her steps back to the point of thought. Fuck, she thinks. Why did she get up? The three steps back to the bed are exhausting.

'*Let the truth be my path!*'

'*S'a braw pie there, lass!*'

What? Was it to take a piss? Did she get up to take a piss? She can't remember. It's not that important, but still. She hovers on the edge of the bed, uncertain, unable to lie back down, just in case it comes back, in case she remembers.

'*A frightnur. That's right, sur!*'

She fixes her gaze on the terrain of patterns on the painted walls opposite. Her walls, all four of them, hers for natural life. Back and forth she rocks, gently, back and forth, back and forth.

'*S'a braw pie there, lass!*'

Back down she goes – down into the stiff black foam. Green rubber squealing as tired bones sigh into a faint impression of life. The bland white ceiling remains indifferent to empty staring eyes – but why? What was the point? Why on earth did he have to say that he believed she was innocent? He had but made an assumption. A personal belief, a hunch – not hard fact. Then again. What if? God please, please.

'Let the truth be my path!'

Angelena stares at nothingness. But yes. Wouldn't it be wonderful, she thinks. A nice glass of cold water. Yes, a nice cold glass of clean fresh water. That really would be wonderful. Cold water to moisten her swollen tongue.

'S'a braw pie there, lass!'

And Jesus commanded – 'Feed my lambs.'

The sweating rubber shroud shrieks as she drags herself from the sticky surface while the greyish-green linoleum rushes up to meet her face. She grips the rounded rails of the bed while the sudden rush of blood returns to the plastic slippers. One, two, three she scuffs before looking back, trying to retrace her steps.

'A frightnur. That's right, sur!'

But she can't remember what it was—

'S'a braw pie there, lass!'

Was it to take a piss? It's not that important, but still.

'Let the truth be my path!'

But what if he is wrong? What if his assumption had been nothing more than that, an assumption? God, no. What if that dead man had confessed to lying about something completely different? God, please, please.

'Feed my lambs.'

But why, she asks herself. Why did she get up from the bed?

Was it to look out of the window? Fuck, she thinks. Back and forth she rocks. Gently back and forth.

'*S'a braw pie there, lass!*'

The ceiling remains indifferent as she stares. But wouldn't that be nice? A wonderful, ice-cold glass of water? Wouldn't it? Yes, she thinks, rising up, but still.

'*Angelena. Angelena. Angelena.*'

Angelena lies still as the spy-hole snaps open – 'How is she today, then?' whispers a voice as an eye blinks – 'Taken any liquids yet?'

The flap falls back into place as another voice replies – 'She's been lyin there aw day, ma'am. Never moved an inch. Filthy tae, nae even wash itself.'

The first voice seems concerned – 'I'm bringing the doctors in tonight. She's slipping into a coma,' continues the voice – 'And I don't want her dying here in my nick.'

Vengeance is Mine Sayeth The Lord. But the fixed grin lying on the steel bed is still.

'*Robert? Robert? O-hh Robert, darlin.*'

Chapter Eighteen

JOHNNY McGINTY'S BEING philosophical in the face of the lengthy interrogation, but you learn to take the bad with the good in this game. After four hours, his most immediate problem is the big come down – withdrawal symptoms – W.S.

Underneath the cool exterior the sweat oozes from his pores, a cold slick crystalising like ice across his prickly skin, the preliminary stages of Cold Turkey.

He needs to negotiate medicine – 'Fifteen stretch?' he drawls lazily while a young detective predicts the length of his future behind bars – 'We-ll. A wunder wit the papurs ur gonny make ootey corrupt cops, eh?' he sneers – 'Aye eh, noa gonny be too pleased aboot it. Yer hearin aboot it aw the time, resignations.'

He cocks his head to the side as the detective looks up – 'S'right. Corruption – graft,' he smiles as the detective leans back – 'Oh, aye,' he continues – 'Your gaffer. Big McGhee – The Hammur. Lauder's Bar? Wi dealurs eh? Know wit a mean?'

The big detective by the door folds his arms: he's there to listen to the body language.

'Technology, eh?' continues Johnny – 'Tape's n video machines, amazin wit ye kin dae wi these things, innit?' he grins – 'Aye. Big McGhee n Pat McGowan, eh. Terrible, dealurs tapin people as well, eh.'

Stewart Street. Johnny's first time here. The police station is relatively new compared to his previous experiences. However, no amount of frosted glass could conceal those age-old attitudes – 'D.C. John Anderson. Interview with John McGinty. Stewart Street station. Ten thirty-five p.m.' Click – 'Right, McGinty, jist state name an address when the machine's on, okay?'

Huge, plain-faced detectives are hoping to clear up some unsolved events – recent and past – bin-bagged bodies and campers with holes in their heads found in the Campsie Hills.

'S'a doctur a wantey see,' replies McGinty – 'N'then wull see aboot ma name n address.'

The detective is becoming frustrated by the potential break-throughs, but the prisoner just won't speak whenever the tape-recorder is switched on.

McGinty needs to get down to the holding cells, there'll be something down there to beat the chills – 'Look, boss. Av told ye,' he says – 'Get the doctur furst. Then al gie ye the full spiel on tape.'

The figure lounging by the door leaves the interview room – 'Dearie me,' he grins, amused by the prisoner's resistance – 'Still the same,' he says – 'Right, then. Think we should relieve Anderson.'

The desk sergeant nods in agreement – 'Yes, sur,' he says – 'V'noa seen that face fur a long time, but he'll talk, they aw dae in the end.'

Chief Inspector Tom Forrest places two long legs apart, twiddling his thumbs behind an erect backbone – 'Talking?' he mutters, rocking to and fro – 'Oh, McGinty's talking alright. S'what he's talking about that's the problem,' he adds, planting a huge palm on the counter – 'Well, better get back in there. Oh, and bring the doctor in. Make sure the prisoner's registered.'

The desk sergeant nods again while reaching for the telephone — 'Yes, sur,' he replies, pausing as the chief inspector turns.

'S'the deputy left yet? Hmm. Oh, well, ask him to wait, will you? Thanks.'

Johnny barely glances up as the chief re-enters the interview room. Anderson has been replaced by another detective, but he too is getting nowhere — 'Look, boss. Am a suspect,' McGinty's saying — 'Am no convicted. So am entitled tae medical attention. So?' he asks — 'A doctur, then al talk tae ye.'

Tom Forrest detects the discomfort, the toe tapping, the trembling, but other than that McGinty appears in control. He's disquietingly pleased there's been no pleading or begging for cigarettes or anything at all like that; he'd have been disappointed by that for some reason. He detested drug dealers in particular, peddling poison to teenagers, kids like his daughter, then demanding deals through bent lawyers, but fate had dealt this man a bad hand. The odds are always stacked against his type. But still — a killer?

Tom's thoughts on the question are interrupted. A knock on the door informs him that the doctor has arrived.

'A doctor's here, sur,' whispers the shirt and tie.

'Fine, fine.' replies the inspector, slipping into the passageway between the interview room and the holding cells — 'Evening, Doctor,' he smiles, taking the doctor by the elbow — 'M'so sorry tae have called ye out so late, but we have a slight problem here,' he whispers, guiding the doctor out of earshot — 'Unusual circumstances, but. Well, if ye would like tae follow me al try tae explain the situation.'

Johnny doesn't believe his luck — 'Things've changed right

enuff, eh,' he grins, rolling up a sleeve – 'S'a fag pushin ma luck, boss?' he asks – 'Don't smoke, mate,' sighs the young detective – 'Aw, don't tell me,' replies Johnny – 'Nae bad habits, eh?'

The doctor's hands are unusually shaky. It's not every day one's called out to administer Class A – certainly not to a murderer.

'Pharmacutical, eh?' murmurs McGinty holding out his desperate arm – 'Good, clean swag,' he continues – 'Ye want me tae dae that maself, Doc? Naw? Oh, well, take yer time, thur gettin shy,' he adds, as the doctor tries to find a suitable vein from the derelict pipeline – 'Whoof. Think wur cookin wi gas, eh. A-w. Ye-esss.'

The inspector thanks the doctor before returning to the interview room – 'Thanks very much. You've been a great help. Kin a have a car take you home? No? Oh, well. But, thanks again,' he smiles apologetically – 'Sergeant'll see you out. Thank you, bye then, night.'

Johnny's dilated pupils have returned to zero pin-points; his demeanor is relaxed, considering the serious nature of the circumstances – 'S'appreciatit boss, thanks,' he winks from behind a trail of smoke – 'Cuppa tea n ad be made man,' he chuckles – 'S'dyin fur that fag there – thanks. Right,' he says – 'Johnny McGinty. Royston Road. C/o Johnstone. Noo, wit's aw this aboot a murdur?'

Inspector Forrest leans against the door. Well, well, well, he thinks. He really is going to co-operate.

'Wait, haud on a minute,' pleads the young detective, pressing down a red button – 'Eh, D.C. Michael Thomson,' he stammers – 'Interview with a Jo-hn McGinty. Stewart Street police station. One forty-five – a.m.' Click – 'Right,

John. Kin ye jist repeat that before the interview? Right, fine, that's it. Noo, ye wur sayin . . .'

Johnny blows a smoke-ring through the air – 'Aye,' he says thoughtfully – 'McGhee n McGowan. Thuv been behind fake bank robberies, two ur three murdurs. McGowan pays five grand a week fur pratection. Blastin guys aw o'er the place, man.'

Five hours and two tapes later, the detectives wipe the sweat from their brows in total silence.

'Johnny?' asks a voice for the first time – 'How do you know all this? These are very serious allegations.'

'Sweeney,' replies McGinty – 'The guy canny haud es tongue,' he adds – 'Derek Sweeney. McGowan's bruther-n-law. A bampot. Noo,' he continues – 'M'a no supposed tae huv a brief here? Av been put in the frame fur murder, so wit's the script?'

Inspector Forrest knows they'll get no further tonight – 'Well, Johnny,' he says – 'Your lawyer's been contacted,' he explains – 'However, I'm sure you can appreciate these are unusual circumstances so we're going to have to hold you here for a few days. I'll have your personal property brought down. Cigarettes and things. Things have changed, but I have to point out we are not running a café. Anyway, how are you feeling?'

Johnny frowns for a moment before replying – 'Eh, brand new,' he says – 'Dae a know you, boss?' he asks – 'Face looks familiar.'

Tom smiles – 'Long time ago,' he says, almost embarrassed by the recognition – 'Was years ago. Anyway, Detective Thomson here will look after you in the meantime. And mind, this isn't the George Hotel. Play the game and we will see what we can do, okay?'

Johnny's frown deepens as he's being led to the holding cell. The George Hotel? he's thinking – 'Nae problem, boss,' he winks – 'Nae problem.' The police won't buy into a deal, he knows, but he'll be happy to reduce the possibility of a recommendation. Ten, twelve maybe, but fifteen to twenty years in the hen house? Fuck that, he thinks – 'Nae problem.'

The inspector is exhausted as he returns to his office – 'Dearie me,' he mutters. What a business, he thinks, picking up the telephone – 'Karen?' he asks – 'S'me,' he sighs into the receiver – 'Aye, late again. Well, I'll have tae fill reports in tae,' he adds – 'Eh? Oh, jist tired a suppose. Well, that sounds nice. But there is an immediate report involvin A10/CIB3,' he continues – 'Oh, they're the big boys fae the Corruption Investigation Bureau.'

The police, he knows, can't have this coming out – politically it's too embarrassing for the force but he has no choice – 'McGhee, aye,' he confirms – 'Be an early retirement, no doubt,' he laughs – 'Eh? Well there's been rumours. Gives us a reputation but we'll see what he has to say for himself. Eh? No, he hasn't been told yet. Well, he will shortly,' he sighs – 'Oh, God knows how he'll react. Anyway, better go, love. Well, I'll do the best I can, but don't wait up. Okay, night night.'

Chapter Nineteen

McGHEE TURNS PURPLE, apoplectic almost – 'Suspended, sir?' he gasps – 'But, but, but. This man's a murderer!' he squeals – 'I'm being suspended?' he whimpers in disbelief – 'Me? Suspended? But, but, but these bloody allegations are totally unfounded. Well,' he declares, rather hollowly it must be said – 'I'll be taking this up with my union members – suspended?!'

The inspector holds up a hand – 'Now look,' he states – 'You are entitled to take these matters up with whomever you wish. But the fact of the matter is that I have no choice but to report these allegations to CBI. I'm sure you are aware of these procedures?' he demands – 'Indeed, I'd strongly suggest you make yourself available for questioning and clear these matters up as soon as possible. However, it is my duty to inform you of your immediate suspension, and if you so wish, make legal representation through the various avenues available to you as a police officer. Oh, and,' he adds a little heatedly – 'Incidentally, a statement was also made by Bert Spears.'

CBI? McGhee feels the floor fall away as he gets to his feet – 'No, sir,' he whispers as he fumbles with the door handle – 'No-thing else.' CBI? God, he thinks. The London Met. police chief had had to admit to 1 per cent of the police force being corrupt – one hundred police officers had to resign, he recalls. CBI? God, he thinks. On the appointment of another new chief five hundred officers had resigned immediately – 'Bert. That little bastard.'

Derek is the first to feel the impact as one of a series of co-ordinated police raids finds him in a telephone booth at Dover – 'Pat? S'Derek,' he's saying – 'A pure cakewalk, man,' he laughs – 'Witsat? Paki Black, Gold Seal.' He adds – 'Fucksake, a think the weans ur aw stoned.'

Pat laughs down the line but picks up a commotion – 'S'a bust! S'a fuckin bust!' he hears his brother-in-law yell.

'Hullo? Pat?' asks a stranger's voice – 'Pat? Ye there, mate?'

Pat breaks the line and immediately dials his brief – 'Hullo,' he says – 'Could you put me straight through to Mr Finlay Muir?' he asks – 'Patrick McGowan, yes.'

He holds the line for a moment – 'Pat?' asks a voice – 'Hullo. What can I do for you? Pardon? Where? Hold on a sec, just make a note of that.'

Pat repeats the message – 'Auckland Street, fifteen, that's it,' he says – 'Witsat? Naw, Possilpark. Right, twenty minutes, right. Am in Lauder's Bar, witsat? Am leavin n a cuppla minutes. Okay, don't be late.'

Pat hangs up the receiver – 'Here, barman, phone a taxi wull ye.' he says, passing a score across the bar.

'Five minutes, mate, okay?' replies the barman.

'Tell McGhee a waited,' continues Pat – 'N'al phone later, okay? Oh n leave they car keys behind the bar, somebody'll pick thum up later.'

The barman watches him disappear through the door a few minutes later – 'Jesus,' he mutters, pocketing the car keys – 'Think that guy wid buy eself a decent suit.'

Operation 'Get the Cunts' had kicked-off to a good start, but like most police plans they blew it with the warrant.

'Who?' demands Janis — 'McGowan? Disny live here. This is my house,' she sneers — 'Witsat? How the fuck dae a know where ey is? You're the fuckin detective, int ye! Noo get aff ma fuckin property!'

One helicopter, two battalions of uniforms — including four marksmen — limp off like the cavalry on the wrong movie set.

'Who n the hell?' blusters one angry voice — 'Contact the bloody station and get this man's fixed abode from his conviction sheet!'

Janis bellows at the row of twitching curtains across the road — 'Nosey bastards! The fuck ye hidin fur?' she screeches, picking up the telephone — 'Eh? Hide that's right ya— Hullo? Angie?' she asks, calming down — 'Listen, hen, shut the shop up an get a taxi,' she says — 'Aye, hen. Am in the hoose,' she continues — 'Coppers've been at the door. S'Pat, hen, aye. Naw, thur away noo, right, okay, hen.' Pat, she thinks — 'Where wull ey be at this time?'

Pat's lawyer looks distastefully around the room — 'Who lives here?' he asks.

'Me n ma shadows,' replies Pat — 'V'hud this place fur years, born here,' he adds — 'Ma Da lived here maistly, anyway. Here, take these. Bills, rent n electricity n other stuff.'

The lawyer takes the receipts, but he's puzzled — 'Fine, fine, but why?' he asks — 'Why the bills? Why the house? I thought you lived in Bearsden?'

Pat folds his jacket over an old armchair — 'S'fur the trial.' he states — 'S'ma address. So keep that stuff,' he adds — 'N'take these as well. Driver's licence n registration fur a second haun van.'

The lawyer's bemused — 'Okay, okay, now,' he says — 'Tell

me. What's this all about? A trial? I'm not with you?' Hearing a knock on the door he adds – 'You expecting any visitors?'

Pat's poker-faced as he opens the door.

'Patrick McGowan?' asks a voice – 'Stand back. Now raise your arms above your head,' the same voice orders, as uniforms fill the room.

'My God. What's going on?' asks the lawyer, as he's pushed back against a wall.

'Name?' barks an armed policeman.

'Finlay Muir,' he replies – 'And this is my client.'

Finlay doesn't carry much sway out of court it seems – 'Excuse me,' he calls after the entourage of visors and bulletproof vests – 'Excuse me! As Mr McGowan's solicitor, I demand to know where he is being taken!'

A six-foot overcoat wheels round on him – 'Stewart Street, sir. You will find your client at Stewart Street! Anything else, sir?' the voice asks – 'Well, don't present an obstruction, sir, otherwise you may find yourself under arrest. Now, will that be all, sir?' the voice continues – 'Thank you, sir.'

Janis is relieved the kids are still at school – 'Bastards,' she mutters, walking round in circles – 'Bastards. Aw Angie, c'mon, hen, c'mon,' she repeats, wringing her hands in frustration – 'S'that hur?' she cries as a taxi draws up outside the house – 'Shite, ma purse? Where's ma purse?'

She's still looking when the doorbell rings – 'Aw, Angie, hen, thanks, come in, come in.' she smiles – 'Fuckin polis've been tae the door. Aye, aw ma neighbours as well. Thur hidin behind thur curtains,' she continues – 'Bastards. Think they'd nuthin better tae dae, wint ye? Nosey bastards the lottey thum.'

Angie hands her the keys — 'Av locked everythin up,' she gasps — 'A jist caught a taxi tae, Je-sus!' she pants.

'Aw Angie. Sit doon hen, sit doon,' replies Janis — 'Ma heid's nippin,' she explains — 'Aye, fuckin polis, guns as well. A helicopter! Wid ye believe it? A fuckin helicopter flyin o'er the hoose? Mad bastards, int they? A thought a wis imaginin it an the next thing thur tryin tae batter the door doon! Honest, ye widny believe it, wid ye?'

Angie's bewildered by the buzz — 'Wit's been happenin?' she asks — 'R'they lookin fur your Pat?'

Janis nods — 'Aye,' she says — 'So look, kin you stay here?' she asks — 'Am gonny try tae find the lawyers an see if es been lifted. The weans usually get hame aboot hauf four.'

Angie nods — 'Nae problem. S'Pat know thur lookin fur um? Aw, right. A thought they'd been chasin um ur sumthin,' she says — 'Right, Janis, a see. Right, well, ye jist want me tae wait here tae ye get back?'

Janis pulls on her leather coat — 'Aye Angie, wid ye?' she asks.

'Aye, s'nae problem, honest,' replies Angie.

'And don't worry aboot wages,' her boss assures her — 'They bastards won't be back either so don't worry. Right, look, hen, thanks fur this. A think the best thing's tae go straight tae thur offices, eh?'

Angie agrees — 'Aye Janis, the lawyers know wit tae dae,' she smiles.

'Right, doll. Al be back as soon as possible,' Janis says, waving — 'Look at thum!' she points, getting into her car — 'Hidin behind the curtains!'

Finlay Muir's trying his damnest, but bail has been blocked — 'But this is absolutely disgraceful,' he claims — 'No formal charges have been made against my client. Why then is he being detained?' he demands.

'Further enquiries, sir.' replies the sergeant behind the counter.

'Further bloody enquiries?' the lawyer muses.

'S'the best a can dae for ye, sir,' continues the sergeant – 'Likely be bailed the morn's morn.'

Janis and Mr Muir leave the police station threatening legal action – 'You haven't heard the last of this,' the lawyer promises – 'The morn's morn?' he mimics – 'I take it, sir, you mean tomorrow morning?' he asks.

'S'right sur – morn's morn,' continues the sergeant dryly – 'Morn's morn, unless of course enquiries continue,' he adds – 'Al hand the cigarettes in tae um the nicht.'

Mr Muir promises to do what he can – 'Yes, yes. I'll be there personally tomorrow.' he says, looking at his watch.

'N'thuv definitely no charged um wi anythin?' asks an irritated Janis.

'Oh, they'll dream up something to hold him,' replies the lawyer – 'He knows that himself, but I'll talk to the procurator to fix bail before he appears in court. Be interesting to see what they come up with,' he says, frowning – 'Did he mention at all to you, anything about an imminent arrest?' he asks – 'No? S'odd,' continues the lawyer – 'He appeared to expect something when we were at his home address. Well, I'll be there first thing tomorrow,' he smiles – 'And he has been legally advised to say nothing, so maybe you ought to just go home now. S'no point in hanging around here, is there?'

Janis agrees – 'Right, Mr Muir, fine,' she says – 'Thanks, two daughters'll be thinkin thuv been abandoned,' she smiles weakly.

'Fine, Mrs McGowan,' replies the lawyer, opening her car door — 'Shouldn't take too long to have this sorted out,' he adds — 'I'll have him home tomorrow.'

Janis finds Angie watching television with her two daughters — 'Awright?' she asks as they look up — 'Uncle Derek's been on television, Mummy,' replies Zoe — 'They said he's been arrested, Mummy,' she whines.

'Where is Daddy, Mummy?' echoes her sister, Laura.

'Right, Zoe,' sighs Janis, turning off the television — learning for the first time the purpose of the police raid — 'C'mon then,' she says — 'Noo, c'mon girls, nae cryin,' she continues — 'Daddy'll be hame the morra, so c'mon. Daddy's noa done anything wrong, wull see um the morra.'

Chapter Twenty

BUT DADDY DOESN'T come home. Both Daddy and Uncle Derek emerge from the bowels of the court to face trial after exactly one hundred and eleven days. The indictment almost passes legality. The C/Hall population had held its breath. The Steel brothers, bank robbers done bang to rights, had been freed years earlier when an astute lawyer had declared that their imprisonment was illegal, after a procurator had failed to bring the brothers to trial within the one-hundred-and-twelve-day period dictated by Scottish Law. But still, the legal precedent had helped pass the time for the 'not yet' convicted experts measuring their own hopes against time – 'Me? M'dun bang ey rights! But av dun a hunner n ten days.'

The bad lads prepare for the long haul ahead and extremely sore arses – seated eight hours a day on a hard bench is no joke; that highly polished mahogany slab's caught many a collapsing arse shrinking away from the terrifying recommendations of a High Court Judge – 'Cor blimey, guv – Oofff!'

Derek shifts his enormous, growing arse around while that frayed black suit perches by his side in an almost catatonic state, staring blankly straight ahead beyond the fifty kilos of hash lying on the productions table.

'All rise!' drones the decrepit court usher as he announces the presence of the dreaded Lord Wheatley.

'Fucksake, am in soapy,' whispers Derek – 'Thought Wheatley wis deid?' He glances out of the corner of his eye – did Pat move away there? he wonders, as a slight gap emerges. He knows Pat is furious with him, but the press had been feeding the public with stories for weeks – it was daft snidey screws, exaggerating and spinning yarns about their affluence behind bars – 'Twelve grand,' they had reported – 'Twelve grand on Pot Noodles!'

The Pot Noodle Two have been given the heavy treatment – high security; helicopters, motorcades and cops everywhere. This guaranteed maximum entertainment and big sentences, and a series of underworld stories milked by the daily tabloids – at least until the coppers came up with the next 'Big Fish'.

Shareen Nanjiani is first to break the story later that day – 'The High Court today heard how two men, posing as anti-drug campaigners, used a mini-bus to smuggle fifty kilos of cannabis through customs at Dover,' she says, before the cursory pause and shuffling of papers – 'Patrick McGowan and Derek Sweeney, both from Glasgow, denied the charges of conspiring to smuggle drugs into the country. However, as related allegations emerge concerning police corruption, calls for an independent investigation into the claims are being demanded by Labour MP George Galloway. Mike Edwards has the story now,' she smiles.

'Yes, Shareen,' replies the reporter, shielding himself from the rain on the steps of the High Court in Glasgow – 'Mr Patrick McGowan, describing himself today as an ordinary businessman, refutes these allegations as the machinations of a fantasist.' He continues – 'John McGinty, himself accused of murder, accuses McGowan of bribing senior policemen and city councillors in Glasgow. McGowan, he claims, ordered the murder of three people. The Glasgow businessman denies similar claims that his private cab company and garage businesses have been used for selling drugs. The trial continues. Mark Edwards, reporting from the High Court in Glasgow.'

The C/Hall population are waiting for them as they return each and every night with up-to-date bulletins on the trial – 'Pat? Happened, mate?' scream the hundreds of heads poking through the rails of the three floors – 'That McGinty's a grass!' they call – 'S'a fuckin canary!' they sneer – 'Gettin tanned, that fuckin canary!'

Pat's black suit reeks of cold sweat while the brother-in-law appears freshly attired in a different suit each day.

'S'a fuckin joke!' Derek informs the mandatory audience – 'Aw thuv got's circumstantial!' he roars – 'Am impeachin the daft driver, takin the derry, so wur walkin! Ma Pot Noodles there, boss?' he asks, chancing a wary glance in his brother-in-law's direction, but Pat's banged his door closed already, not interested in answering the stream of questions and well-meaning predictions – 'Aye. S'a fuckin joke. Shood finish n a cuppla days,' continues Derek – 'S'a fuckin canter!'

Fifty-three days later no amount of new suits – or veiled threats – can convince a certain witness to implicate himself – 'No, sur,' wavers the voice in the witness box – 'The bus is Derek Sweeney's. Yes, sur,' it adds – 'The drugs had tae be his. A didnae know thur wis a secret compartment. Am the driver, that wis aw.'

Pat's Q.C., Mr John Simpson, leans across the bar to whisper in his client's ear – 'Pat. There's not a shred of evidence against you on any of these charges,' he winks – 'Do have a word with your co-accused. I don't want you in that witness box otherwise you may become entangled.'

Pat doesn't have to be told twice, he nudges his partner –

'Get yer hauns up, you,' he whispers – 'Yer dun anyway,' he adds.

'Here boss, eh,' sighs his co-accused without any hesitancy – 'A wee minute,' he says, signalling his defence counsel – 'Am changin ma plea. Guilty, aye.'

Lord Wheatley observes the court while both counsellors reach an agreement on whether the plea is acceptable or not – 'Derek Sweeney,' he says, on receiving a slip of paper stating the Crown's position – 'These are very serious charges,' he continues – 'Drugs are a scourge upon society and it is the inclination of this court that those peddling in death should be sent to prison for a very long time. You have deliberately wasted the time of this court at the expense of the tax payer and shall go to prison for twelve years with the court's recommendation that parole be forfeited in this case. Do you have anything you wish to say?'

Shareen Nanjiani breaks the news before the prison van arrives at Barlinnie – 'Violent clashes erupt as drug dealer Derek Sweeney is sentenced to twelve years,' she says, shuffling papers around – 'In what is being described as one of the longest court trials in legal history, costing tax payers over two million pounds, there were angry scenes as police guards fought to restrain a man as he tried to attack court officials. Earlier,' she adds – 'Lord Wheatley freed Patrick McGowan. Allegations of police corruption in relation to the case were dismissed as Mr McGowan was cleared on all charges. Mike Edwards has this report.'

Mike Edwards presses a microphone close to his mouth as newspaper photographers jostle each other for shots outside the buildings of the High Court – 'Yes, Shareen!' he shouts – 'As you can see, the excitement that has been building throughout the trial has reached a climax' he continues – 'But today, friends of the convicted man were angry as he began his twelve year sentence. Derek Sweeney, described as an evil man, shouted at Lord Wheatley "I'll do this standing on my head," then had to be restrained by police officers as he tried to attack solicitors and court officials.'

Shareen interrupts with more questions as she reappears on screen – 'Mike?' she asks the reporter – 'Has Mr McGowan said anything? Have the police said anything?'

Mike grips the microphone tighter – 'No, Shareen,' he blusters, pushing back – 'No, he has refused to talk to reporters.' He continues – 'Police have said the allegations were unfounded, although it is believed that the Detective Chief Inspector, Ron McGhee, has since retired due to ill-health. Mr McGowan was seen leaving a few minutes ago with a woman, apparently telling waiting reporters 'You don't see me in Armani suits,' before driving off at high speed in a black BMW,' he smiles – 'Mark Edwards, reporting. Back to you at the studio.'

Shareen smiles wryly and looks up from her papers.

'Mrs Thatcher today told party members that law and order must play a key role in future policy, as the run up to the general election began at the Blackpool Tory Conference,' she says – 'The Prime Minister, determined to silence critics, told her supporters, "There is no such thing as society. There are individual men and women." She later received a standing ovation.

'You have been watching *Scotland Today*, bringing you all the up-to-date news around Scotland. I'm Shareen Nanjiani.'

Chapter Twenty-one

THE WEE GLEN is heaving; the patrons of lager frown deeply, searching intensely for an answer – 'Now, take your time,' teases the television game show host – 'For three points, and a chance to take away tonight's star prize,' he continues – 'Can you tell me, for the three points,' he chuckles, glancing again at the gleaming new car – 'What age is the Duke of Edinburgh?'

The silence reaches critical stage; half-filled pint tumblers hover, hanging crookedly in mid-air as cigarette clouds stretch into eternity, until finally – 'Is it – sixty-six?' stutters a voice, quavering with terror.

'Sixty-six-a?' taunts the host.

'C'mon! Ya fuckin bampot!' a voice yells from the bar.

'Sixty-six, you said?' again the quiz host teases.

'C'mon! Fucksake!' roars another.

'Sixty-six – and the answer is . . .' continues the host, swivelling on his heel – 'SIXTY-SIX!' he roars – 'A-n-d! You willa take home with you tonighta! Tonight's star prize! The ASTON! MAR-TINNNN-A!'

Tumblers bang and clatter in a cacophonic cheer; fingers relax their tight grip in envy and desire as the punters covet the new convertible panty-puller.

'You! Have won yourself this new CAR!' cries the host – 'AND-A! You also take with you – eight hundred POUNDSA!' he roars – 'EIGHT HUNDRED POUNDSAAA!'

A blue-ish hue darkens the bar; the television channel

is flipped over, changing the atmosphere as national news recreates murder and mayhem from around the world – 'The Duke a fuckin Edinbra?' sneers a voice – 'Turn it o'er fur the news, listenin tae this pish. The Duke a fuckin Edinbra.'

Shareen Nanjiani's face transforms the daily bludgeoning; hands dig deeper into back pockets, searching for the remains of a giro, while more manicured fingers drum on a table top.

'S'keepin this cunt?' wonders the thinly built, bespectacled figure sitting at the table. The Coca Cola glass rattles as ice cubes crash impatiently inside the frosted beaker while he watches the door – 'S'keepin this cunt?'

The drumming persists; he pays little attention to the presenter directing her audience to the result of an isolated score in the national body count – 'A jury heard today how a killer gunned down a priest in cold blood,' she begins – 'At Glasgow High Court, the jury returned a verdict after two hours,' she continues – 'John McGinty was found guilty of the murder. Lord Elmsley, on sentencing, said that McGinty should serve a minimum of fifteen years. Describing McGinty as a dangerous thug, the judge said the public had to be protected,' she adds – 'Mike Edwards has more news.'

Mike Edwards hugs his microphone outside a small chapel – 'Ye-es, Shareen,' he says solemnly – 'Father Joseph Kennedy, a popular figure within the local community, was gunned down as he prayed. Police described how the priest had been discovered by his housekeeper as he lay dying on the steps of the altar.' He pauses – 'As you can see,' he continues, glancing over his shoulder – 'flowers have been left by a community mourning the passing of a man known for his passion for football. Locals say he will be sadly missed.'

The reporter coaxes a young face onto the screen – 'Eh, eh,

ye used tae see um gaun tae the fitbaw, every Saturday, ey, see Celtic.'

Catholic feeling spills onto the bar – 'S'terrible, so it is!' declares a voice – 'A priest?' it roars drunkenly – 'Fuckin polis! Dae they gie a fuck aboot us? Naw!' he continues regardless of sly looks in his direction.

'S'up wi him?'

'A-ch, jist bevvied,' someone replies – 'Musta tanned es giro.'

Shareen Nanjiani doesn't hear the tirade – 'Police investigating allegations of bribery and corruption made by McGinty said today they had carried out a thorough investigation into the matter and were satisfied that the claims could not be substantiated.' She adds – 'Detective Chief Inspector Ron McGhee has since retired after a career spanning twenty-three years with the police force. A police spokesman said he had retired due to ill-health caused by stress.'

The drunken voice erupts and a glass is slammed on the bar – 'Stresh?' he roars, laughing – 'Eh? The fuck dae theshe people know aboot stresh?' he demands.

'Right, Tommy. Oot,' says the barman.

'Oot?' asks the drunkard – 'Wit fur?' he asks, puzzled – 'Aw, John. Ye'v got it aw wrang, shun,' he smiles – 'M'no pished, shun, gen up,' he continues.

'Right, Tommy, c'mon, yer steamin,' replies Big John.

'Shsteamin? Who me?' he retorts in drunken disgust – 'Shsteamin? Me?' he repeats as he's led to the door – 'Right! A kin fuckin walk masel!' he exclaims angrily – 'The fuckin hauns aff, ya fuckin bampot!' he repeats earnestly.

'Aye, Tommy, right, c'mon,' replies the big barman.

'Al knock you out, ya cunt, ye!' threatens the drunk, as he

careens straight into the jukebox by the door – 'Aw!' he roars – 'Pumpin iron, urye? Al pump iron intae ye! Aye! A hunner mile an hoor, ya fuckin haufwit!'

The other drinkers burst into laughter as Tommy batters straight through the door face first and still growling, but no one can hear him as the jukebox deafens the whole bar with punk.

'AM PRE-ETTY! PRETTY VAY-CANTA! AND NOWA!
COS WE DONT
CA-AAAARE!'

Pat McGowan leans back, unmoved by the nonsense, and watches the door until the person he's been waiting for arrives.

'Awright, Pat?' asks Wullie Brodie.

'How're ye doin, Wullie?' replies McGowan – 'Ye drinkin?' he asks, signalling the barman – 'Two Cokes, John,' he orders.

'Right, Pat. Ice, Pat?' asks the barman.

'Aye, John,' grins Pat – 'Good tae see ye, Wullie. How's things?'

Wullie leans back – 'Ach, noa bad,' he replies – 'Promotion's through,' he chuckles as the drinks arrive – 'Detective Sergeant William Brodie noo,' he winks – 'Big man stuck through the recommendation afore ey left,' he adds.

'Congratulations, Wullie. Never know, might come in handy,' suggests McGowan.

'Aye, well, thuv fired me intae the vice squad, so-o . . .' laughs the cop – 'Thought the two ey us might get thegither, an see wit wi kin dae. Wid'ye think?'

Pat pushes a bundle of bank notes across the table – 'Here,

Wullie,' he smiles – 'Back pay, eh,' he sniggers – 'McGinty, eh, tryin tae be wide.'

Wullie pockets the wedge – 'Aye,' he sighs – 'S'in Barlinnie the noo,' he says – 'Know a cuppla screws in there so al get um nipped.'

'Sound, Wullie, sound,' grins McGowan – 'How's the big yin?' he asks.

'McGhee? Ach. Bounce back, been offered jobs abroad so es okay, rajin as usual, but es okay.'

Pat signals the barman – 'John,' he drawls – 'S'Wullie Brodie. Free drinks whenever es in, okay?' he orders.

'Right, Pat,' replies John – 'Nae bother, Pat,' he adds as the detective sergeant offers his hand – 'Right, Wullie, pleased tae meet ye, Wullie.'

Brodie's impressed – 'Got this place tied up, eh?' he winks.

'S'mine,' replies Pat – 'A own it. Right, Wullie, listen,' he adds – 'Janis n the weans ur waitin in the hoose an am late. That parcel's behind the bar. John'll gie ye it. Tell Derek Janis'll be up in a fortnight when we get back fae Spain.'

Brodie takes the proffered hand – 'Right, Pat,' he says – 'Am headin doon the road as well. Huv a nice holiday n al see ye when ye get back,' he adds, watching his new partner jump into his car – 'Okay, Pat, catch ye later.'

Pat turns the ignition key – 'Sound, Wullie, sound,' he smiles – 'Al phone as soon as a get back. Okay, see ye in a fortnight,' he calls out the window – 'Aye, Wullie, see ye,' he continues, slipping the tiny tape machine from his inside jacket pocket – '*Detective Sergeant William Brodie noo.*' Click – 'Sound, Wullie, sound.'